RS03

D1192199

MAR 2009

THE HORSE TAMER'S CHALLENGE

THE HORSE TAMER'S CHALLENGE

A ROMANCE OF THE OLD WEST

G. K. AALBORG

FIVE STAR
A part of Gale, Cengage Learning

GALE
CENGAGE Learning

Detroit • New York • San Francisco • New Haven, Conn • Waterville, Maine • London

GALE
CENGAGE Learning

LIBRARY OF CONGRESS CATALOGING-IN-PUBLICATION DATA

Aalborg, Gordon.
    The horse tamer's challenge : a romance of the old west / G. K. Aalborg. — 1st ed.
        p. cm.
    ISBN-13: 978-1-59414-742-5 (alk. paper)
    ISBN-10: 1-59414-742-6 (alk. paper)
    1. Frontier and pioneer life—Montana—Fiction. I. Title.
PR9619.3.A22H67 2009
823'.914—dc22   2008043343

First Edition. First Printing: February 2009.
Published in 2009 in conjunction with Tekno Books.

Printed in the United States of America
1 2 3 4 5 6 7 13 12 11 10 09

This for Deni—who believed!
And my sister Rudi, who shares the history.

A good editor is a pearl beyond price, and Brittiany Koren is—by that definition—a priceless necklace all by herself. I am suitably thankful for her patience and expertise.

Merci, indeed!

1

Montana Territory: 1876

The ancient Indian trail twisted like a faulty memory along the contours of the high country, visible much of the time only as a shadowy trick of the light. But to Lucas Swallow, the tall rider on the blue roan Appaloosa stallion, the trail was almost as obvious as the coach road below.

Still, it was the stallion who caught the sign of recent travel on the ancients' track. The stallion *whuffled* and shook its head at the scent. Muscular thighs clamped against its ribs as the rider steadied it with a whispered, guttural command that was immediately followed by an even quieter hiss of surprise when he saw what the horse had smelled.

Blood! And fresh . . . this morning. Thick, viscous clots of blood, imperfectly covered by a hasty attempt to disguise the traveler's passage. The blood brought the rest into focus for eyes long trained in the art of reading sign.

One man, badly injured but still mentally alert enough to try and hide his trail; a man experienced in wilderness travel; a man wearing moccasins, or what was left of them, but no Indian, and no longer young. As the rider carefully guided his sure-footed, mountain-bred horse along the almost invisible trail, his eyes read the signs before him with growing certainty. The man he tracked was doing his very best, and it was a damned good best, to hide all signs of his passage. Was he fleeing somebody?

Something? Whatever, he'd been successful thus far. There was no sign of any pursuit . . . yet.

That thought caused the rider to shift his weight and guide his stallion uphill, away from the track and into cover. He sat there, silent, his eyes patiently scanning the countryside, his ears tuned for any foreign sound, before he finally returned to the trail, which he then followed until it swung round a hillside and brought the coach road below into view. He was moving into cover again when the sound of a whiplash drew a snort of surprise from his horse.

The rider was equally surprised, but less alarmed. He knew the difference between a cracking whip and an exploding firearm, and the whip wasn't close enough to offer any threat. Nor was the voice that followed the whip, even though the pure air of the high country made the voice as clear to the rider as if he'd been down there beside the speaker, several hundred feet below.

Crack!

"You are a fool and a damned coward, Turner."

Crack!

"If Otis Bennett wasn't so near to dying, he'd not only horsewhip you, he'd shoot you for the cowardly, mangy dog you are!"

Crack!

The rider had only to move his mount a few yards forward to get an unobstructed view of the scene before him, and again he hissed with surprise.

"And if you dare lay so much as a finger on one of these horses, Mr. Turner, I'll shoot you myself!"

Crack!

This assault gained a reply, albeit a whiny, cringing one, from the obvious victim of the affair, a hulking, bearded teamster who was at least twice the size of the tall, lanky, but obviously female figure. She wielded her whip with surprising skill in an aura of anger as vivid and tangible as the roughness of her voice.

But the teamster's reply was overridden by the woman's voice as she flung down the whip and replaced it in her hands with a rifle.

"You can go to Helena or go to Hell, Mr. Turner," she retorted, and her voice fairly dripped with anger and contempt. "But by all that's holy, you'll go on your own and you'll go without being paid. You contracted to drive this team to Helena, and if you're too much of a sniveling coward to fulfill that contract, it might as well be Hell for all I care!"

The rider on the slope watched a younger woman step into view. A young and beautiful woman—that much was clear even from the distance. A woman whose mane of auburn hair flowed like sunset fire down her back. Her softer voice didn't carry well enough for him to hear what she said, but the gestures of the slat-thin woman with the rifle made it easy to follow what was transpiring, and *her* words sizzled in the high country air.

"He isn't worth a bullet," she spat, her voice still acid with contempt as she spoke to the redhead. "And he isn't worth feeding, either. I won't have him around, and that's that. I am quite capable of driving your wagon myself and I will, but not until we've tended to your father. Turner can go to blazes, provided he damned well walks, and if the rest of you want to leave us here, then go ahead and do it."

She shook the rifle at the still-departing teamster, then swung back to where the rest of the party waited in the shade, many of them clearly undecided about the issue they now faced. As the rider watched, even that situation became obvious. The group halted on the coach road was a mixed party of miners—probably headed east toward Helena and the new diggings farther east in the Black Hills—and immigrants heading . . . somewhere, for reasons that likely made sense only to them.

The rider sat silent on his big stallion, knowing himself invisible, his faded, travel-stained clothes blending easily with the underbrush. He wore buckskin, although his flat-crowned black hat was felt, and both he and the horse wore nothing that would catch the eye—no shiny metallic objects, nothing that jingled or rattled. The horse wore a hackamore of soft, smoke-tanned leather. The saddle was hand-made in the Spanish mold, but without the traditional silverwork.

He, himself, was tall and lean as a winter wolf, with darkly tanned skin. His eyes, a pale ice-green color, narrowed as he continued to watch the proceedings below.

The mining contingent, which included the disgraced teamster, seemed intent on leaving the red-haired woman and her injured father. The emigrants were obviously disposed to stay and offer, if nothing else, assistance in burying the man. The older woman who had intervened seemed important among them, and she was on the side of the redhead.

Turning his horse, the rider began to move back along the trail, pondering as he backtracked. Had the blood been left by the redhead's father? Certainly by a man who, from his tracks, was skilled in wilderness lore; a tough, cunning and experienced plainsman who had escaped . . . what?

"Something bad enough to near kill him," the rider muttered to his stallion. "And something to make me curious enough to go looking and see what. They aren't expecting us in Helena for a day or two, but somehow I don't think it'll take that long, even being as careful as we'd better be."

And careful he was, as he painstakingly unraveled the injured man's back trail. Alert to every sound, every movement, he held to deep cover and kept as tight a rein on his impatience as he did on his Appaloosa stallion.

The horse, actually, was easier to curb. There was something about the red-headed woman that prodded at his subconscious, and it was more than her obvious attractiveness. Something . . . that hair . . . the color of a mountain sunset . . .

Whatever it was, it eluded him and disturbed his concentration at the same time. But the effect only made him more alert than usual.

2

"Lord, but I hate this country, Mattie," Rebecca Susan Bennett sighed, as the miners straggled out of sight around the first bend of the road. "It's no place for decent folk, no place for anything except Indians and wild animals and things that kill and maim and torture." Her mother's voice, though Rebecca didn't consciously realize it nor recognize her mother's words. She'd grown up with them, absorbed them without thought or question.

She'd been brought up to hate the West and anything to do with it, an attitude easily maintained by her memories of the childhood wagon train episode in which her father had been scalped and almost killed, and her twin sister Amy stolen by Indians. She had been hustled back East by her mother, whose attitudes had colored Rebecca's every conception.

But here she was, lured after her mother's death by a father she loved—a father insistent on making one last attempt to find his missing daughter. Rebecca's sister. She'd been unable to refuse him. How could she? But she'd *wanted* to, despite a conscience that demanded otherwise. Amy couldn't possibly still be alive, and even if she was . . .

Now that the crisis with the recalcitrant teamster was over, Rebecca was showing the strain. Her fingers shook and her eyes were bright with more than anger. Not fear, or at least not the expectable fear of unseen Indians, but fear of something else.

No, she found herself thinking . . . just a vague sense of uneasiness.

Even as she spoke, she darted quick glances at the surrounding hills, unable to shake off the certainty, not of being watched exactly, but of having stirred some . . . awareness . . . out there in the wild country. And there was no real reason for the feeling. She hadn't felt it when her father crawled into camp earlier that day. It had come upon her only in the last few minutes, like a sun-shadow or an attack of conscience.

She shivered, feeling the goose bumps creeping along her arms. Childhood memories and her mother's acid recall flooded unbidden to her mind, where they fought with adult logic and did nothing to cure her unease. She reached up to touch the bear-claw pendant, her talisman. Seeking comfort.

"It does seem as if everything that walks, crawls or flies is out to get you," said Mattie. She was a tall woman in her early forties, gaunt to the point of emaciation, and her now-soft voice belied the rawhide toughness for which Rebecca had admired Matilda Holmes ever since their first meeting. Thrice widowed and childless despite her first marriage at the age of sixteen, Mattie was as tough as the wilderness around them.

"Nothing wrong with the country," she continued in a voice that was hardly past a whisper. "It's the people. Although I guess the country is what makes some of them what they are. It's no place for weaklings, and that's sure."

"It's no place for civilized people at all!" Rebecca turned away so that neither her friend nor anyone else could see the tears that now threatened. The burly teamster's reaction to her father's injuries—an immediate diatribe about Indians and their dangers, used as an excuse to try and abscond with one of the Bennett wagons and stock—had thrown her off balance. As had the blunt, inhumane response of the miners who formed such a large portion of the expedition.

Maybe Indians, maybe not; to the miners it made no difference. Otis Bennett had been tortured, almost to his death. It
was a known risk, a gamble he'd lost. Nothing to do with them.
They were headed for the gold fields and her father's problems
were his own . . . and hers.

"You've got to see their viewpoint," a matter-of-fact Mattie
Holmes had said in a bid to try and explain to Rebecca the
tenuous links that could so lightly bind travelers in the vastness
of the West. "They'd have helped defend him if they'd known
he was being attacked. But it's done, and they reckon it's not
their fault, so why should they lose traveling time just to end up
burying him anyway?"

"It was *their* bellies he was trying to fill," Rebecca had replied.
"If he hadn't gone hunting yesterday to get meat for the camp,
he wouldn't have been attacked. He'd have been here where he
should have been."

"Men like your father don't hold to most folks' rules. He
knew the risks and I reckon even if he'd known for sure there
were Indians or . . . whoever . . . out there laying for him, he'd
have gone anyway. Sure we needed the meat, but it's not that
far to Helena. We could have got by without. Your father hunted
because he wanted to get away from being with folks for a while.
Too many people around made him testy and irritable. You
know that, child."

Despite her initial denial, Rebecca did know it. She also knew
that her father was, in the eyes of many people, as crazy as a
loon on his good days and worse on his bad ones. Most old
trappers and mountain men were. Their oddness came from being alone for so long that they forgot what civilized society was
all about, if they'd ever understood it in the first place.

Otis Bennett had wandered the western mountains for as
long as Rebecca could remember, and his occasional brief visits
"home" to the civilization he'd rejected had inevitably ended

sooner than planned. Without fail, he'd start feeling cooped up, edgy, suspicious. Downright peculiar. Exposure to his wife didn't help.

Given his druthers, Father would have made their passage to Helena without company. He'd have preferred the isolated Indian and renegade-infested country to the crowds of miners and settlers he despised.

"They's too dang many of 'em, Becky," he'd said a dozen times. "Swarming over the country like locusts, they are, ruining it. Most of them shouldn't be here. It's no place for 'em. This country's too tough. It chews 'em up and spits 'em out like so much rotten meat. If the Injuns don't get 'em, the country will. But they'll keep coming. It be human nature, I reckon, but there's nothing in it I like. 'Cepting of course that there's safety in numbers, and I reckon to see us safely to Helena in time to meet Cope, like I promised. 'Sides, with these wagons we're forced to the road anywise."

So they'd joined the mixed party of emigrants and miners, even though, from the first moment, Otis Bennett had retreated into a shell of obstinate surliness and suspicion that encompassed virtually all of their traveling companions. He made it only too clear that he was joining them for his convenience, not theirs, and as a result had made few friends, despite his ability to keep them in meat even while passing through country most men would have thought to be hunted out.

But he'd brought no meat from yesterday's hunt. Only his own tortured, bloody carcass, an incoherent nightmare that had crawled into camp just past dawning, barely recognizable as human, raving in shattered syllables not one of them could understand.

Turner, with plenty of backup from the miners, had immediately begun fomenting panic about Indians, though it was clear enough to Rebecca he was only using the excuse to try and make off with far more than he was owed for having driven their wagon this far. Helena was within easy reach, and the teamster, while far from brilliant, had an eye for the main chance.

Well, let him go and good riddance, she thought. She had other things to worry about. Her father was dying—not even such a tough old mountain man could survive the tortures he'd endured—but damned if she'd let him die without doing all she could to save him.

It took Otis Bennett three days to die, and for almost all of it he was insane, or close to it. Rebecca got very little sleep and even less peace of mind. The firelight brought forth memories from her childhood, some pleasant, others less so.

Like when her father had returned from the West, and stayed home a full month to the day, almost a record for him. Most of the time, he spent lounging on the porch of the family's modest home, recounting his adventures to a less than enthusiastic wife and two spellbound children.

He told them of the vastness of the Western plains, the splendor of the Shining Mountains and the vast rivers that plunged to the Western sea, rivers with gold as bright as the dreams of the thousands who flocked to find it. But it was his tale of the hidden canyon and the bear-savaged Métis boy that captured the imaginations of his two girls. Especially Rebecca . . .

3

The last Spaniard died alone, but rich.

A Franciscan friar, he was close to his God but almost a year's hard travel from the nearest of his religious brethren, who were in Santa Fe, 1800 kilometers as the crow flies to the south and east. Black-robed or not, the friar was no crow. He and his soldier companions had traveled more than twice that distance in their wandering search for the gold they'd finally found. When winter prowled south along the mountains like a rabid wolf, driving away the game and making travel impossible, the gold they had smelted couldn't feed them. The friar was the strongest, so he died last and therefore alone, but he died of the same natural causes that had inexorably taken his companions. He starved.

The place of his death had no name. It was a high, tiny valley on an unnamed tributary of an unnamed creek, merely one of a myriad of mountain meadows nearly a mile above sea level in what would someday be called the Rocky Mountains of Canada.

The friar and his party, driven to the high, hidden valley in their need to escape the notice of a roving Peigan war party, were almost certainly the first white men to the see the valley, and the last for more than two hundred years, by which time the only evidence of their visit was the arrastre in which they had crushed the ore, the crude smelter they had used to melt and mold their gleaming treasure, and the good friar's silver crucifix. And, of course, the rough ingots of almost pure gold for which they had died. Dozens of ingots, enough to have overloaded the Spanish mules, had they survived that tragic winter and the appetites of the foolish men who had brought them so far north to die.

Metal tools and accouterments rusted. Porcupines and other rodents gnawed away wood and leather. And all manner of scavengers laid waste the bones of man and mule alike before the harsh mountain climate completed the destruction. The friar's crucifix, hand-fashioned of pure Mexican silver, somehow ended up at the entrance to the shallow mine shaft where the gold had been stored, uniquely placed to catch a ray of evening sunlight when Otis Bennett scrambled into the hidden valley.

He was trying, as the Spaniards had done, to avoid a roving party of Indians. And, like the Spaniards, he was looking for gold. Otis had become separated almost a week earlier from his party, a group who'd already spent half of 1859 on the long overland trek from Upper Canada, headed for the British Columbia gold fields. He wasn't exactly lost, but he was in trouble and he knew it.

Unlike the Spaniards, Otis had no mules. He didn't even have a horse, his having spooked and thrown him two days before and then compounded the offense by running off to leave him with only the clothes on his back, his knife, and his Hawken plains rifle.

Also, unlike the Spaniards, he didn't starve in the valley. He was able to club an incautious porcupine on his second day and cook it over a very small, very carefully hidden fire. But he took none of the Spanish gold with him when he left, having no way to sensibly carry even one of the heavy, crudely smelted ingots. He did, however, take the silver crucifix, and the secret of the gold's location.

Two days later he set out afoot, and the day after that, he found the wounded Métis boy with eyes the pale, pale green of winter ice, and hands that could carve beauty into what had almost killed him.

Rebecca's mother, Pauline, had wished Otis would stop filling the children's heads with such tales, especially when he spoke of them all going West in search of "his" golden valley and perhaps a new life by the western ocean. St. Louis was, in her opinion, already too far west, too close to the fierce, untamed frontier she feared as much as her husband loved it.

She'd raised her first objections immediately, then piled caution upon concern upon worry until she could raise a litany of objection whenever Otis brought up the subject. Indeed, she had raised such a mountain of denial and opposition that it overshadowed the far more immediate—and equally dangerous—outbreak of the War Between the States. Otis enlisted almost immediately, this time heading in the wrong direction, for him, and seeking not gold but glory.

His leaving provoked a confusion of memories, no less clear now to Rebecca, in hindsight.

The morning of his departure, smartly dressed in a new blue uniform but riding the same scrubby nag which had carried him out of the West, he paused long enough to bestow hugs and presents upon his two daughters.

He hung a bear claw mounted on a silver chain, around Amy's neck, and a friar's crucifix around Becky's.

"This is to help you remember me, although I doubt I'll be gone so long this time. Now go play while I say good-bye to your mother."

Rebecca's response was typical, spoken as tears streaked her cheeks. "Be careful, Daddy. Come back safe."

Amy had no tears when she fiercely demanded, "Kill all the rebels, Daddy."

She also had no tears when she confronted her twin in the back yard. She had removed the bear claw from her neck and held it at arm's length, her lips pursed in a sneer of disgust.

"I'm the oldest; I get to choose."

Becky was still upset by their father's departure; she didn't want a fight. But . . . "Daddy gave this to me . . ." she began.

Amy grabbed at the crucifix, dragging Rebecca to her knees

19

before finally wrenching the chain free. She wasn't gentle; didn't intend to be, and when the chain snagged in Becky's fiery hair and brought a squeal of pain, she laughed.

"You're such a baby, Becky Sue."

She placed the crucifix carefully around her own neck, then dismissively flung the bear claw into her sister's face, causing even more tears.

"Bears are baaaad," she sneered, and scampered off to see if her father had gone yet.

He had, but it was far from the brief sojourn he and so many others expected when they set out to fight the War Between the States. More than five years passed before he saw St. Louis and his family again, and he stayed only long enough to sell up, pile them into a wagon, and set off in search of a new future in the West.

Pauline Bennett objected, of course, but as well try to harness the wind as dissuade Otis from his chosen path. He had returned from the war changed, hardened in many ways, and more fixed in his ideas. He acknowledged her objections, but ignored them, as he did her incessant fears for their safety in the wilderness ahead.

4

Otis' suffering was tremendous, made worse by the sheer futility of his daughter's labors to save him. But equally bad, from Rebecca's viewpoint, was the sobering realization that perhaps her father hadn't been sane since he'd been scalped and left for dead in the Indian attack nine years earlier; the attack in which her twin sister Amy had been taken captive. Or maybe he'd *never* been sane in the truest sense. Take his paranoia about the "Spanish" gold he'd supposedly found when she and Amy were children, and his insistence on their memorizing the map which could locate that gold. She and Amy had each been taught half the map and sworn to secrecy. At the time, it had seemed a lark, a childhood fantasy. Later in life, she had occasionally wondered if he wasn't merely seeking some means of bringing his disparate daughters closer. But now the possible reality of that gold seemed confirmed by her father's torture. Rebecca simply didn't know what to think.

That he had been tortured because of the gold seemed indisputable; during one of his few lucid moments he had said as much, and said also that he hadn't told, would never tell.

"Jayhawkers," he'd whispered, then repeated that single, damning word in a scream of agony. And there had been something in his ravings about a small Spaniard with a knife, the evidence of that tortuous instrument all too clear on Otis Bennett's ruined body.

Rebecca had never been totally comfortable about joining her father on this expedition. It had seemed questionable in the extreme, giving up her teaching career after her mother's death to participate in the pursuit of a dream he'd already wasted the past nine years of his life on. Her twin sister Amy was dead; everybody said so. Had to be. And if not dead, then better off dead . . .

Even her father had seemed to agree with that in his dying moments, moments in which he had raved against his pain, although he often seemed to lose all ability to distinguish between Rebecca and her sister, calling her by name one minute and by Amy's name the next. But, most disturbing of all, demanding of her that if she could not manage to rescue her sister, she should kill her, rather than leave her a captive of savages.

Rebecca knew the logic behind his thinking. There were dozens, hundreds of tales of white girls captured by Indians, forced to become Indians themselves, to actually mate with savages, to produce half-breed children who, everyone said, were worse than Indians. It was a bleak picture, but when compared to her father's dying request that she kill her own sister . . .

It had been her father's plan, a plan that seemed so sensible at the time, that they would accompany the Philadelphia paleontologist Edward Drinker Cope on his journey east from Helena to the Bear Paw Mountains. Cope needed a reliable guide; none better than Otis Bennett, who had been providing the Philadelphian with fossil information and specimens for several years. And the Bennetts needed the security of a larger party if they were to venture into the hazards of Indian country. The eastern and northern part of Montana Territory was the traditional buffalo country for Indians of many tribes, all of them hostile. Peigan, Blackfoot and Bloods roamed down from Canada to compete with their traditional enemies, the Assiniboine and the various branches of the Sioux nation, hunting the buffalo that were the very lifeblood of the tribes, but also raiding and warring upon each other and especially upon the whites, who were the common enemy.

It was the Bloods who had taken Amy, so long ago and far to the north, across the "medicine line"—the international boundary with Canada. But Otis Bennett was now convinced his daughter was with the Minniconjou Sioux, although how Amy might have made the transition between two such hereditary enemy tribes he could not, or would not, explain.

"If we travel to the Bear Paws and the Judith Basin with Cope, maybe we've got a chance to find her," he'd said when they started out for Helena. "And if all else fails, it will get us far enough to be able to cut north to the Whoop-up trail out of Fort Benton. There's a man in Tail Creek Town who can help us, can we but find him, if he's the same man I think he is, and if he remembers. I'm a fool for not having tried to contact him years ago. He surely could have helped, if he but would."

"L'Hirondelle, you mean?"

She had asked the question mechanically. There was nobody else he could have meant. Luc L'Hirondelle, the Métis boy, now obviously a man . . . if he existed at all . . . had featured heavily in Otis Bennett's Spanish gold tales. The boy whose life he had saved, the boy who had carved the bear claw that, along with the silver crucifix, was the only tangible evidence her father's tale had any basis in fact. Rebecca wore the bear claw, now set in silver, around her neck, and it seemed, at least to her, that she'd always worn it.

Although . . . it had originally been given to Amy. Rebecca had been given the silver crucifix at the same time, when Otis Bennett departed to do his part in the Civil War. She could still remember Amy's tantrum, her sister yanking at the crucifix, dragging Becky to the ground in tears, ripping the trinket from Becky's neck to place on her own, then flinging the bear-claw

23

necklace at Becky . . . a thing of no value in Amy's eyes. Typical of Amy; she had always wanted whatever Becky had.

Had her father always known about Amy's cruelty, her selfishness? He hadn't seen that particular incident, of course, but . . .

"Never thought of L'Hirondelle before." A barely perceptible hint of softness had shaded Otis Bennett's wary eyes. "Wouldn't have but for a chance meeting I had with one of his people up north of here a ways. Seems Luc's big medicine now he's growed, and he's been around the traps a bit, too. He'd know how to take up Amy's trail."

"And surely he'd help us. You did save his life, after all."

Rebecca hadn't been really keen, even given this new information, but she couldn't help wondering why her father insisted on joining Mr. Cope when there seemed a more logical way to go about things.

"Maybe he'd help, maybe not," her father had responded. "Injuns is notional. There's some, maybe most, would have thought me weak for saving Luc when I had the chance to take his hair. He was only a boy then, sure, but old enough to be called a warrior. His coup stick said he'd met an enemy or two before I found him."

That discussion had taken place some many days earlier, when Father had met her at Franklin, where the Utah and Northern Railroad ended and the long coach road led north and east to Helena and, eventually, Fort Benton. They had discarded the idea of waiting at Franklin for Edward Drinker Cope. Father had arranged to meet him at Helena and was determined to hold to that plan, despite his near certainty Cope would have to travel the same road they were taking.

And now, two days out of Helena, Rebecca watched as her father's body was lowered into a grave dug by men who didn't know him, had words spoken over him by a preacher he'd never met, and she was left with two good teams and wagons, her father's weapons and equipment, and a memory of what he'd asked her to do about Amy . . .

"You decided what you're going to do?"

Rebecca had been staring at the starkness of the scarce-covered grave when Mattie Holmes spoke, and she was startled, not so much by the question, but the accuracy, the . . . exactitude . . . as if the older woman had read her mind.

Dry-eyed—Rebecca had, inexplicably, found herself unable to cry at the graveside—she turned to meet the gaze of her new friend. Around them, the emigrants were already moving to strike camp, obviously glad to be shed of the need for further delay. They had done their duty by Otis Bennett, a man with them but not one of them, and now wanted only to get on with their trek.

"I haven't got all that much choice," Rebecca replied. "I must take these wagons to Helena and wait for Mr. Cope's arrival. After that . . . we'll just have to see, I guess." She hadn't confided in Mattie about her father's dying wishes, and would not. Mattie, a woman of the frontier, would think her mad.

"You ought to pick up with a party heading the other way," Mattie said. "Go back to the end of steel and make your way back East, is my advice. Nothing here for you now, and this country's no place for any woman with the choice, and the sense to leave it."

Rebecca could only stare. Choice? She had to deliver the wagons, at the very least, and to report her father's torture and death. Just what the authorities in Helena might be able to do about it, she couldn't imagine, but surely they would do something. As for the rest . . . she couldn't run away from her promises. No matter that they had been gained under duress, under the strain of trying to ease her father's dying. She had promised to try and rescue Amy. One final try. And she would! As for the gold, well, all her befuddled mind could conceive at the moment was that it might, if she could find it, aid her in the task of seeking out her twin.

"I am going," she said as firmly as she could manage, "to Helena."

5

Dover Sugden well suited the nickname given him by the northern Indians and Métis he had abused and cheated during his relatively brief years of trading north of the medicine line. *Le Carcajou,* they called him, and he was very much like the wolverine in both looks and temperament. Especially temperament. Except that where the ferocious, ill-tempered and cunning wolverine was notoriously fearless, Sugden preferred having all the odds in his favor, if he was to fight at all.

Which was why he took one look at the well-armed emigrants awaiting Otis Bennett's recovery or death, then signaled his men to follow him away down the coach road. By his perverse standards of fairness, the odds were wrong. Only when his outlaw band was out of sight and hearing did he snarl his fury.

"You should have grabbed her while we had him," Sugden growled. And later, while the band relaxed around the fire of their carefully chosen and well-hidden camp—far from where they had unsuccessfully tortured the old man—Sugden's temper was hotter than the campfire.

"He's told the girl. By God, he has, and it'll be a pleasure getting it out of her," Sugden snarled, glaring wild-eyed across the fire to where his two companions lounged against their saddles.

The men rested, but warily. Sugden's animal rages were common enough, but they could never be viewed with complacency.

"We should grab her before she can get to Helena," Sugden

continued, the words spat through broken teeth as yellow as the evil little eyes that glinted past the greasy beard covering most of his face. "But those damned movers are all stirred up and Indian-shy. They'll be sleeping with cocked rifles, the lot of them. No chance on the trail now. Too risky by far."

"I think we risk too much, anyway. I think there *is* no gold. The old man was mad. It is a known thing."

The speaker was half Sugden's size, a slender weasel of a man dressed entirely in black and with deceptively soft, almost liquid eyes of the same color. He leaned back against his saddle, one hand idly scratching the queue of ebony hair at the back of his neck, and that gesture—more than anything else—prohibited Sugden from spitting out more vehement oaths.

Luis Sebastian's fingers teased the haft of a throwing knife, a knife he could—and would—use with more speed and deadly effect than most men could manage with a gun. Sugden was the band's leader; Sebastian his most trusted subordinate for many years, but the larger man knew how difficult and dangerous a tool the small killer could be.

Sebastian combined the worst aspects of a mixed ancestry that included New World Spanish, French, even a trace of Lipan Apache, if the rumors were true. He was a natural for Sugden's gang; no leader himself, but a quicksilver, bloodthirsty killer; an almost perfect lieutenant. Although small, he was so handsome as to be almost pretty, but he thrived on blood like the weasel he resembled, and would face anyone, regardless of the odds, if it meant work for his knives.

"He's told the girl," the brutish leader repeated. "And the gold does exist."

"The gold, it may exist." Sebastian's shoulders moved in a barely perceptible shrug that served only to settle more comfortably the throwing knife between his shoulder blades. "But I do not think the old man knew any more where to find it again. He has been loco, they say, ever since he was scalped, when his party was raided by the Bloods up in Canada, when the other daughter was taken. It is a known story, and it is this other daughter the old man has been seeking over the years, not the gold. Nine years! We have all heard the stories of this, and of the gold, but they make no sense."

Deep thinking was not Sugden's forte. He was a cunning tactician, a skilled and ruthless terrorist who had brought his gang through the Civil War without joining either side. Instead, he'd raided and preyed upon isolated, helpless families, left defenseless to predation from the likes of Bloody Bill Anderson, Quantrill, and Sugden himself.

"It's there, I tell you," he insisted, shooting a glare at the small Spaniard. "The old man might have been crazy, but he found that gold. I know it."

"And heard his crazy tale about teaching each daughter a different portion of the map leading to the gold? *Mon dieu!* If he had done so, would he then go about telling everybody? It is madness, the whole thing."

"He drank, you fool. And when he drank, he talked. You'll see, when we get our hands on the girl," Sugden growled, rolling his piggy eyes with savage anticipation.

Sebastian's own eyes glistened with a soft luster, a deceptive gentleness that couldn't totally disguise the cruelty behind them.

"When we get the girl," he said, "it will not be gold that I will think of. It is a long time since I had a woman. Too long." One hand waggled in a gesture that should have been casually simple but relayed an aura of obscenity.

"When we get the girl, it will be the gold first and pleasure later," Sugden said firmly, then bared broken, crooked teeth in a grimace of a smile. "Although a little physical persuasion will be called for, I'm sure. But if it is, by God, it'll be me that takes care of it first, and don't you forget it, you little Spanish bastard.

I remember the last time you had first go at a woman. You broke her mind so badly there wasn't anything left for the rest of us. Like screwing a corpse, it was."

Sebastian shrugged again. "To argue is of no sense until we do take the girl, and now she will go on to Helena where it will be even more difficult, I'm thinking. You cannot be seen there. I, myself, would not visit during daylight, and . . ."

He need say no more. Sugden, truly enough, did not dare to be seen in Helena. Even in Fort Benton there was always the risk he might be recognized, but in Helena the risk was greater and such an occurrence would mean, at best, a short trial and a quick hanging. More likely, it would mean being shot down like a dog in the street by any one of dozens who had survived his predations over the years. His back trail was strewn with corpses and blood and rapine, but only in his soberer moments, which were few, did he contemplate that life would be easier if he'd left behind only corpses. No witnesses, no one to point him out to a lynch mob or simply shoot him where he stood.

The biggest problem was that only Sebastian could be trusted with any undertaking that required intelligence. The other members of Sugden's motley band could not, in his own estimation, pour piss out of a boot without written instructions. Or even, if truth be told, read such instructions if they existed in the first place. And it was nearly as dangerous for Sebastian to be seen in Helena as it was for the outlaw leader himself.

"I also am concerned," the black-garbed Spaniard continued in a voice directed only at Sugden, "about the rumor that L'Hirondelle is in Helena, or at least south of the line. The old man, he spoke of L'Hirondelle, did he not? If he is involved in this matter of the girl, it could mean problems."

Sugden tensed, then shrugged, his perfunctory motion conveying an indifference that didn't ring true. "L'Hirondelle is just a bloody half-breed. He may get about the tribes a bit, but even among his own he isn't that much. Not important like Riel, or even old Gabe Dumont. Besides, the old man said nothing about meeting him here. He mentioned going into Canada to find him."

"L'Hirondelle's name is strong among the tribes," Sebastian replied, ignoring the last part of Sugden's statement. He wasn't arguing, merely sticking to his own thought pattern. His Indian blood gave him a different appreciation for how a man's reputation could register among savage tribesmen, and he knew L'Hirondelle was highly regarded everywhere on the plains.

"Many names, he has, but always the same meaning . . . tamer of horses. They say he is wilder than the horses he pursues, cunning as the wiliest of mustangs, savage as the worst stallion there is. I would like to meet this L'Hirondelle." Sebastian gave Sugden a smile that was almost shy and yet totally, eerily evil. "A stallion can always be tamed . . . with the knife."

"Forget about L'Hirondelle! He's not a part of this and he won't be. You just concentrate on finding a way for us to lift that girl and get her off someplace where we can discuss her father's gold . . . quietly." His grin suggested anything *but* a quiet discussion.

"Williams and the boy should be back soon," Sebastian said calmly, refusing to be drawn into further argument. "Let us wait to see what they report."

"Williams is a drunk and the boy's a bloody half-wit. Neither of them's worth feeding, and I was a damned fool for letting them go on into town after the girl. They're most likely both in jail by now, and that's if we're lucky."

"Better they should go in daylight than us." Sebastian rose up from the ground with the fluid ease of a cold-eyed, deadly snake. He had been watching the third member of their trio, a one-eyed brute named Harrigan, whose chief asset was his animal-like sensitivity to noise, scent, and anything else

31

significant to his own safety. "They are coming now, I think," Sebastian said, following the one-eyed man's mindfulness to where the sounds of two slow-moving horses could only just be made out.

The report from Williams and the half-wit boy was less than encouraging. The Bennett girl had arrived in Helena, and had first of all gone straight to the governor of the territory, Benjamin F. Potts, whose reputation held little to frighten the Sugden crowd. Of substantially more interest was the news that Edward Drinker Cope, the bone-hunter, had arrived, and was to be guest of honor at a huge soirée that very evening.

"The girl will be there," Sugden said, "and with every fool in town celebrating, we might just get the chance to grab her."

"She may be at the soirée, but you and I cannot be," Sebastian responded in a nonargumentative voice. "And these . . ." he indicated the remainder of Sugden's gang ". . . would not be allowed inside the door. So what are we to do? Stand outside and watch?"

"Exactly. Only it won't be 'we.' It'll be you. Nobody'll notice you with all the goings-on, and if there's a soirée, there's likely as not to be a fight or two, or some such doings. Might give you a chance to grab the girl, might not, but I want you there just in case."

It took a long time of sour silence before the smaller man spoke, but when he did his voice revealed no sullenness. "I will do what can be done," he said, stooping quickly to pick up his saddle and move to where his horse was tethered.

Never once, Sugden noted, did Sebastian entirely turn his back on his companions. It was something he'd never done, not in all their years together. Smart . . . Sugden didn't and wouldn't deny that. But it was spooky, too . . . unnerving even to Sugden, who would go to his death denying he had any nerves to bother about.

"Luis," he called as the slender *mestizo* glided into the saddle and walked his horse slowly around the edge of the camp. "If L'Hirondelle is in town, leave him alone. Understand? The girl is what we want, so don't go starting off on any of your private little feuds."

Sebastian's reply was the merest of shrugs. He knew what Sugden meant, knew also that the warning was irrelevant. All he had heard about the Métis horse tamer over time had served only to whet his appetite for a meeting. A true professional himself, he admired similar qualities. The only problem with his admiration, although he himself did not see it as a problem, was that his nature was such that admiration had to be earned, tested, proven.

Sebastian was as much a man of caution as his leader, except when it came to the personal proving ground, the ground where his *macho* instincts would override any caution, any logic. Ever since he had first heard of L'Hirondelle, north across the line at the lonely outpost of Spitzee on the Highwood River, Sebastian had been enchanted by the possibility of meeting and almost certainly killing the horse tamer.

There was no logic to this obsession, nor did Sebastian need any. L'Hirondelle was a tamer of horses, while he, Sebastian was a tamer of men. He would someday meet this man and kill him. He would do it this very night if the opportunity presented itself. Or not, as his fancy dictated. But he did not say this to Dover Sugden. To say this would provoke another, different killing, and he did not want to deprive himself of the most satisfying leader he'd ever had.

Sebastian didn't really think L'Hirondelle would be in Helena, but it was possible. Nor did he think L'Hirondelle was involved in the fantasies of the crazy old man and his gold, the ludicrous fable of twin daughters and divided maps and Indian captives.

Nor did Sebastian care. He had seen the red-haired daughter of the old man, and if he could follow his leader's wishes and capture her, he would have his share of the fleshy spoils. More than his share.

L'Hirondelle would be a bonus.

6

Rebecca Susan Bennett found the governor's soirée everything she might have expected—and then some. It reflected the status of former General Benjamin F. Potts and his famed paleontologist guest, but it equally reflected the raw newness of Helena itself, the isolation both physical and spiritual of Montana Territory.

Most of the men in attendance looked uncomfortable wearing suits to which they were obviously unaccustomed. White shirts and collars held tanned necks in strangleholds. Broadcloth was a new form of dark rigid armor, with creases.

The guest of honor suffered no such problems. Edward Drinker Cope had been raised a Quaker, and his stilted, rather formal way of speaking quite suited the ease with which he wore formal clothing.

He was also a most charming and interesting character, widely read, broadly educated, if perhaps too arrogant, too certain of his own place in the paleontological scheme of things. His professional rivalry with Professor Othniel C. Marsh of Yale University was known, apparently, even in the wilds of Montana, and the urbane Cope lost no opportunity to disparage his rival scientist.

But the demands this put on his accessibility created a problem for Rebecca . . . a problem exacerbated by her own situation. Not that she could have done much about this particular problem, even if she'd predicted it. Being young and attractive and eligible in a community where all three attributes of womanhood were seldom combined in a single person was sufficient to make Rebecca nearly as popular an attraction as the guest of honor.

Not that she was exceptionally well dressed. On the contrary; she lacked white gloves and she had left her bustled petticoat back East. She had, in fact, packed only one festive gown, and while it flattered her petite figure and its blue-violet color matched her eyes, it was velvet rather than silk or satin and hopelessly out of style.

Furthermore, she had no jewelry, only the bear-claw necklace her father had given her so many years ago, her talisman. It was, by any standards, barbaric and eye-catching, the reason why she'd tucked it beneath her bodice. A bear claw from a grizzly bear, its shiny outer surface intricately carved to portray a rearing wild stallion defying capture. The rope around the stallion's proud neck wound down along the shearing edge of the tooth, and when her father had—years later—arranged for the curio to be set in silver, that rope design had been incorporated into the setting.

But it was not the gown, nor yet her talisman that caused her to be so noticeable; merely the circumstances, the time and the place. From the instant she walked in the door, men of all ages, sizes, and positions in the community had begun to flock around her like bees drawn to some fragrant flower.

Except, of course, Edward Drinker Cope—busy living up to his unusual middle name, with the governor doing the pouring.

Aside from Cope, one other man captured Rebecca's attention. This man didn't appear the type to need or even consider wanting an excuse to do exactly as he wished, or might wish, as the mood might take him. And while he made no attempt to meet her or be introduced to her, that omission belied an obvious interest in her that he made no attempt to disguise.

Rebecca could *feel* his interest, tangible as a physical touch whenever their paths crossed in the milling crowd.

Tall and lean in the manner of a winter-starved wolf, his hunger was not, she somehow felt, of the purely physical variety. This man walked with hungers of the soul, hungers as sharp as his pale eyes, as the knife-blade beak of his strong nose. He was perhaps thirty, maybe a bit older. His hair was black with auburn tints and just the hint of a fine wave, long, gathered behind his neck in a queue. His strong, rugged features might have been carved from dark, fine-grained wood. Like some predator, his nose seemed to seek out the invisible messages from the room about him. And his eyes . . . unusual, brilliant against the dark tan of his face. Eyes the color of spring sea ice, so pale a green as to be almost without color, yet all the more striking because of it.

His clothes were more or less typical of the gathering—a dark broadcloth suit, white shirt, string tie, shiny boots. Still, he was different from the others. There was a proud, wild quality she couldn't quite put into words—but could feel. Perhaps it was just that he moved differently, Rebecca thought, her gaze diverted from the guest of honor once more by the stranger. A diversion she didn't need! Despite her father's horrible death— something she had yet to deal with emotionally—she'd come to the soirée specifically to try and meet with Cope. And it wasn't working out that way, much to her frustration.

Cope had been monopolized by the governor the instant he'd arrived in Helena, after a speedy, nonstop coach journey from Franklin with his assistant, Charles Sternberg. They had, Rebecca discovered, arrived at the Idaho border town to find there was no hotel, so they'd slept on the depot platform before embarking on the four-day, three-night coach trip with stops only for food at the relay stations along the way. The experience didn't seem to have fazed the paleontologist. He was clearly enjoying himself immensely as the center of attention. But she had been given no opportunity whatsoever to even meet the celebrated scientist, much less discuss her plan to take over her father's role in his expedition.

The governor had, admittedly, been quick to issue an invitation to the soirée—about the only thing he'd done for her. He had been able to offer no aid in apprehending her father's killers, or even an investigation into the matter. Not surprising, really, without a single clue to go on. Montana Territory was filled with gold-seekers, would-be settlers, outlaws and transients of all sorts, strangers to the territory and to each other.

The stranger with the ice-green eyes seemed foreign, even amongst the elite of the mining town's inhabitants. He was self-contained and, even in repose, stood out from the crowd like a racehorse amongst pack mules. His expression hardly seemed to change, but he gave Rebecca a sense that he was twice as alert as anyone around him, ever vigilant, ever watchful.

It seemed to her that he followed her own movements about the room without even using his eyes. He was simply . . . aware. And when he did look at her, his slightest glance seemed capable of capturing her attention whether she was trying to fend off the attentions of some persistent suitor or trying to focus her own mental powers on Cope.

She could feel the stranger's pale eyes tracking her through the crowded room, their touch an almost tangible caress along the length of her throat, the rising swell of her bosom. And the sensation felt so real she had to look up and meet those damnable eyes, just to be sure he stood on the other side of the room, not close to her.

Eventually, she could stand it no longer. The man's regard had been intriguing at first, even flattering in a strange way. But now it was just too distracting. Not offensive, she thought. How could it be? He hadn't so much as spoken to her, hardly even looked at her directly enough so that she could justifiably take any offense. But distracting, yes . . . that, certainly, and she couldn't afford such distraction. If she didn't find some way to separate Edward Drinker Cope from his now boisterously drinking host, if she couldn't at least find some way to arrange a meeting and talk to him . . .

"I do not think you will manage it."

The voice whispered into her ear, pitched so low as to be almost inaudible. Yet every word was crystal clear, and Rebecca didn't even need to turn her head, didn't need to look to know who had spoken. The voice was as distinctive as the eyes, as the man himself, and even as he stepped round to face her, thus freeing her from the need to turn and force a confrontation, she found herself thinking how such a deep, gravelly voice befitted him. Rough and yet smooth. Hard-edged and yet mellow. With just a trace of an unfamiliar accent.

"Manage what?" she asked, aware that it was a futile and perhaps even silly question, because she knew exactly what he'd meant, knew also that he expected her to know.

One dark eyebrow lifted imperceptibly. Strong white teeth flashed in a grin that could as easily have been a sneer. A wolf's grin, she thought, dangerous, predatory, too knowing by half.

"I doubt if you could pry our guest of honor away from the governor with a crowbar," he said. "Not that I can see why you'd want to. Mr. Edward Drinker Cope of Philadelphia is too wrapped up in his old bones and dignitary status to pay more than passing attention to any woman, even one as striking as you. Your bones, delectable as they may be, are not quite old enough, I fear, to attract the attention of Mr. Cope."

"None of which, I suggest, could be any of your affair," she countered, keeping her voice cold, using the color of his eyes as a guide. Yet she poised the remark as something of a question, not really understanding why. She hadn't been properly introduced to this man, not that such an omission seemed all that important at the moment, nor had he bothered to introduce himself, as rightly he should have done.

"Probably not," he replied, continuing the name omission with an almost deliberate arrogance. "I just find it curious, is all, same as I find it curious that you're being tracked by a couple of men I'd shoot, were I to find them on my own back trail. Makes me wonder about your intentions regarding the good Mr. Cope."

"You're being quite ridiculous," she retorted, honestly confused by his allegation. Suddenly fearful, she began to move away from him, although still holding his gaze with her own. Followed? Tracked? She wondered idly if he might be drunk, despite an inner certainty that he was not.

He merely shrugged, somehow making even that gesture so smooth, so incredibly vital, so . . . predatory . . . that she felt an inward shiver of awareness, warning. Drink was not this man's problem.

"They've been with you since you hit town, and, I suspect, long before that," he said. "Followed you to where you're staying, then the governor's office and back again, and likely all the way here tonight, though I admit I haven't seen them here. Wouldn't expect you to have noticed unless you're involved with them . . . they've been almighty cautious."

"I don't know what you're talking about, truly I don't. And even if you're right about . . . about me being followed, I can't imagine what it would have to do with Mr. Cope."

Again the shrug, this time accompanied by a slow grin that just barely revealed his white, even teeth. "If it isn't Cope, then it must be you," he said, and again she was reminded of a wolf, pale-eyed and hungry. Menacing. "Might be that dress that's attracted them," he added, his eyes flowing like quicksilver across her gown and her skin. "But then you weren't dressed like this when you arrived. All you seemed to have was a bit of luggage, your wagons and horses, and a couple of guns. Are you carrying a particularly well-stocked poke of gold?"

Again, his gaze roamed down her body, touching with an almost fiery arrogance at her throat and breast, waist and hips.

"Can't imagine where you'd hide it if you were," he said.

Rebecca had managed, she thought, to effectively stifle the instinctive spurt of alarm she'd felt at his mention of gold. Here in Helena, even with the crest of the gold rush in the surrounding mountains more or less over, such mention was probably logical enough, certainly not unreasonable. But there was too much at stake, too much at risk, in having anyone suspect her secret, much less this man who seemed able to peer into her very soul with his icy eyes and alert, predacious manner.

"I think, sir, that you are being insulting," she said, forcing into her voice a haughtiness she didn't really feel.

She turned away, refusing to allow him to recognize how much his visual caresses had affected her. While a part of her had shrunk away from his mention of gold, another part had reacted with animal clarity to his gaze upon her, to the way he had somehow caressed her, touched her without touching her. She had felt a strange softness in her stomach, her knees had turned to jelly, and her spine tingled as if a ghost walked the nubbins of her backbone. Predatory, his look, and totally . . . stimulating. Desiring, demanding, blatant.

"I did not mean to be insulting, ma'am," he said, "and my apologies if I seemed so."

That declaration was followed by a slight but very formal bow. Rebecca thought he was going to reach out, take her fingers, and lift them to his lips. It wouldn't have been unseemly. This man had the manners and élan to carry off such an overblown gesture.

Worse, she wished he would.

Whereupon, quite to her astonishment, he did! Lean fingers, long, strong and callused, reached out to take her own small hand and lift it to where he could touch his lips to the back of her hand, without for an instant losing eye contact.

"I'll leave you alone now," he said. "Please understand that I would not have approached you in the first place except that it will be my job to look after Mr. Cope's interests, and I take my work seriously. Perhaps too much so in this case. I happened to notice the men following you and made an illogical link between that situation and your obvious interest in Mr. Cope."

Which explained everything and nothing. Except . . .

"You work for Mr. Cope?" The question popped out even as Rebecca's brain was whirling, seeking some way to turn this incredible coincidence to her advantage. She had already discounted his absurd tale of her being followed. It simply made no sense, had no logic. But if this strange, wolf-like man could aid her in becoming attached to the Cope expedition . . .

"In a way," he said, the words abrupt. "I have agreed to guide him to where the best of the bones he seeks can be found."

His teeth were bared in a half smile that Rebecca thought could be either threatening or inviting. Whichever, he had the instincts of a wild animal and she would be foolish to fabricate her intentions.

"*I* have the wagons he'll be needing and the horses to pull them," she found herself saying with equal candor. "And it was my impression that my father had been hired to guide Mr. Cope."

"I know nothing of your impressions. But then, like you, I've had little chance to consult with the great man. Time enough for that tomorrow, I suppose, assuming we all survive this evening."

"I expect you may find yourself out of a job," Rebecca

42

retorted, a small coal of anger fanning inside her. How dare the illustrious Mr. Cope engage someone else to guide his expedition? Had her father been here, he would have . . . have . . .

"I'm sorry, but I don't understand your anger. Are you annoyed that Mr. Cope would hire two guides, or is it that I am one of them?"

"I'm angry because my father is dead and I'm here with the wagons and the horses and I can't even manage to *talk* to Mr. Cope."

Rebecca felt her eyes brim with tears. She bowed her head to at least try and hide them, only to find that this pesky stranger still held the hand he'd kissed. Furthermore, she could feel the imprint of his mouth where it had touched her hand.

"I'm sorry about your father," he said softly, "but I don't see the problem. Mr. Cope will be well financed and you should get good returns, once you provide him with your wagons and stock."

"It was my father's intention that we accompany Mr. Cope." Rebecca kept her voice steady, wishing she could summon up the resolve to pull her hand free, unable to combine that with the sheer willpower she now needed to curtail her tears.

"You cannot be serious." His voice registered astonishment, and for some strange reason Rebecca found gratification in that. "Cope is going into the very heart of Indian country. And even though he poses no threat, he risks being attacked, a very high risk. Especially since I expect we shall have difficulty getting good men to accompany us. I've heard that Fort Benton is booming. There's no shortage of easier, safer work. But that aside, it's no place for a woman, if you don't mind me saying so."

"I do mind," Rebecca replied, under control now. "I have reasons, very good reasons, for wanting to accompany Mr. Cope's expedition."

She finally yanked her fingers free, gaining a brief flicker of his wolf's grin at her gesture.

"I'm sure you have," he said, although his reply was tinged with sarcasm. "And would it be too . . . insulting . . . for me to ask what those reasons might be?"

"I would prefer to relate them to Mr. Cope. Not that I expect there to be much of a problem. As you have said, there's a shortage of men in Fort Benton. But my understanding is that there's an even greater shortage of wagons and stock. And if my horses and wagons go with Mr. Cope, I go with them. Is that so difficult to understand, Mister . . . ?"

"Swallow. Lucas Swallow. At your service, ma'am, if I possibly can be."

"The only service I can imagine you providing would be to find some way for me to talk to Mr. Cope."

Rebecca marveled inwardly at her cheek, but was certain this unusual man would respond to directness better than any other approach. "That," she added in a deliberate move to soften the brusqueness of her remark, "would be truly wonderful."

"I hardly think wonderful is the word for it, any more than I can imagine Mr. Cope agreeing to take you along into Indian country."

"Even if I have the only horses and wagons he's likely to find?"

"That is one reason for him to consider taking you, but I'm more concerned at your reasons for wanting to go. They must be powerful reasons indeed, I reckon."

"They are. They are also Mr. Cope's concern, not yours."

His shrug was casual, deceptively so. Rebecca almost, but not quite, might have believed she had scored a minor victory.

"You tell him, he tells me, can't be any other way if my services as a guide are important to him," Swallow said, and again there was that flash of a grin. "Might save a lot of trouble if I knew it all first. I might even be on your side, which couldn't hurt."

"Are you saying that you would take a woman into Indian country, provided you thought her reasons for going were acceptable? Or that you might assist in persuading Mr. Cope on my behalf?"

"I'm saying my curiosity bump is itching like crazy, that's all. You seem damnably determined to risk that pretty hair, and you do not strike me as a complete and utter fool. So I'd admire to know what's so important to you out there. Some cavalry officer take your fancy, for instance, or maybe you've got missionary tendencies, Miss . . . ?"

"I am Rebecca Susan Bennett, and I have tendencies in neither direction, I can assure you," she replied, still unsure, wanting to trust him at least part of the way, for reasons she couldn't fathom but instinctively accepted.

"Now that we have been more or less properly introduced, Miss Rebecca Susan Bennett, may I suggest we take a glass of the splendid punch they're providing here and seek just a trifle more privacy?"

Without waiting for a reply or assent, he took her arm and guided her, first to the punch bowl, then to one of the glass doors leading out from the governor's function room. Rebecca followed, her mind six steps behind the positive certainty of Swallow's movements. It wasn't until they were outside on the verandah of the building that she began to wonder if she was doing the right thing.

Lucas Swallow seemed amused at her obvious consternation.

"Take a swig of your punch, Miss Bennett. I expect it will ease the burden somewhat." Reaching inside his suit coat, he extracted a thin cheroot. Nodding for her approval, he scraped a match on his boot sole and lit the cigar.

Then he listened, his silence a force that drew the words and emotions from her first in a trickle, then a torrent.

The coulee was a river of mist, and the Indians emerged as if rising from beneath it. First the heads of the ponies with feathers plaited into their forelocks, eyes ringed with vermilion. Then the gleaming scalplocks and hideously painted faces of the Blood warriors, eyeing the slumbering wagon camp like wolves.

An even dozen in all, most of them seasoned, battle-hardened warriors stripped nearly naked but for their war paint. Only a few had rifles; most were armed with bows, war lances, tomahawks and war clubs.

They moved their ponies forward at a slow walk, guiding them with legs bowed by a lifetime on horseback, and they moved toward the circle of wagons with the dawning sun at their backs and death in their eyes.

They paused at their leader's signal, waiting with deadly silent purpose until he raised his rifle to the pink-tinged sky. Then terror erupted from a dozen throats as they kicked their ponies toward the circled wagons.

A nervous dog had wakened Otis. He was given precious seconds of warning, and leapt from his wagon with a loaded rifle in one hand and a pistol in the other as the Indian ponies leapt fair into the center of the camp . . . and into his sights. One or two other men were less fortunate; they leapt from sleep to death as war clubs smashed them down.

Then the Indians were gone, for the moment, having ripped through the circled wagons like a whirlwind of screaming death. Otis screamed, calling Pauline and the girls to him, then shoved them under the wagon.

"Stay there! Keep down," he shouted over his shoulder as he turned to the renewed assault. He was struggling to reload when the second wave struck, and got off only a single shot before a passing warrior struck him down from behind. The youthful Blood was off his pony,

knife in hand, and sawing at Otis' hair when a bullet lifted him into oblivion.

Beneath the wagon, Pauline could only cower, girls held in her circled arms and her eyes closed against the terrifying sounds and smells of the battle. She was blank with shock, didn't even notice as Amy wriggled free and crawled to the outside edge of the wagon, peering through twelve-year-old eyes that were wide with excitement.

Medicine Calf was wise in the ways of war. He had led his party in that first surging charge through the circled wagons, but not the second. And there was no third charge aimed at the inside of the camp; instead he led his warriors in a furious charge round and round the circled wagons, each man taking what shot he could with arrow or bullet, firing from beneath their ponies' necks.

The Blood leader saw the flicker of movement beneath one wagon on his first circle of the camp, but not until the second did he realize it was not a threat but an opportunity. On his third circuit, he slipped from his rearing pony, reached a strong brown arm under the Bennett wagon and grabbed at the calico-clad figure he'd spotted.

Amy barely had time to scream before Medicine Calf was back on the horse's back, her small figure flung across his lap as he turned the pony away from the battle. They were a mile away before Pauline even knew her daughter was gone, several miles away before the awful realization that the twelve-year-old was an Indian captive. And hours away before the disorganized people in the wagon train could attempt a timid and futile search for the missing child.

The Bloods vanished like morning mist into the sea of grass from which they'd emerged, taking with them their single casualty—the youth who'd foolishly paused to try and scalp Otis—and leaving behind a wagon train in chaos and panic with two men dead, several wounded, and all the women terrified and angry.

Otis was no help; he recovered quickly enough from the blow on the head, but the bullet-interrupted scalping streamed blood at the slightest movement. All he could do was rage at his impotence and endure his wife's acid tongue.

The fury of the Indian attack was nothing compared to that of Pauline Bennett, Otis' head wound notwithstanding. She cursed the Indians, she cursed the timidity of her traveling companions, she cursed the empty, vast land in which they found themselves. She even cursed God. But mostly she cursed Otis.

"This is God's revenge on you for bringing us here," she said in a voice shrill and ragged with terror and long-suppressed anger at her husband's golden dreams. Which, she said, were over now and forevermore—"not another step West will I take, nor my remaining child, either."

She was good at her cursing, and she proved persuasive with the women who shared her grief and loss and terrors. In the end, she had her way; never did she take another step westward. Mostly at her urging, the party turned back, heading south to rejoin the main emigrant road they'd left at Otis' suggestion several weeks earlier. Easy enough, then, to link up with others disgruntled and defeated by the West . . . Pauline Bennett and Rebecca were home in St. Louis by autumn. And there Pauline Bennett stayed, slowly but surely killing herself with resentment and frustration and bitterness.

Otis, predictably, returned West as soon as he could, using the search for Amy as his excuse. He saw St. Louis only three times in the next nine years, never found his missing child, never got back for his hidden gold, and never overcame the scorn and rejection of his wife.

He used the lure of his golden secret to finance his wanderings, and became increasingly isolative, moody and taciturn, a cantankerous enigma traveling light and alone across the mountain country and high plains on both sides of the international border. Some declared him a madman; others deferred to his knowledge and experience, but as the years passed he became a legend in his own time without even realizing it.

Swallow guided Rebecca through her carefully contrived tale, prompting her whenever she hesitated. She was extra careful not to even think of the gold and the map she shared with her sister. This man was too astute, too quick to pick up on every detail. But she managed to get through the rest of her recitation, including her father's obsession with making one last try to rescue Amy, and her own acceptance of his dying request.

"So after all you've been through already, you still think you have some chance of finding your sister, even rescuing her? Have you no idea of the sheer *size* of the country out there? You could wander around as long as your sister's already been a captive and never encounter the band she's supposedly with. Never even see an Indian, for that matter, although for my money the problem would be the reverse."

"I promised my father on his death bed," Rebecca argued, but it was a faint echo of her fiery tirade in the governor's office earlier that day. The magnitude of it all had finally begun to sink in, although she couldn't imagine why this stranger's blunt speech should have that effect when the governor's identical opinion hadn't fazed her. Ever since her father's death she'd struggled to go on with only two lodestones of purpose: find Amy and find her father's gold.

"You might be keeping that promise on your own death bed," Swallow said. "But you've got sand, Miss Bennett. It takes a whale of a lot of guts to even contemplate what you intend, given how terrified of Indians you are."

She shied at the truth of his comment, but refused to voice the obvious question of how he knew that, knew it so surely, when she had managed to deny it . . . even to herself . . . until now.

She made one last attempt to avoid facing up to it by breathlessly adding to her story, as if words alone could dispel the

truth of his insight. "I simply must try, if there is any way possible. The only other option open to me is to seek out a man my father helped, a man who, if I could find him at all, might be persuaded to help me. And to find him, according to my father, would mean going north into Canada. That is where I thought Father and I were going to travel, once he'd found the bones for Mr. Cope, but now he's dead and I . . . I . . . just don't know anymore."

Swallow smiled, the wolf-look gone from his eyes. It was a gentle smile, almost tender, as his hand reached up to touch at her left temple. Merely a touch, scarcely long enough to be felt, but there was an element of a caress in the gesture, such as one might offer a frightened child. If he had listened to her babble, he didn't show it, still intent on what he, himself, had said earlier.

"Every time the word Indian has been spoken, by either of us, there's a little vein here that throbs," he said. "When you talked about the massacre where your sister was captured, I could smell the fear in your memories, and that, too, comes out whenever Indians are mentioned."

"You could smell the fear in my memories?" Rebecca could only shake her head at the concept, the reality beyond her comprehension, beyond any logic she could deal with. She might have laughed, but Lucas Swallow sounded serious.

The noise from within faded, subdued by an atmosphere, an aura that hung like smoke around the two of them. It was as if the world outside had been shut away from them, as if they existed only in themselves, only in this eerie, half-lit, timeless moment. A fear welled up inside Rebecca, nameless, formless, unlike anything she had ever experienced. She felt as if she had walked outside with a dog, a creature tame and predictable, and now found herself facing a wolf, or worse, a werewolf. Certainly there seemed to be something almost supernatural about this

tall man whose icy eyes looked into her soul.

Trembling and hating herself for it, she felt herself drawing away from him, not moving her feet but forcing what little distance she could manage. Her hand rose and drew upon the chain that secured her bear-claw talisman, which she fondled without thinking as she sought the strength to free herself from the grip he held upon her with his eyes. Winter-sea-ice eyes, only now they were pale fire, flickering like the green flames of the northern lights. As a child, she'd seen the aurora borealis, washing the sky with that same intensity, that same power.

A hand shot out to grip her fingers and pry them from the bear claw. A hand that moved so quickly, so fiercely, she had no chance to resist or refuse. The chain holding the talisman became a leash as he dragged her over to where he could examine the object in the light cast through a nearby window.

"Where did you get this?"

She heard no gentleness in his voice, just a humming tension that seared like lightning through the air between them. A fierceness, held in place the way a predator would contain itself before launching at its prey.

"My . . . my father," she stammered, wanting to flee, but held by his grip on the silver chain.

"Your father gave you this? Where? When?"

There was a thread of urgency in his questions, an insistence she couldn't fight against. "When I was a child . . . years and years ago . . . I can't remember exactly," she managed to reply, reaching up with one shaking hand to try and free herself, to make him release the talisman, to release *her*.

"But where did it come from? You must know that."

His voice, no louder, seemed almost a shout, the words striking out at her like physical blows, bullets fired from his lips and eyes.

"From an Indian boy. No, a *Métis* boy he helped, a boy whose life he saved." Frightened by Swallow's intensity, she had trouble getting out the words. The tale in its entirety was there, in her mind where it had been since childhood, repeated over and over in her father's own words. But against this man's . . . vehemence . . . she couldn't function, could hardly speak at all, much less repeat her father's admonition concerning the bear-claw talisman.

"You must keep it with you always," he had said more than once. "It may be even more important than the map you share with Amy. Because if all else fails, and if you can manage to find L'Hirondelle, it may convince him to help you. He knows where the Spanish gold is, but doesn't know he knows. And being Indian, or near as damn-it, it mightn't matter to him anyway. But keep the bear claw, Becky. Keep it always!"

Suddenly the intensity was gone, fading like smoke in a breeze. Lucas Swallow's fingers released the talisman almost reverently, lowering it to Rebecca's breast so gently that even though his hand touched her breast briefly in the process, there was no insult in the gesture, no threat.

"Miss Bennett?"

"Yes, Mr. Swallow?"

"This Métis boy, this is the man you would now seek out in Canada, the one you mentioned earlier?"

"Yes."

"And his name?"

Rebecca told him, and in her agitation thought she imagined he repeated the name not only as an echo of her reply, but somehow in conjunction with it. *L'Hirondelle.*

Lucas Swallow didn't move. His masculine physical presence was right there in front of her, undeniable. But *he* was not. Even though his ice-green eyes were still locked with her own eyes, no bond existed between them. It was as if the man behind those eyes had vanished, leaving his eyes alive . . . but empty.

Then Rebecca saw that intense life force which had so initially attracted her flow back into his eyes with a visible, almost audible snap. And if Lucas Swallow was aware of his momentary trance, if that's what it had been, he gave no sign of it.

His eyes now blazed with a force that could have been passion, anger, almost any violent emotion save sorrow, then shifted from her eyes to rove casually along the planes of her face, then down along her throat and the lines of her body. It was not a particularly erotic assessment; he even stepped back a pace, his gaze encompassing every detail of her face and hair and figure, as if he were memorizing her, composing a mental image as real as she was.

And all in silence, a silence that seemed to hang round them as tangible as the night, unbroken, untouched by the raucous sounds from within the building.

Swallow looked at her, his gaze probing, assessing, calculating. But he said nothing during that intensely private appraisal that was in one sense intimate and in another so totally impersonal she might have been a horse examined for purchase.

"I must think on this," he finally said, the words followed by a small but distinct bow, hardly more than a nod. Then his strong hand flashed out to grip her elbow, and he was turning to guide her back inside the soirée, moving as easily through the crowd as if he was water in a boulder-strewn stream. Rebecca went with him, a leaf floating in the current without control or understanding, until he stopped and she found herself face to face with the guest of the evening, Mr. Edward Drinker Cope.

Swallow's introductions were formal, brief, and courteous. As was his departure a moment later, although his final words to Rebecca seemed more instruction than farewell.

"Until the morning, Miss Bennett," he said, his lips once again touching her fingertips. "By then, perhaps, I shall have an answer for you, if you'd be good enough to wait that long."

Which told her that tonight would not be the time to broach her suggestion about accompanying Cope on his expedition to the Bear Paw Mountains.

Leave it to me, Swallow had silently said. Demanded. *Trust me!* His eyes had repeated the message as his lips scorched her fingers. And even as she turned her gaze from his lithe, swift-moving figure to meet those of the soirée's guest of honor, nobody could be more surprised than Rebecca Susan Bennett at how certain Swallow had seemed that she would obey him.

7

Luis Sebastian had less trouble than he would have expected in making his way through the boisterous streets of Helena to where he could watch, from a position of some inconspicuousness, the governor's soirée.

Whatever his faults, the small Spanish mixed-blood was no fool. His presence in Helena could all too easily become the focus for a shooting or hanging, so he moved quietly through the shadows, once he had secreted his horse on the outskirts of town.

He was also, he firmly and suspiciously believed, a lucky man. It was to this luck he attributed the good fortune of finding himself in the right position at the right time to view Rebecca Bennett emerging onto a side porch in the company of a man Sebastian didn't, at first, recognize. Or even pay much attention to.

At first . . .

"*Mérde*," he muttered to himself, his fingers involuntarily reaching to the throwing knife at his neck as the young woman's companion lit his cheroot. For an instant the flame revealed a face Sebastian knew he should recognize, though he'd never before seen it, knew he should be able to put a name to, but couldn't. And then could.

Or thought he could. Half his mind said he could not be right, this could not be the man, but his instinct said it *was*, and

Luis Sebastian trusted his instincts almost as much as he trusted his knives.

Enough, at any rate, so that when the couple eventually returned inside and the man emerged alone a few moments later, Sebastian abandoned his surveillance of Rebecca Bennett without a second thought. Dover Sugden's orders were forgotten as Sebastian focused his entire attention on the tall, lean figure who walked slowly and thoughtfully toward the center of town.

Sebastian followed, a darker shadow among many, his attention so strongly focused, he became oblivious to everyone else who moved upon the crowded night streets. The man he followed seemed equally oblivious to Sebastian's presence. The man walked slowly, seemingly without any specific purpose or destination, so lost in his own thoughts that Sebastian's task became too easy, losing for the Spanish *mestizo* any sense of personal challenge.

He could only follow, muttering beneath his breath, cursing the man ahead for not realizing he was being followed, for not giving Sebastian the opportunity for the violence his bloodthirsty temperament so badly craved.

Unnerving. Unsettling! If this was the man Sebastian thought he was, he could not be so oblivious to the atmosphere of danger that followed him. Could it be possible that this was not L'Hirondelle? Had Sebastian abandoned his ordered task to follow a figment of his imagination? Even if this was L'Hirondelle, Sugden would not be pleased. But if he, Luis Sebastian, was wrong . . .

His quarry continued to stroll along the street, seemingly unaware of his surroundings, much less to the potential danger that stalked him. He paused on one corner and appeared to be stargazing, or staring into the face of the moon. Some minutes later he paused yet again, and Sebastian halted in mid-stride, fingers on his knife haft, certain this time he had been observed. But no, again it was the stars, or the moon, or perhaps the sky itself that had claimed the tall, lean man's attention.

The third pause was potentially more significant. The man slowed, then stopped to exchange remarks with an ancient, drunken Indian, slouched in his ragged blanket near the mouth of an alleyway. Sebastian heard the murmur of their voices, but couldn't pick up the words. The tone, the cadence, however, was clear to him, and even though he didn't know the language, his instincts told him it was Peigan . . . Blackfoot . . . and his heart soared with an obscene sense of rightness. Surely this incident justified his instinctive move to follow the tall, lean man.

Except . . . what if it *wasn't* L'Hirondelle?

Sebastian shrugged away the thought. Better to trust his instincts.

A flash of silver as a coin was tossed to the huddled figure, and then the pursuit began again, only now his quarry had changed direction, still moving aimlessly but heading for the part of the town where the livery barns loomed dark against the night sky. Sebastian's stalking became both easier and harder. Most of the barns, he thought, would be empty of humans; even the hostlers had either bedded down or were off visiting the various saloons. He quickened his own pace. It was darker here, making it easier to follow closely but more difficult to keep track of the man ahead of him.

Sebastian crept closer, moving like a black ghost in the now-silent street, hugging shadows as black as his own clothing, placing each foot with exaggerated care, his fingers never far from one of his razor-edged knives. He had discarded his spurs at the beginning of his stalk, tucking them beneath his shirt where their large rowels were silenced, and he might as well have discarded the gun at his hip, for all the notice he paid of it.

Ahead, the tall figure continued to stroll unhurriedly, nothing in his demeanor suggesting the type of wariness Sebastian would have expected. Perplexed, he began to doubt his judgment once again. How could this be L'Hirondelle? Surely a man of such stature and reputation could not be so unobservant, so little a challenge!

L'Hirondelle, if it *was* L'Hirondelle, sauntered through a maze of cloud-spiked moonlight, his eyes peering lazily upward. Then he disappeared into an indistinct patch beside one of the more remote livery barns. Ahead loomed another stretch illuminated by the moon, and Sebastian paused, waiting.

Too long, his mind cried as his fingers leapt to his knife haft. The man had simply vanished! He had stepped into a patch of shadow and then melted away as if he had never existed. Sebastian gripped his knife tighter, the hair at his nape bristling with the certain knowledge that all was not as simple as he had thought, that something could very well be going horribly, terribly wrong.

He stayed, poised in silence, ready to fight or flee, but unsure which would be called for, knowing only that his original feelings had been validated. The proof was in that empty pool of shadow which should have disgorged a human figure into the moonlight beyond . . . and had not.

Luis Sebastian was, for all his faults and his hot-blooded Spanish ancestry, a patient man. In his world, patience often meant the difference between life and death, and he had survived where many had not simply because he understood that fact. So now he waited, all his senses alert, his curiosity piqued but held closely in check. When he moved forward, one painstaking step at a time, to investigate this shadow which could swallow a grown man without so much as a whisper, he was himself a shadow, a study in silence.

More than ten minutes it took him to travel as many steps,

and when the answer to his question was revealed, he swallowed an instinctive grunt of surprise and relief. Inside the shadow was an archway, a doorway without any door, hardly more than another shadow inside the larger one. Clearly a little-used side entrance to the livery barn, through which he could now detect the sound of stabled horses in a darkness thicker than that in which he stood.

Sebastian relaxed minutely as he focused his eyes on the blackness inside the doorway, his ears on the rustling and rubbing noises of the animals within. Again he waited a long time before he dared slip through the nebulous entrance. Instinctively, he hugged the row of stalls nearest to him, his throwing knife in his hand.

Lucas Swallow's silent warning lasted about as long as the bubbles in Rebecca's glass of champagne.

Surely, she thought to herself, there could be no better time to approach Edward Drinker Cope than now, this very minute! The paleontologist was in an effusive, undoubtedly receptive mood, and his political companion was literally awash with it.

What did she know of this Swallow person anyway? He was a stranger, come from nowhere and vanished so abruptly she could almost have imagined him. Almost. She had to force herself to forget the lambent touch of his lips on her fingers. And if he did have influence with Mr. Cope, why hadn't he put it into practice, instead of merely providing an introduction and then removing himself from the scene with an almost indecent haste?

She wrinkled her nose as the champagne bubbles lifted her optimism, and at the first reasonable opportunity began to plead her case with the scientist. The opposition was more or less what she had expected and she was able to formulate her own arguments around that expectation, despite an unexpectedly sober series of arguments from the governor himself.

"Of course I realize there will be Indians," she replied to the first obvious objection, depending heavily upon bluster to disguise her inner fears. "And I realize, too, the threat of possible trouble with them. But you will be a strong force, Mr. Cope, well armed. And my understanding is that the Indians are really only at war with the cavalry, the army. Isn't that right, Governor?"

"Only because there's hardly anybody else out there to fight with," Potts replied. "Over in the Black Hills, where the latest gold rush is drawing civilians like flies because of reports from that damned . . . excuse me, ma'am . . . fool Custer, the Indians are slaughtering miners whenever they get the chance."

"But we will not be in the Black Hills. And you will not be mining, either," she said, turning her most enchanting smile on Mr. Cope, whom she presumed to be the least obstinate of the two. Cope's assistant, she decided, had already succumbed to her feminine charms, and the great man himself would follow suit if she played her cards right.

"We shall be digging. Does an Indian know the difference, I wonder?" Cope said, and in his eyes was no immediate sign of capitulation. Rebecca straightened her back, unable to resist the challenge, but careful now to watch the scientist's reactions.

"As to how strong a party we shall be," Cope continued, "it may depend a great deal on what men Lucas Swallow can muster when we reach Fort Benton. There are no men for hire here, and my friend the governor informs me that things could be even worse there. Do you know what they want for horses? And not good horses, either . . . just rough-broke nags! Sixty-five dollars, Miss Bennett! And despite my offering wages of one hundred dollars a month, I've had no takers here and may find none in Fort Benton."

The governor, his sodden attention wavering between Cope

and Rebecca, nodded solemnly, but thankfully stayed silent. "All the more reason for you to find a place for me with your party, sir," she insisted. "I have, as I've said, the horses and wagons my father promised you."

"And they will be most welcome, I assure you. As you would have been, had your father not met with his unfortunate accident, and had he been with you, responsible for your care and safety. But you must realize, Miss Bennett, that I cannot assume such responsibility, and cannot even consider your request without consulting Mr. Swallow, who is to be our guide."

"I suppose Mr. Swallow is among those who are demanding such exorbitant wages," she retorted, and immediately wished she could have bitten her tongue.

"Lucas Swallow is part of the expedition by his own choice, and it is glad I am to have him," Cope replied in a voice as firm as it was gentle. "Your father, I must remind you, had not replied to any of my later communications, and I was not even certain when I arrived here if he planned to be with us at all. Lucas Swallow has vast experience of the country we shall be traveling, knows intimately the Indians we cannot help but encounter, and has not a little knowledge of the specific scientific criteria which must be met."

"I did not mean to be critical," Rebecca said, backtracking as she realized that her own, essentially visceral response to the mysterious Lucas Swallow was partially to blame. Damn the man, anyway! He had caught her at a vulnerable time, in a vulnerable situation, and even without being there was *still* manipulating things. It helped not at all to have the governor suddenly decide to include his own views at this precise moment.

"The whole idea is ridiculous," he asserted with a punctuating belch. "Even if your father had not been killed, Miss Bennett, I should have insisted against your inclusion in the expedition. It's nothing short of madness!"

"I tend to agree with thee," Cope said, subsiding into his Quaker formality and, Rebecca could see, mentally dismissing both herself and her proposal to accompany his party.

"I certainly respect your opinions," she said with her most dazzling smile. "But given that Mr. Swallow's opinion is so highly regarded by you both, could I be indulged to the point of being given no firm refusal until you have talked with him?"

The governor's whiskey-reeking snort was obvious enough, but Cope was clearly made of stronger, fairer stuff. Either that, or she had underestimated his need for her horses and wagons.

"We shall see what Mr. Swallow thinks in the morning," he agreed. "Thee would have to be ready early, mind. We must lose no more time, and will be away to Fort Benton at dawn."

His final remark, a reiteration that he would be interested in Lucas Swallow's views on Rebecca joining the expedition, put an end to their discussion. She was left to her own contemplations on how Swallow would react. Would he, she suddenly found herself wondering with not a little concern, be angered by her approach to Cope? Would he have been on her side anyway?

She spent the rest of the evening consumed by those concerns, although her popularity made it difficult to give them adequate consideration. Being courted by half the men in the place was, she reflected between exhausting forays onto the dance floor, wonderfully good for a girl's sensibilities. And it would have been even more enjoyable if Lucas Swallow's handsome but enigmatic features didn't keep roaming into her mind to criticize her decision to approach Cope, and to manage, even in her memory, to look at her quite differently than did any other man in the room.

Lucas Swallow would have taken little comfort from Rebecca's confusion. He had concerns and confusion enough of his own, and no throng of admirers to take his mind off them.

Recognition of Rebecca's talisman had struck him like a thunderbolt, smashing up out of his past to throw his entire future into chaos with an unexpectedness that served only to accentuate his problems.

"Damn it!" he muttered. "Damn it all to hell anyway!" Followed by an equivalent remark in Peigan that lacked the profanity but was, if anything, even stronger in literal meaning.

Bad enough to have found himself so unexpectedly attracted to the entrancing, auburn-haired creature. Any normal man would be, he thought. The girl was, after all, stunningly beautiful and intelligent, however foolhardy her plan to seek out her Indian-captive sister. But there was more to it than that, for him. Far more!

Her father had saved his life, a blood debt he'd carried ever since. A debt he could not, in any conscience, now ignore. A debt handed down from father to daughter, but no less inviolate. The fact that Rebecca Bennett didn't seem to know the true extent of the debt, did not know and *could not* know that Lucas Swallow was in fact the very Luc L'Hirondelle whose aid she sought, was irrelevant to the issue.

For an instant he wondered what her reaction might have been had he admitted his double life, told her that he was Luc L'Hirondelle, the now-grown-up Métis boy whose life her father had saved, the very person whose much-younger fingers had carved the bear's claw she wore around her slender neck, snuggled between her exquisite breasts. There had been a moment when he might have said so, perhaps should have said so. But he had not, and now it became a matter of conjecture how he would manage that task when it would have to be met. And he never doubted for an instant that such a time must come, would simply have to come.

Luc L'Hirondelle . . . Lucas Swallow. The same name in two languages. And the same person, he found himself thinking. But also two very different people, and the difference was as much created by the language involved as anything else. In Canada, use of his French name, his Métis name, was acceptable, even preferable under many circumstances. The Métis were treated far better by white society in western Canada than the half-breeds so despised south of the medicine line by almost all white Americans. So for Luc L'Hirondelle it was simply good sense to use the literal English translation of his name . . . Swallow . . . when traveling among Americans as a white man, which he often did, although explaining *that* to the delectable Miss Rebecca Susan Bennett would be even more of a complication.

It took no great powers of observation to realize that Rebecca had what could only be termed a phobia about Indians, not surprising given her experience as a child in the raid which had seen her father scalped and her sister abducted. And, given her feelings and noticeable terror when she merely talked about Indians, he thought it took an amazing element of courage for her to have accompanied her father on this trip in the first place. To want to go on and try to rescue her sister, under the circumstances, was even more astonishing.

During the earliest of his thirty-one years, Luc's life had been governed almost entirely by the Indian one-eighth of his ancestry. He had roamed the Rocky Mountain foothills from Fort Edmonton and Rocky Mountain House to the Missouri, spending summers always with his mother's people, the North Peigan, the *aputoxi-pikuni* of the Blackfoot confederacy. As a youngster, he'd spent winters with his parents, French-Canadian fur trader Phillipe L'Hirondelle and his quarter-blood Peigan wife with the Cree name of Ilona, *Climbing Woman*.

Here, too, the issue of a name was relevant. At home he was Luc, and spoke both French and English while being educated by his father, who was himself quite well educated. But among his mother's people, where he had been given the childhood name *Eyes-like-ice,* he had spoken Peigan Blackfoot and lived entirely the life of the people.

His mother had died when Luc was only nine. And her death was perhaps the first major step in the transformation of the Métis child into a man whose complicated history and personality was now about to become even more complicated by his involvement with a white woman whose violet eyes had haunted his dreams for half his lifetime.

Luc had been sent to Montreal by his father after his mother died, and stayed under the caring but strict discipline of the Oblate fathers for nearly five years, proving himself an apt if erratic student with an uncanny gift for languages and a strength of personality and will that had both amazed and frustrated his mentors.

Then his father had been killed by a roving band of renegades. Luc had returned to the mountains—educated, virtually penniless, and with no family left but the roving Peigan whose nomadic lifestyle, he was astute enough to realize even then, was certain to change dramatically during his own lifetime.

"You are a direct descendant of Etienne Brûlé, one of the greatest explorers ever," his father had told him time and time again. "Your great grandpére Phillipe was with David Thompson when he discovered the Athabasca Pass to the Big Bend on the Columbia. True, you are Métis, but you must become more than that. The time of the Indian in this land will not last, and neither, I'm thinking, the way of the Métis. Education, Luc. You must have it, and you will!"

And I have, he thought with a wry grin that encompassed both the present and the past. But it was not exactly in line with the vision his father had held. Nor even the vision he, himself, had expected when he'd gone off as a youngster to seek his medicine in the Peigan fashion, to dream himself into manhood on a lonely promontory during the last few days before Otis Bennett had come into his life.

Pausing on a Helena street corner, Luc stared upward at the cloud-whipped moon. He saw the moon with his eyes, but in his mind he saw snippets of the vision that fasting and primitive belief had given him during his medicine dreams in the remote Rockies so long ago.

Mountain Chief, the wise old leader of his mother's people, had sympathized with the young L'Hirondelle's passion to avenge his father's murder. But the old Peigan had insisted the fourteen-year-old must first find himself, before setting out on such a vengeful mission.

"You are not yet a man, Eyes-like-ice," he had said. "There is bravery in what you intend, but it would be wrong for you to go about this in the white man's fashion . . . and it would get you killed. You must first purify yourself, then travel alone into the mountains to fast and seek your medicine. Without that, you would be going into battle not as a man, but as a boy. And a white boy, at that. Better you go with wisdom, strength, and a proper name . . . a man's name; a warrior's name."

Luc had remained mute, torn between his desire for vengeance and his desire to become a man.

"Do not be discouraged," Mountain Chief had told the disconsolate boy. "I will help you to prepare for this, and when it is done, when you have dreamed your medicine, I will be here to help you seek out the enemies who killed your father. They were men of the Chiniki Stoney. We know that. And already they are back north of the Bow River, safe among their own people. Alone, you would have no chance in this, but once you have your medicine, I will help you to find assistance from the Blackfoot and the Sarcee. There will be vengeance, Eyes-like-ice. I promise you. But first . . ."

First had been the rituals of purification, the lonely journey into the high country, the fasting, and—after hours that seemed like days, and days that seemed like seasons—the dreams and visions his fasting had produced. The educated Luc L'Hirondelle, even at fourteen, had recognized that what he would experience would be hallucinations brought on by his fasting, but the one-eighth pure Indian in his makeup could only *believe*. Horses . . . Wild horses of all sizes, all colors; these were the essence of Luc's dreaming. But through it all, two stood out from the rest with a startling, almost frightening clarity and intensity.

The first was a stallion, perhaps the most magnificent animal of its type in the world. Certainly more splendid than any horse the fourteen-year-old boy had ever seen, or even might have thought existed, and Luc L'Hirondelle had been raised amongst the Peigan—nomads who lived by the horse—who virtually worshipped fine horseflesh and whose horses were the equal of any on the prairies.

But no horse among the Peigan, or among the Blackfoot, the Bloods, or their enemies the Sioux and the distant Cheyenne, could equal the stallion of Luc's vision. He was an unusual blue roan color, but added to this was the distinctive blanket of white spots across his rump, the rump spots intrinsic to the famed buffalo runners and war ponies of the Néz Percé. A blue roan Appaloosa! And to further add to his uniqueness, he was a single-footer, a horse whose gait, could he ever be caught and broken, would provide the smoothest of rides, the greatest of endurance.

And he *could* be broken, *could* be caught. That was the wonder of Luc's medicine vision, that he, Luc L'Hirondelle would do that, would actually find the medicine horse, track it, follow it, capture and ride it.

Again, the tall Métis stared up at the moon. That much of his vision had indeed come true, although it had taken nearly half his adult life to accomplish it. That self-same stallion was in the livery barn only a few streets away at this very moment. And Luc had followed and captured the medicine horse exactly in the fashion related by his vision. Which could not explain why he had always assumed that the other horse significant in the dream was only that, a dream, a spiritual mystery that was intrinsic to his vision but . . . somehow . . . different.

Perhaps it was because the red mare in his dream had never seemed real even then, not in the way the great stallion had. She'd drifted in and out of his fasting visions, a dream within a dream, a racing mare with the cleanest, finest lines imaginable. A spirit mare, a magic mare, perhaps. He hadn't known then, and until tonight hadn't really considered the possible reality of his vision. Who, after all, had ever heard of a mare with a coat the color of a mountain sunset, the color of Rebecca Bennett's hair? Or a mare with violet eyes?

Luc had never in his dream captured the red mare; had never so much as tried. The mare possessed some fey quality that had dissuaded him, and that same quality struck him even more forcibly as he stared upward at the silvery shimmer of the moon. A moon that suddenly seemed tinged with violet. Like the eyes of the spirit mare. Like the eyes of Rebecca Susan Bennett, a vision stepped from his past to bind him to a blood oath and a debt she didn't know existed, and he couldn't forget.

A high wind whipped clouds across the sky to obscure the moon. Luc shivered, then bared strong white teeth in a derisive grin as he tried to laugh at himself. His white blood and education told him to dismiss such nonsense as superstition, but his Peigan heritage was strong, his memories stronger.

His spirit vision had taught him the ways of horses, taught him without real words or any visible, tangible instructor. Memory couldn't even tell him how many days and nights he'd spent under the spell of the fasting vision . . . four, five, six? . . . only that when it ended he had wakened thirsty, starving, limbs stiffened from immobility, cold from the exposure to mountain nights, and he *knew* that he now understood horses better than any man alive, Indian or white. Knew it, and as the years passed, came more and more firmly to believe it because it was nothing less than true.

No less true, but infinitely more important at the time, had been the scream of agony from a living horse, a scream that had yanked the fourteen-year-old boy back to a reality so terrifying it still had the capacity to give him nightmares. The scream had come from his own, real-world horse, a shaggy aging pinto about as far removed from the horses of his vision as could be imagined. The pinto was elderly, hammer-headed, rump-sprung and ugly—but his! Or so it had been until the roving grizzly bear had stumbled upon the hobbled, and therefore helpless, animal and staked its own claim with massive claws that smashed the Indian pony to the grass.

Body stiffened by his fasting ordeal, mind only half alive, the young Luc had rolled clumsily to grasp with fumbling fingers at the bow and quiver of arrows that lay beside him on his elk-hide robe. The arrows, his own, were only somewhat better than might have been expected from a craftsman of his age. But the bow was a gift from Mountain Chief, and as fine a weapon as could be found amongst the tribes. It was a heavy, horn-and-sinew-backed buffalo bow, a weapon so strong it was all Luc could do to string it, let alone draw the bow to its full power. But somehow he managed, and put four arrows into the bear before it could gallop close enough to smash the bow from Luc's fingers with one immense forepaw. Then the grizzly slashed ribbons of flesh from Luc's left upper arm and naked shoulder.

The blows drove Luc backwards, and he was doing his best

to scramble free when the now-dying mountain giant's head shot forth to grasp at his left thigh with fangs that had been designed to shear through the flesh and bone of moose, elk, or mighty buffalo. Only the luck—it hadn't been anything else and young Luc knew it—of his marksmanship saved him in the end. The fourth arrow had severed an artery. As the bear's great mouth gnashed at Luc's thigh, and as another blow from a forepaw laid gashes in his scalp and on down his back, the animal's roar of rage had faded to a grunt and died even as Luc fainted from the pain of his wounds.

He had wakened much later to find his legs still imprisoned by the immense bulk of the great bear, and the ground beneath them awash with both their blood. In the meadow below, his dying pony wheezed and whinnied in agony, but Luc was incapable of freeing even his own feet. Just the effort of raising his head to look toward the horse caused him to fall unconscious again.

When he *was* conscious, he maintained enough of a hold on reality to understand he would die, could do nothing else if he could not somehow free himself and find water. He wasn't going to bleed to death. He knew he would have done so already if that was the problem. But the thirst! Coupled with the privation of his fasting, the injuries caused by the bear were almost beyond tolerance. He could feel the infection raging through his wounds, could see the bad color surrounding the deep punctures in his thigh and the scratches across his arm. And try as he would, he simply could not find the strength to free himself from the great bear's deadly embrace.

He was conscious for the tenth, or perhaps hundredth time, trying to force his own death chant through thirst-thickened lips, past a tongue that seemed ready to choke him, when Otis

Bennett emerged from the forest and swore with shock at the scene of carnage.

The boy's camp was on a ridge top, and Otis was almost on top of it before he even knew it existed. There wasn't much to see, and most of that was dead. Otis didn't even see the boy at first, buried as his slight, teen-aged frame was beneath the body of a gigantic mountain grizzly that lay like some grotesque fur rug across the shattered remains of a primitive lean-to. And when he did see him, the prospector was certain the lad must be as dead as the old pinto pony sprawled nearby. His injuries were horrific.

The bear had slashed a sunburst pattern of deep gouges across the boy's neck and left shoulder; another blow had laid gashes in his scalp and down his back. But it was the bear's final, dying gesture that was the worst—the boy's left thigh was still crushed in its massive jaws.

Otis, stepping cautiously around to where he could see better, grunted at the sight, then grunted even louder as the boy's eyes flashed open at the sound. They were bright with fever. They registered something like recognition, then unfocused and closed again almost immediately. But clearly the boy was alive!

Whether he could survive having Otis drag the bear's carcass off him was another matter, but one without many options. The best Otis could manage was to be as gentle as possible in dislodging the animal's huge fangs from the lad's thigh before he started.

What followed was bush medicine at its most primitive. Otis got a fire going, found a battered tea pail in which to boil water, plundered his own meager supplies and the boy's camp for whatever might be useful, and began the laborious job of closing the wounds. He plucked hair from the dead pony's tail and used it to sew up the worst wounds, beginning with the ghastly thigh injury that went right to the bone.

The boy opened his eyes once during the process, then fainted again from the pain. In the days that followed, he mostly slept, half waking occasionally to rage and rave and wander through fevered dreams, hovering twixt life and death.

But he lived! So Otis had no moral choice but to nursemaid him, boiling broth from the meat of both pony and bear, sponging away the fever sweat, using the bear's thick pelt to warm the boy when he lapsed into chills. And finally, more than a week later, the pale eyes opened without the fever brightness, and the boy looked around, wary and cautious as a wild animal.

"Not fair if you die on me now, boy. Waste of time I could be using to get out, put together a new outfit and come back for that gold," Otis said, speaking his thoughts aloud.

The boy's silence hung between them as the pale eyes locked with Otis' own, then flickered in a series of glances that took in the makeshift camp, the thigh wound, the arm and shoulder bandages.

Unnerved by the feral stare, Otis pointed to himself. "Otis. Otis Bennett." Then he pointed to the boy, and waited.

Finally . . . "Luc. Luc L'Hirondelle."

"French?" Otis made no attempt to disguise his surprise.

"Métis."

That was about the extent of their verbal exchanges during the weeks that followed, weeks in which the boy slowly crept from near death to recovery. Otis spoke no French and the boy, Luc, apparently spoke no English. Indeed, he seldom spoke at all, save for a soft *Merci* where such was appropriate. He had the silent, enduring patience of some captured wild thing, ever alert, always watching.

Not that he was afraid; never did he show a single sign of fear. Of *anything*. Once the fever passed, he never once revealed a sign of pain—though there were times he must have been in agony—nor the slightest evidence of concern at his situation. Silent, stoic. But always alert, always . . . aware.

Gradually, life between them fell into a sort of pattern. Otis hunted; they both cooked; the boy tended the fire with wood Otis brought. The days passed and Luc became stronger; he managed to crawl, then to move upright, if falteringly. The makeshift crutch Otis made didn't please him; he crawled into a nearby thicket and emerged with a branch that suited him better after some whittling. The knife he carried was of better quality than Otis' own, and he kept it honed to a razor edge.

During the long recovery, Luc spent many hours using the knife to etch designs into the claws he had removed from the bear. Otis paid little attention, assuming he was merely making the claws into a necklace of some sort. Luc also repaired the fletching on the arrows damaged in the course of slaying the giant, painstakingly making new shafts to replace those broken in the animal's death fall.

This was something Otis could appreciate, and he did.

"You've got good hands, boy," he said one day. "Real talent, I'd say. 'Spect you're good with horses, too; your old pinto was sure enough well kept."

Luc appeared not to understand, indeed seemed uninterested. A crude sign language sufficed for both to get their messages across.

Otis was more voluble than Luc, although mostly he talked to himself in the way of men too long alone. Often, he spoke to the boy as he would have to his dog, or horse, speaking in a gentle, companionable voice and expecting neither interest nor understanding nor reply. Talking to himself, but . . . different.

And most of what he said, as the days dragged by and his impatience to be away intensified, focused on his desire to rustle up a fresh grubstake and return for the gold he'd found. He was unsure whether to continue on now to British Columbia or go straight home to St. Louis—a lengthy walk in either direction—but at least if he went home he would see the twin daughters he'd not seen in more than a year.

"Six of one; half a dozen of t'other," he said to himself and the silent Luc. "Be easier, I reckon, to get across these damned mountains to the gold fields whilst the weather holds, but then . . ."

He was no closer to a decision when the day of departure arrived, but the impatience remained. Luc still limped, but he, too, seemed eager to be on his way, so one morning they just . . . went, although not without an unexpected bit of ceremony.

Luc made no big show of presenting Otis with the finely etched bear claw he'd been working on so long, a dramatic scene of a wild stallion fighting a rope that snaked round the point of the claw. He just handed it over, almost dismissively.

Otis was touched, however, though unsure how to respond.

"Well thanks, boy," he eventually said, meeting the pale green eyes with a sober gaze of his own. "I will treasure this . . . 'pon my word I will."

Luc's soft *Merci* followed him as Otis plunged down off the ridge, heading mostly south to where he could re-establish his orientation and make the ultimate decision to then head west, or south and east.

Luc had watched the prospector go, then made a slow, thoughtful show of gathering his own meager possessions, glancing round the soon-to-be-abandoned campsite as if to fix it in his memory . . . the place of his dreaming . . . the very spot where he had become a man.

Once he was sure Otis was really on his way, however, he took on new energy, hobbling swiftly in a wide-ranging scout that focused on the direction Otis had come from originally. For one of Luc's experience, it was no great feat to pick up the other man's spoor; despite his injured leg he made it back to where the gold was hidden almost as quickly as Otis had originally moved away from it.

Then it was somewhat more difficult. His leg still caused him pain and upset his balance; he took longer than he would have expected to move the crude ingots into a hiding place of his own choosing. Not a great distance . . . still within the tiny valley. But hidden now so that neither Otis nor anyone else would find the gold except by the most astonishing luck.

Then Luc, also, departed the place of his medicine dreams, hobbling north by northeast toward the camps of the Peigan.

Luc could now grin at the memory. It had been a toss-up who had been more surprised. The white mountain man or the almost-delirious Métis boy with the pain-raddled eyes. But when Otis Bennett began to kneel beside the injured boy, gabbling to himself in sheer astonishment that the boy lived at all, Luc had been just aware enough to hide the fact he could understand the prospector's English.

And help had been given. Bennett had spent more than six weeks with him there on the tiny, isolated knoll, tending Luc's wounds, nursing him through the fevers of the infections that literally melted the flesh from his young frame, feeding him, bringing water and more water and still more water. Luc didn't remember much of it, certainly had no memory of the white man dragging the bear's carcass from him, or of the way he'd first treated the ghastly wounds by crudely sewing them shut with hairs plucked from the now-dead pinto's tail.

Luc did know that Bennett had dressed out the bear, saving the best cuts of the strong-flavored meat, knew Bennett had done the same with the pony, even to the extent of rigging frames of saplings on which to dry the meat and smoke it. But of the first fortnight, Luc had no proper memory, except of being too hot, too cold, too hungry, too thirsty; of bear-shaped demons that chewed upon his flesh and horse-shaped demons that trampled upon his broken, fang-gnashed thigh. And of other, formless demons whose talons ravaged the flesh of his chest and head and back.

There were vague, jumbled memories of fighting those demons, of screaming with pain and terror, of thrashing against the older man's efforts to hold him down, hold him motionless without re-opening the wounds. Eventually, Luc awoke to find the prospector squatting across the fire from him, humming a tuneless dirge before he'd looked up and smiled in his surprise that Luc had finally thrown off his fever and infections.

"You're tough, lad, I'll give you that," the prospector had said. "I did think for a time there that you'd go under, but I guess you'll live."

Which, Luc now reflected, was perhaps the longest single speech Otis Bennett made during their entire time together. Whatever else the old man had been, he wasn't much of a talker, except when he muttered to himself.

Otis Bennett was solitary, peculiar like so many of his breed, and definitely hiding something . . . something that accentuated the old man's usual paranoia beyond his normal caution. At the time, Luc had noted it and ignored it. Among his people a man's privacy was his own, to be recognized, understood, and above all, respected.

Now Luc found his memories of that time surprisingly clear. He could reconstruct Otis Bennett's face, almost hear the man's voice, could remember his complaints about being cut off from his companions while heading west to the British Columbia gold fields. Luc could remember filling in those long, idle hours while his leg healed, could even feel in his fingertips the effort that he had put into carving the bear's great claw, the one he had given to Otis Bennett, and had been mildly surprised at how much the white man seemed to appreciate the gesture.

To find the bear claw around the slender neck of Rebecca Bennett was a coincidence beyond superstition, beyond logic. She would have been . . . what? Perhaps four at the time he'd carved the claws. How unusual to find that Bennett had placed so much importance on Luc's gift. Almost as unusual as the girl's unique sunset hair and violet eyes.

And what was Luc supposed to do with her now? The decision to try and intervene with Cope had been a spur-of-the-moment one, ill-considered and, with hindsight, damned stupid. He'd have been better to concentrate on convincing Miss Bennett to hasten back to wherever she'd come from, taking her fear of Indians and her unruly nature with her.

Cope would help, of course. No way in the wide world would the great man consent to having Rebecca accompany his expedition, much-needed horses and wagons or not. Especially if Luc had a chance to put a word in the great man's ear before Rebecca started fluttering her eyelashes at him.

If she refused him her horses, we could always get others, he thought. And wagons, too, come to that. Or maybe we could take her as far as Fort Benton, put her on a downriver boat, and be done with it.

Luc heaved a deep sigh. It would not, could not, be that simple. He was blood-bound to assist her, one way or the other. Even if he could convince her to go back to civilization, he'd be honor bound to try and rescue her sister, and given the fact that Otis Bennett hadn't been able to find the girl in all these years . . .

"Well I can go where he could not," Luc muttered. "Risky, but better than seeing all that sunset hair on some Sioux war lance."

Alone, Rebecca had no chance at all. Given specific information about her sister's whereabouts and six regiments of cavalry to accompany her, she might succeed in finding Amy Bennett. But there was every chance the Sioux would kill their captive in the face of such odds.

Maybe, Luc thought, taking Rebecca with the Cope party wasn't such a bad idea after all. Cope would be seeing his share of Indians and more before the summer was out, and given Rebecca's fears, that alone might persuade her to change her mind. Even without Indians, the sheer hardships of the journey would be daunting. Getting to the headwaters of the Judith and the foothills of what the Blackfoot called *Kiyayo-otsii-stukists*, the Bear Paw, or Bear Hand Mountains, promised to be anything but an easy trek. Especially with wagons.

And if she wouldn't give it up? Luc shrugged inwardly at the knowledge that he would still have to help her.

"Horse-tamer, is it you?" The guttural question in slurred Blackfoot came from a shrunken figure huddled beneath a scabrous, filthy blanket just inside the entrance to an alley. "It *is* you," the wheezy voice continued without waiting for a reply. "Have you any whiskey for me?"

"Have you not had enough of the crazy water, grandfather?" Luc knew the answer before he spoke, knew the futility of even trying to argue. He recognized the old man, and knew there was no sense trying to free him from his addiction to the white men's liquor. It was all the old man had left in life.

Sleeping Fox was *Amiskapi-piskuni,* South Peigan, and had lost his entire family during the Baker Massacre six years before, when the American cavalry under Major Eugene Baker, seeking the winter camp of Mountain Chief and several suspected murderers, had made a stupid, deadly mistake. They had attacked the peaceful camp of South Peigan, led by Heavy Runner, and by the end of the slaughter, 173 men, women and children lay dead in the January snow.

Luc had been with neither band. Instead, he had been farther to the south, wintering in the Grand Canyon of the Colorado with a band of Havasupai. But he could have been, and in any event, the old man's suffering touched him.

"The crazy water will kill you someday, grandfather," he said sadly, but tossed a silver dollar to the shrunken figure. Grief would kill the old man anyway, with or without the whiskey to ease his pain. Sleeping Fox no longer cared about living. He had lost too many of his family, too many who were important to him.

"The one who follows may try to kill *you*, Horse-tamer." The guttural reply was accompanied by a hacking laugh. "You wear the white man's clothing . . . have you given away your Indian ears as well? I have watched this one coming along behind you like a hunting weasel, but all you can do is look at the ancestors in the sky."

"I thank you for the warning, grandfather," Luc said, forcing himself to keep his voice soft, his words in the same conversational tone he had been using all along. But he was far less calm as he made his polite farewells and continued moving down the street, keeping his pace casual, looking behind him with every sense but sight.

His ears were alert to any sound, but his mind also heard the mental curses he cast at himself for having gone to the governor's soirée unarmed. There was a knife in his boot-top, but if attacked from behind, he'd have no chance to reach it with his trousers worn outside his boots, and to make any move to change that situation might serve only to provoke such an attack. And why was he being followed in the first place? He had no enemies in Helena, or at least none he knew of.

Switching direction but maintaining his ambling pace, he began to lead his follower toward the darker edge of the town, where the livery stables were. It was a risk. Luc had thought first to wander back to the center of town, perhaps even enter a crowded saloon. But he discarded that plan almost immediately. While he could lose his follower by moving into a crowd, he wanted to know who was behind him and why. The other risk was that, even in a crowded saloon, a determined assassin might reach him too easily. Innocent men died all too often in mining-town brawls.

Strolling along his chosen route, he could now *feel* the presence of his pursuer, was at last certain the old Peigan hadn't been indulging in fire-water fancies. Again, Luc cursed himself for a fool. He'd let his mind get so bound up in memories, he'd forgotten about the men he'd noticed earlier on Rebecca Bennett's trail. Was this man from the same crew? Unlikely to be anyone else, Luc thought, as he stepped into the shadowy stretches beside the livery barns. Of course, there was always the chance it was a simple case of someone seeing a well-dressed stranger, an easy target for a mugging. No. There had been ample opportunities for that already. Whoever followed him had something else in mind. But what?

And who? That's what he really wanted to know, he thought, reaching the side of the barn where his blue roan stallion was held in a strong box stall for its own safety and that of anyone visiting the stable. The roan was a trained Peigan warhorse, and had no tolerance for strangers of any color. He had almost trampled a curious stable hand down in Wyoming territory the year before, and Luc now took great care to avoid such problems.

He whispered to the stallion as he slid through the open side door of the barn, his voice inaudible to human ears, but sufficient to alert the stallion to his presence and carry a warning of impending danger. As Luc tiptoed past the stallion's stall, silently lifting the latch rail as he passed, he heard the horse turn to face the front, heard the low *whuuff* as it tested the air.

Luc sped to the far side of the barn, moving silently on soft straw to where his memory told him a pitchfork was racked on the wall beside the main doors. Then he slid into the shadows and waited, silently inching his hand down to free the knife from his boot-top, his senses alert to the shadows behind him.

It wasn't much of a plan, he realized, but it was all he had available, and the primary requisite—patience—he held in abundance. In the end, it took less time than he'd expected, given the expertise of his stalker.

A small man slid through the arched doorway, knife in hand. Luc saw only a shadow among others, caught only the faintest glimpse of the knife blade. But his stallion had much more finely tuned senses and could see better in the dark.

The stallion saw the man, saw the knife, and was raging his way through the loosened stall gate before either human realized what was happening. The abruptness of the stallion's screaming charge and the fact that the gate was hinged on the small man's side was all that saved the man. The gate smashed him back through the open doorway, which stopped the stallion—and Luc—from following.

The small man cried out in surprise and fled before Luc could get past his still-raging stallion and attempt to give chase. Nor did he bother. It might be vaguely possible, he thought for just an instant, to let the stallion pursue the attacker. The horse had a better nose than most hounds and would have relished the idea, but it was hardly a practical notion.

Instead, Luc re-stabled the animal and spent time talking quietly, calming, soothing. Then Luc barred the stall gate behind him and knelt to gather up the knife the man had dropped when the heavy gate had flung him backwards, inches ahead of the stallion's furious teeth. Luc had gained only the briefest glimpse of his stalker, but that sighting, combined with the evidence now in his hand, was sufficient to provoke a good deal of speculation.

Cautious, alert to any attack, Luc took time to examine the spurless boot tracks outside the doorway before taking a roundabout route to his hotel. The tracks were unquestionably among those he'd seen when he'd backtracked to where Otis Bennett had been tortured.

"I should know that man," Luc muttered under his breath as he walked swiftly but still cautiously. "I should know him, but I can't think why, except that he was among those who crucified Bennett. And probably with this very knife."

So there was the link, tenuous at best, but solid enough to make him wonder. The torture of Otis Bennett, marauders tracking Rebecca Bennett's every move—and now this attack— was enough to make Luc change his plans again. Moving quickly, he made his way to his hotel and belted on his revolver.

8

Seated inside the governor's carriage, Rebecca arrived back from the soirée just as Luc reached the front of the boarding-house, and he sighed with relief.

"Damn it, I should have gone straight back to the soirée and stayed with her," he murmured under his breath. "It's her they're after. It has to be!"

It was stretching coincidence far too much to have it any other way. She had been watched ever since her arrival in Helena, if not before. She had been at the soirée, which was the only place Luc, logically, could have picked up his own fol-lower. The two things had to be intertwined.

But why? What on earth could Rebecca have that would war-rant such interest in the first place? A dead father, a couple of guns she might or might not be able to use, her wagons and livestock, and a sister captured by Indians so long ago as to be irrelevant now.

It had to be more than that . . . And then he knew . . .

It was ridiculous, but there could be no other explanation. Bennett's gold—a legend created by the old man himself, usu-ally discounted and scoffed at, but like all treasure legends, granted a life of its own just through the telling and retelling. And this time, of course, true—Luc knew that all too well.

Luc reached up to hand Rebecca down from the carriage, engulfing her small hand in his own, but meeting her eyes for only a moment before instinct had him scanning the street around them for some sign that either or both were still under surveillance. Which they were. There wasn't a red-blooded man within sight of Rebecca's gleaming hair and petite figure who wasn't fixated on the vision of her descending from the carriage. Even the governor's youthful driver was intent on the scene, the expression on his face clearly revealing his envy that another man should be greeted with such a dazzling smile.

And dazzling her smile was. Caught in its radiance, Luc allowed himself the briefest indulgence, a moment to drink in her youthful beauty. Then he tore himself free from her gaze and resumed his suspicious scanning of the late-night crowds. He was so intent on that, he might have missed what she said but for the excitement in her voice.

"I've spoken to Mr. Cope, Mr. Swallow, and I'm sure . . . almost sure, anyway . . . that he'll find a place for me."

The words were uttered as soon as her tiny, booted feet touched the boardwalk. Luc could have kicked himself for it, but his response shot out before he could curb his tongue.

"And I suppose you did it right in front of the governor. You're a damned fool, Miss Bennett. If Governor Potts demands it, and he very well might, Cope will drop you so quick it'll make your head swim. Why do you think I wanted you to leave it to me? Damn it, woman, haven't we got enough trouble?"

"*We* have no trouble at all, except I'd prefer you keep your hands off me," she snapped, wrenching herself free from his grip. "I am fully capable of doing my own negotiating with Mr. Cope, or the governor, or anyone else."

"Including whoever's been following you, and who not twenty minutes ago tried to stick a knife in me? You have all sorts of trouble, Miss Bennett, and half the problem is that you don't even know it."

"Knife?"

She gasped, and Luc could see the fear that shrouded that

single word. At least the haughty antagonism had been washed from her features.

"This knife," he said, deliberately keeping his voice low and shielding the gesture with his jacket as he lifted the throwing knife from his belt. "The man didn't connect, so you needn't worry about that."

"But . . ."

"But nothing. Except I'm moral certain you've got something to do with it, even if you don't know why. Your father was tortured with a knife, the way I heard it, and whoever went after me did so after I'd left the governor's party. I don't know what the hell's going on, but I'd bet my saddle you're at the center of it."

His fingers closed firmly upon her hand as he turned and began moving her toward the entrance to the building. He would get her tucked away safely in her room. Then he'd find Sleeping Fox and pray he'd been sober enough to have noticed more about Luc's assailant than Luc had. Pray the old Indian was still sober enough to divulge that information. Pray . . .

"Mr. Swallow? Mr. Swallow!" Rebecca had to repeat herself before she could be certain of gaining her surly escort's attention, or at least the portion of it not devoted to scanning the street. "You are hurting me," she said, tugging against his steely grip to emphasize her words.

His handclasp eased slightly, certainly not enough to release her, and Rebecca was suddenly conscious of the way his other hand hovered near his thigh, where the butt of a revolver was evident.

"I'm sorry," he said, clearly not sorry in the least. "I'll see you to your room, now. And quickly, if you don't mind."

"And then?" There was no tremor in her voice, nothing like the tremor she could feel inside her. Lucas Swallow was serious, deadly serious. Prepared to accept his tale of her being followed, she was equally afraid of what it might portend.

"And then I have things to do," he replied. "A man to see, for a start, and preparations to make for tomorrow, assuming my employer survives tonight with enough energy to make his early start. And you, Miss Bennett, had best get what sleep you can. Dawn isn't that far off."

"Sleep?" She made no attempt to keep the fear out of her voice, and it rose as she tried to free her hand and talk to him at the same time. "How can you tell me I'm in danger of being attacked and expect me to forget it and go to sleep?"

Swallow stood there, ramrod straight, still holding her hand, his face . . . his nose . . . probing the breeze. It took only an instant before she could smell it, too, and only a brief moment longer before the shambling, blanket-wrapped figure of an old Indian reeled into sight behind his unwashed, whiskey-sodden odor.

The Indian's eyes were bleary, yet somehow ferocious in the dim light. They seemed to glare with madness, to project such vehemence that Rebecca found herself leaning into the protection of Swallow. Then she gagged against the old Indian's smell as his mouth opened to reveal his teeth and intensify, were that possible, the overpowering odor of him—the smell of filth, of whiskey, of rancid grease and dry, dusty age.

But it was more than the old man's repulsive appearance, more than his repulsive odor. Rebecca was suddenly shaken by pure, simple terror, the same terror Lucas Swallow had claimed he could smell in her memories. In the old warrior's eyes she saw no humanity, only raging flames and murderous hatred. No mercy, only madness of fire and terrorizing war whoops. No compassion. Only flashing knives and powder-smoke and rearing, snorting ponies. And blood . . . so much blood . . .

Words, guttural and totally incomprehensible to Rebecca,

emerged from that awful mouth, but they were cut off as a rumble of comparable gibberish came forth in Lucas Swallow's distinctive voice. And now, finally, Swallow did release her, so that his hands could be free to flutter some spell at the apparition who faced them.

The old man replied, or so it seemed to her. Certainly he nodded as if he'd understood Swallow. Then his own aged hands danced a waltz, a quadrille, perhaps even a Virginia reel, creating incomprehensible patterns, fanning the air between the two men.

Lucas Swallow's incantations must have been stronger, because the old man abruptly turned and stumbled into the narrow alleyway beside the building.

"What was . . ." She got no further before Swallow's hand once again captured her own, before he tugged and towed her toward the door. Impatience was obvious in his grip, in his entire attitude.

"Bedtime, Miss Bennett," he growled.

When she attempted to protest, tried to free her throbbing fingers, he only clasped her more tightly, using the sheer power of his strength to silence her objections.

"You are going to your room now," he said, his voice as patiently firm as if he were addressing a child. "You are going to do it without any further arguments, and you are going to stay there until I come for you. Is that clear?"

The street door had opened to his thrusting shoulder, and when Rebecca angrily tried to hold herself against the opening, to pit her flimsy strength against his, he merely yanked, then gathered her into his arms as she popped through the doorway like a dizzy cork.

"Which room?" he asked.

Through her gown, she could feel the hard, rippling muscles of his chest. "I . . . I . . ."

She couldn't give him the right directions. It was as if he had stolen her intellect and was crushing it along with her ribs. Her tongue fluttered inside her mouth and her brain fluttered with it, incapable of reason or logic.

"Which room, damn it? I'm running out of time here," he snapped. Somehow, she managed to point. Somehow, she managed to guide him as he maneuvered his way down the corridor, up the rickety stairs to the second floor. Inside the small room, he shifted her weight only enough so that he could thrust her into the room's single chair, still hanging onto her, still holding her attention with his pale, vivid eyes.

"Your father's guns . . . are they here?" he asked. "Could you use them if you had to?"

"I . . . well . . . yes . . . of course. But . . ."

"Show me!"

He waited with a predatory patience as she crossed the room, fumbled through her luggage, and emerged with her father's revolver, gigantic in her hands. She was amazed to see it almost disappear in the comparative largeness of his grip. He spun the cylinder, checked the weapon over carefully, then returned it to her in a gesture both cautious and thoughtful.

"If anyone but me tries to come through that door, you use this," he ordered in tones that brooked no argument, no opposition. "If you don't know who it is, just shoot and keep on shooting until this gun is empty. Although . . ." he favored her with a quick, brittle grin ". . . I doubt you'll need to worry. I won't be very long and I don't expect any problems."

"But can't you tell me what's going on?" she cried as he turned to leave the room. "You chastise me in front of the governor, or the governor's driver, which is the same thing. You say *I'm* being followed and *you're* being followed. Damn it, you can't just walk out and leave me without any explanation!"

"I don't have any explanations, Miss Bennett, just a whole lot of coincidences that shape up to trouble. I'll be back soon, and hopefully I'll be able to tell you more. For now, keep your father's gun handy and use it if you have to, only not on me when I return, if you please."

The door shut behind him. Rebecca looked down at the huge revolver in her hand, and all she could think to do was prop the chair against the door and retreat to the far side of the room.

Seated on the bed, the gun by her side, she closed her eyes to ease the whirlwind of her thoughts, then opened them again because the darkness her shut eyes created wasn't darkness at all, but brilliant, searing memories of . . .

"The Indian!" As she cried out the words, she realized where Lucas Swallow was going, and who he was going to see. She rose from her bed and crept through the dim room until she'd reached the window that overlooked the alley where the old man had disappeared.

It took only a moment to ease the window upwards, which gave her access to the muted, unintelligible sounds of the conversation below.

Carefully, she eased her head through the opening to where she could see, but the tableau beneath her only added to her confusion.

Sleeping Fox huddled in a malodorous slump against the wall of the boardinghouse. Only his eyes, bright in the reflected moonlight, revealed that he was even alive. His eyes and the almost inaudible chant he crooned beneath his breath. Luc stiffened as he drew close enough to hear the sound . . . the old man's death chant.

"I am ashamed, Horse-tamer," Sleeping Fox said, abandoning the chant as Luc approached. "I must beg for help from you, which is not as it should be, but I am an old man and there is no other way."

"Are you drunk, grandfather?" Luc stepped closer and settled on his heels to bring him to the old man's level.

"I am drunk with anger, Horse-tamer. There is one I must kill, and these old hands are not enough, I think. Have you a gun, a knife, any weapon you can spare me?"

The old eyes were lowered in what Luc realized was indisputably a sense of shame, and the old hands were trembling as much from that as from age and the ravages of drink.

"I do not like to beg, but . . ." Sleeping Fox's voice trailed off.

"They will hang you if you kill somebody here, grandfather. Can you not tell me more of this? I truly do not understand."

"It is the one who killed my wife, Grass Moving." The old man's voice was harsher now, his breath exploding in foul-scented gasps. "The one who killed her and the children, the man who cut off her breasts to make a tobacco pouch. He is here, in a saloon not far away. I am going to kill him. If they hang me, it does not matter."

"Are you certain it is the same man? It was a long time ago, the massacre, and many of the whites look alike."

"I am sure. Six years is not so long when you are my age, Horse-tamer. I have waited with his face always before me in my mind. It is the same one, and I am going to kill him."

"Still a soldier, a long-knife?" Luc played for time. He knew that any attempt Sleeping Fox might make to kill a soldier in downtown Helena would serve only to speed the old man's own death.

"No, Horse-tamer. The soldier who butchered Grass Moving is a wolfer now. A stinking poisoner of carcasses." The old man spit his disgust through his teeth. "And maybe one of those who seek the yellow metal. It does not matter. I have waited these many seasons, and I must at least try to kill him. You know this is true, Horse-tamer. Will you help me? Not to kill him, of course, but can you give me a weapon? I am afraid my old hands are not strong enough."

The decision was more instinctive than thoughtful. Even before he realized what he was doing, Luc reached beneath his coat for the haft of the throwing knife he'd picked up in the livery barn.

"I cannot give you my gun," he said, fingers adroitly spinning the knife to send it quivering into the ground at the old man's feet.

"This is enough," Sleeping Fox grunted, reaching out to retrieve the razor-sharp knife from the dirt. He lifted it for a brief inspection, then tested the edge against a callused thumb. "This you took from the one who followed you," he said, and it wasn't a question.

"What can you tell me about him, grandfather? My war horse won the knife, but I did not get a good look at the one who carried it. Do you know him?"

"He is one who follows *Le Carcajou*. He is the little *mestizo* who dresses always in black and who carries many knives. They are whiskey traders and thieves, you must know this. I do not think he wanted to kill you tonight. He had many chances to do that before you knew he was there. But I think he would like to fight you, Horse-tamer."

Of course! The throwing knife made some sense, Luc thought, if not the kind of sense that would provide him with all the answers . . . but yes! *Le Carcajou.* Dover Sugden. And the little Spanish half-breed? Sebastian? Yes, Luis Sebastian, whose reputation had been built upon his knives. And blood.

The verminous blanket rose as Sleeping Fox lifted himself unsteadily to his moccasined feet.

"It has to do with your sunset woman," the old man mumbled. "I do not know why, but others of *Le Carcajou* have been watching her."

"She has a sister who was taken by the Bloods many years ago and is now supposed to be with the Sioux. Have you heard of this?"

"Yes, Horse-tamer. She is . . ." Sleeping Fox made two abrupt gestures in the sign language of the plains Indians. One signified madness, the other evil. "Even for Medicine Calf's people she was too . . ." Again, he gesticulated, this time the signs for evil and blood. "Medicine Calf traded her to the Sioux to get rid of her." The old man shivered. "She is very bad medicine, Horse-tamer. But that is all I can tell you now. I must find the wolfer I am going to kill."

He lurched past Luc, aiming unsteadily toward the mouth of the alley, his death song reforming beneath his breath. Luc let him pass, but spoke quickly before the old man turned into the shadows along the street.

"Good luck, grandfather. If the white soldiers do not hang you for killing the wolfer, come to the valley of the Judith, the *Otachkui-itachta,* or to the Bear Paw Mountains, the *Kiyayo-otsii-stukists.* I will be there with the one who searches for the old bones."

"If I live, I will perhaps be there before you," the old man replied. "And if I do not . . . well, it does not matter so much as long as the wolfer I seek does not live, either. Do you want this knife back, or can I leave it in his belly?"

"Do what you will, grandfather."

Luc watched as the old Peigan slid from sight into the shadows, leaving only his odor and the shadowy tendrils of his death chant. Then Luc walked swiftly in the other direction, to where Rebecca Bennett waited for answers he couldn't supply. And, he thought, probably waited with answers of her own, whether she knew it or not. There was something here he felt he should understand, and when he reached the front of the building he paused to smoke a cheroot. At the same time, he watched the street around him and considered the situation.

The name Dover Sugden was known to him, although he had never met the man or his half-breed lieutenant. Sugden was a former jayhawker, an outlaw, a whiskey trader, and a scoundrel by any standard. But why would he have an interest in Rebecca's movements? The gold? Surely not.

Luc suddenly snapped away the almost-finished cigar. It could be nothing else! Ridiculous, perhaps, but given Sugden's reputation and his relative newness to the northern mountains, it made just enough sense.

Rebecca eased shut the window of her room after Lucas Swallow and the Indian left the alley. Then she slumped back onto the bed in her darkened room. Her mind still whirled with confusion and her nose still twitched from the Indian's noxious odor. It was a stench she couldn't help contrasting with the unusual but strangely compelling smell of Swallow when he had gathered her so closely against him. His smell was clean, fresh, and yet . . . different. Like fine old leather, she thought, but not quite.

However, what bothered her the most was the extraordinary scene she had just witnessed, the quite illogical but undeniable liaison she had seen between Lucas Swallow and the old Indian.

She found herself half ready to disbelieve that she'd heard such animal sounds in Swallow's distinctive voice, even less ready to accept that she'd seen him treating the repugnant figure of the old man with such obvious respect. And she simply could not believe he'd actually given the old man a knife!

"But he did," she whispered. "He did. I saw him." And this, she thought, was the man she had so readily accepted as a protector, as someone who had seemed ready to help her. A civilized, maybe even cultured, man.

Now she was disconcerted, her entire response to the tall,

pale-eyed Lucas Swallow thrown into question. The fact that earlier she had felt so attracted to him in a physical sense didn't help. It only made her perplexity worse.

When she heard his quiet knock at the door, knowing it was his knock even before she heard him whisper her name, her first response was panic. Plucking up the heavy pistol, oblivious to the lack of logic in opening the door at all, she flung away the chair and was back across the room, pistol aimed, before Swallow entered the room.

"I think," she said grimly, pointing the heavy revolver at his lean, narrow waist, "that you owe me some sort of explanation."

"No question of that." His gaze flickered to the wavering gun muzzle, and yet he seemed to ignore the danger, even to dismiss it. "But I reckon you have more answers than I have. Let's start with the name Dover Sugden. Mean anything to you? Anything at all?"

"I've never heard the name before. Should I have?" *You're supposed to be afraid,* she thought, astonished that he could ignore her weapon and slouch comfortably against the doorjamb.

"What about Luis Sebastian? Little, Spanish-looking fellow, not much bigger than you, always dresses in black, carries enough knives to carve up half the country?"

"No." She took a deep breath. "But while we're on the subject of knives, perhaps you'd explain why you gave a knife to that filthy old Indian. And don't bother to deny it, either."

His glance at the window was so swift she almost missed it, but his wry grin lasted a moment longer.

"Watching, were you? I thought so. Well, let's put it this way, Miss Bennett. If your grandfather came to you and asked to borrow a knife, would you not give him one if you had it?"

Nothing in his demeanor had prepared her for such a reply, for the shocking mental images it provoked.

"Grandfather? I don't understand. Are you telling me you're

related to that filthy, stinking old man?"

"That filthy, stinking old man is human, just like us," Swallow said in a voice chillingly calm, chillingly accusatory. "And you're being extremely judgmental. You'd be filthy and stinking, too, if you'd spent nearly six years trying to drown your sorrows in drink. But to answer you directly . . . no, we're not related. For me to call him grandfather is a term of respect among his people, and he is a man worthy of respect, regardless of present appearances. If you should see old Sleeping Fox again, which you may before the summer's out, I expect you'll see a different person."

Taken aback by his attitude, Rebecca could think of no logical reply, could only repeat herself. "I don't understand. Why did you give him the knife?"

"Because he asked for it. I just hope he uses it wisely and doesn't do something that will get him hanged."

"Hanged? You gave that old man a knife knowing it could get him hanged? What do you expect him to do with it, for goodness' sake? Kill somebody?"

Swallow shrugged, but the gesture didn't contain the sort of indifference it would normally have implied. Rebecca thought there was an elemental, almost eternal weariness, an acceptance of the inevitable.

"Hopefully, Miss Bennett, he'll manage to do what he has to do in such a way that he doesn't get caught."

"Kill somebody," Rebecca repeated, her own mind going strangely numb at this extraordinary conversation. She looked down to see that she'd allowed the gun to slump into her lap, and she raised it again. "I suppose you have someone specific in mind for him to kill, Mr. Swallow! Or will anybody do?"

"Someone very specific, but his choice, not mine. And someone who damned well needs killing. I'd be inclined to do it myself if I knew who the bastard was, but I wouldn't want to deprive old Sleeping Fox of the satisfaction. He's waited long enough."

Rebecca felt her own eyes widen at having correctly read the savage intensity that seemed to glow from Swallow's eyes like . . . like foxfire. There was no mistaking that look. His eyes had gone colder than ice, colder than death itself.

"I believe you would enjoy it," she snapped.

"No, I would not enjoy it. No sane person enjoys killing another human being, no matter how justified. But I'd do it, just as I'd put down a rabid dog. For your information, Miss Bennett, Sleeping Fox won't enjoy it, either. I used the word satisfaction, not pleasure."

"As if there was some significant difference! And if this person is so deserving of being killed, Mr. Swallow, then surely it is a matter for the law, the authorities, not . . ."

"Law? There is no law here if you're an Indian. The man Sleeping Fox wants to kill *was* the law, in the sense that he was a soldier when he slaughtered the old man's wife and children, slaughtered and mutilated them as if they were animals . . . less than animals."

"Slaughtered?"

"The Baker massacre, Miss Bennett, where the illustrious American cavalry raided a peaceful camp of South Peigan and wiped out one-hundred-and-seventy-three men, women and children. Not all that far from here, I might add, and not that long ago, at least not to Sleeping Fox. He saw a cavalry man cut off his wife's breasts, saw the same man smash his youngest child's brains out against a lodgepole. Law? Don't make me laugh."

Rebecca closed her eyes, as much to try and shut out the images as to free herself from the derision in Swallow's voice. She could comprehend vengeance, but this was beyond vengeance. It was too real, too bloody.

Opening her eyes, she looked up again, half expecting to find Swallow transformed into the beast his voice portrayed. But he still leaned against the door frame, his chest heaving as if he'd run a mile.

"Wouldn't you want to kill someone," he asked, "if you found yourself up against those who tortured your father?"

"I don't know." Without information and opportunity, retaliation was hollow thinking, unrealistic, unreal. "If what you say is true, I can sort of understand the old man's attitude. What I don't understand is how you fit into it all. You say he's your grandfather, but then you say he isn't. And he can't be. He's an Indian!"

"It's not anything *you* would understand."

Luc was suddenly aware that he might have said too much. Or perhaps not enough. These were not the right things to be saying to this beautiful young woman with her instinctive fear of Indians. For an instant he wished he had already revealed his true identity, had cleansed the air of the suspicion he could still see in her eyes. But now was not the time.

"You're hiding something from me," she said. "And it's more than just this business of me being followed by people I've never heard of, isn't it?"

"You are being followed," he replied quickly, thankful for any chance to change the subject, to get back to the real and present danger he perceived. "Sleeping Fox told me that, even told me who. And it makes sense, in a peculiar sort of way."

"To you, perhaps, but I honestly don't . . ."

"Sugden and his gang are after your father's 'Spanish' gold," he interrupted, and watched her expressive face register astonishment, fear, then suspicion. "Don't tell me you thought it was a secret? Good lord, woman, everybody in the territory knows about Otis Bennett's lost gold mine. What amazes me is that Sugden's band of cutthroats would take it seriously enough to have tortured your father. And now, I reckon, they hope to get the secret out of you."

Rebecca could only sit there, mute, her mind spinning. Her father's secret was no secret at all?

"It's almost as well-known a tale as the Lost Lemon Mine," Swallow continued, then bending the truth considerably, "And about as likely, I would have thought."

The silence drew round them like an inky blanket in the dimness of the room. Only Swallow's pale eyes seemed untouched by it. They glowed with an unholy light. Dangerous eyes, knowing eyes.

"So," he finally said, "there is something to the story, and you know what it is, and Sugden knows that you know, or at least thinks you do, which is just as bad." He chose his words carefully, hiding his own real knowledge in a bid for more information.

Rebecca said nothing, could say nothing, wouldn't have trusted herself to speak even if her numb brain could have found any words. She could only watch Swallow unexpectedly grin.

"Well, Miss Bennett, if nothing else you've convinced me to find some way to make sure you have a place in the expedition. I have no choice but to go with Cope, and I can't leave you here, not with a clear conscience. Unless, of course, you're prepared to abandon this foolishness and put yourself under the governor's protection until you can safely return to wherever you came from."

He didn't make that suggestion a question, not really, and it seemed he knew even before Rebecca herself what her reply might be.

"Didn't think so," he muttered, although nothing in his features registered the disapproval obvious in his voice. "Well then, my dear Miss Bennett, I can only suggest you plunk yourself back on that bed and get some sleep while I try to figure out how we're going to convince the illustrious Mr. Cope to take you with us."

Still ignoring the gun in Rebecca's hand, Swallow flung himself into the room's single chair. Then, propping his booted feet against one wall, he leaned back into a precarious balance.

"Are you quite mad?" The words emerged almost as a squeak, but that was nothing compared to the astonishment Rebecca felt rising inside her. "Surely you can't expect to sit *there* all night!"

"I could join you on the bed, but I believe you might find that even less acceptable. Or would you?"

"You are being quite ridiculous, as well as insulting. Just leave, please, or would you rather I used this?" She glanced down at her revolver, clenched in both hands, aimed directly at his middle.

Swallow's movements were like that of a striking snake. One instant he was balanced on the chair with his feet against the wall, the next he stood in front of her. His hands held her hands . . . and the gun, which was now turned away from them.

"What I'd rather," he said grimly, "is that you didn't damned well lie to me. You said you knew how to use this gun, but you've been sitting there waving it around, trying to threaten me with it, and it isn't even cocked. What were you going to do? Throw it at me?"

Rebecca's silence was answer enough.

"Do you, or do you not, know how to use this gun?" he demanded, the weapon in his hand, plucked from her nerveless fingers before she could resist.

"I . . . I . . . of course I do. I just . . . forgot . . . that's all."

"You forgot. Has it occurred to you that such a convenient lapse of memory could get you killed? Or worse?"

There was no sensible reply and they both knew it.

"No final word, Miss Bennett? Good. Now go to bed. Dawn

will be here soon enough and I think you'll need what sleep you can get."

"But I can't sleep in this!" Her hand gestured along the lines of her blue velvet gown.

"Take it off. You'll have to sometime. Unless you plan to wear it on your journey to Fort Benton?"

"But—"

"I'll turn my back. There . . . does that suit you?"

"I'd rather you left the room."

Rebecca might as well have spoken to the wall.

Getting out of her gown, at best not an easy task, became an ordeal. Her fingers trembled, and she didn't dare take her eyes off Swallow's broad shoulders and rugged back. It seemed to take her ages, but eventually she managed to get the gown over her head and was buried beneath the covers almost before the crumpled velvet landed on the foot of the bed.

Swallow didn't move.

"You can turn around now," she said, and could have kicked herself. What difference did it make to her if he wanted to sleep standing up? Damn the man anyway!

"Took you long enough," he said. "I hope you manage better on the trail or we'll be a long time getting anywhere. You sure you don't want me to tuck you in and kiss you goodnight?"

"I've given you the benefit of the doubt in everything you've told me so far, Mr. Swallow, so don't start playing the dunce!"

He flashed her a cat grin, then threw himself back into the chair. An instant later his feet were propped against the door, his hat over his eyes.

When, or even whether he slept, she didn't know, but sleep came slowly to Rebecca. She kept sneaking peeks at his lanky figure, as aware of him as if he had been in the bed with her, and yet strangely certain she was in no immediate danger from this enigmatic man.

Just before she fell into a troubled slumber, she wondered what he might have done had she reacted differently to his final suggestion, and such thoughts were not conducive to peaceful slumber. She found her undergarments . . . prickly, her skin beneath them supersensitive—and too warm by half.

It was disconcerting to glance over at Lucas Swallow and immediately feel her nipples throb against the weight of the dress fabric against them, to feel her thighs suddenly tingling, the pit of her tummy adrift in a sea of butterflies.

She reached down beneath the covers, her fingers guided by instinct, the gesture somehow enhanced by the excitement—she was watching *him* . . . was he also watching her? She couldn't know, but she could imagine, and she did. Vividly.

The entire experience was new to her, and she could only be guided by instinct. She didn't exactly trust her instincts, lest they—like her body—betray her, lead her into forbidden places, forbidden thoughts.

9

The sun at dawn bloodied the sky, as if some gigantic cat had swiped at its paling features then swished the bloody lines into intricate patterns with one huge paw. Rebecca saw nothing ominous, and was reassured by the promise of fair weather.

Lucas Swallow had awakened before her, assuming he'd slept at all in what must have been an uncomfortable makeshift position.

"You look like a child when you're asleep, did you know that?" he asked before her eyes were even properly open, before she'd had time to notice the bleeding sky. And while it may have seemed like a question, he didn't give her time to respond before he continued, "You kept hugging your pillow, Miss Bennett. Did you think it was me?"

She was certain he could see the pink rising along the column of her throat, sneaking up from a bosom which thankfully he could not see. "I hardly think so, Mr. Swallow!"

"Believe me, I almost made it so. That is without doubt the hardest chair in creation. I've ridden ridge-backed, ornery nags over broken ground with less discomfort."

"Had you tried to climb into my bed, you'd have found it even less comfortable," Rebecca managed.

"I'd have been warmer, and horizontal. And now that we've settled that question . . . for the moment . . . might I suggest you get yourself out of your warm bed and organized for our departure? *I'm* going to organize breakfast. Then I'll track down my employer and see if I can convince him we have little choice but to take you along to the Bear Paws."

There was no hint of a tease in Swallow's voice.

"I suppose I haven't made it any easier for you," she said bluntly, aware that her attempts last night might well have made his task more difficult.

Swallow only shrugged as he stretched his lean body upward, shaking his head as if to relieve a crick in his neck. "We'll just have to see. It was never going to be easy."

"What if you can't do it?"

"I've either got to make sure you're with us or safely back where you came from, and I'm committed to Mr. Cope. I gave my word, and I don't break it lightly. On the other hand, I can't, in all conscience, leave you to deal with Dover Sugden and his cutthroats, which is what would happen if I just up and left. If they've got the idea you know the secret of your father's gold mine, you won't be safe anywhere west of St. Louis."

He looked down at her, his eyes roving along her slender figure as if her bedclothes and nightgown didn't exist, and Rebecca couldn't help the immediate reaction his attitude caused—mixed excitement with a strange form of panic that wasn't from fear alone.

"Fact is, Miss Bennett, you might be temptation enough for them without the gold, and even here in town there's a limit to what protection the governor can provide. And, of course, I'd expect that as soon as we were two miles down the trail you'd be looking for a way to follow, or go off on some harebrained scheme of your own, either of which would suit Sugden and his crew just fine. A logical person would remember what they did to your father, but you're a woman and logic doesn't enter into it much."

"Now you are being insulting again," she said hotly.

"I'm being honest. Get yourself together and we'll continue

this discussion over breakfast. At least in public I'll be able to keep myself from paddling your pert little rump."

With which words he sauntered out of her room, pausing only to cast a suspicious glance up and down the hallway before he gently closed the door behind him. Rebecca could both sense and see the change in him, the subtle shift from man to predatory animal as he seemed to sniff the air, his hand only inches from his holstered revolver.

She shivered slightly in the wake of his departure, then shook her mane of long hair as if that action alone could remove his aura within the suddenly larger room. Man or animal, it made no real difference. Lucas Swallow was no gentleman, although he gave a mighty fair interpretation of the role when he chose to.

Which, not surprisingly, was the choice he'd made by the time she joined him and the illustrious Mr. Cope and his assistant Charles Sternberg at the breakfast table. Even Mr. Cope's genteel Quaker manners were nothing compared to the veneer of sophistication and breeding Lucas Swallow displayed. He was on his feet at her appearance before either of the others could even move their chairs. Then he was holding *her* chair with a superficial bow, as much the perfect maitre d' as the perfect host, his smile broad and welcoming, his voice smooth and charming.

None of this was quite enough to offset the sudden appetite the sight of bacon, eggs, fried tomatoes—even croissants—created as she replied to the other men's greetings.

She suddenly realized that while she'd dressed and packed her few belongings, Swallow had found the time to change into his trail gear, shave, *and* organize breakfast. And he'd obviously found time to seek out Edward Drinker Cope, who not only accepted Rebecca as part of his expedition, but even welcomed her, though she thought it might have been done with more genuine enthusiasm and a touch less grace.

Mr. Cope seemed to have weathered the effects of the partying without any noticeable effects. His associate, however, looked somewhat the worse for the previous night's debauchery. In fact, Mr. Sternberg looked as if another day in bed would suit him far better than their departure for Fort Benton at this unseemly hour.

Lucas Swallow's warnings about Sugden still rang in Rebecca's ears. She didn't know what to make of that, but Swallow's linking of the man with her father's torture was enough to take him seriously.

She had never seen Sugden or his band of desperadoes, but she had seen what *somebody* had done to her father, had witnessed for herself the almost unbelievable ferocity and callousness that had caused his wounds and killed him. And she'd vomited more than once while trying vainly to comfort him as he died.

Indians? Outlaws? Did it really matter? It seemed part and parcel of this horrible, primitive, violent country. Were it not for her promise to her father, she would . . .

No! She damned well wouldn't! She was going to fulfill that obligation to her father, but not just because of him. She would try her best to do what he hadn't been able to do. She would find Amy somehow, one way or another. And then, her sister in tow, she'd go back to where she belonged . . . to civilization. To where every man didn't wear a gun. To where every man didn't look at her as if she was a dainty morsel to be devoured. To where it was safe, within reason, to walk down the street without . . .

"Would thee like some more coffee, Miss Bennett?"

Edward Drinker Cope's question disrupted Rebecca's thoughts. The excited announcement from the grizzled old miner who burst through the dining room doors drove them from her mind entirely.

"Damnedest thing you ever seen," he was screeching. "Cooley Roberts . . . scalped and skinned and bloody well butchered, he was! They're getting up a posse, but it won't do much good, I reckon. Injun what done it took Cooley's horse and his guns . . . and his scalp . . . and he'll be halfway to Canada by now."

Rebecca listened in silence as the miner related in gruesome detail the butchery which had been inflicted on the person he described as "a wolfer, used to be a soldier." The remains had only just been discovered near the livery barn, where Roberts had been sleeping off a drunk. But the details were all over town, told and retold. Death, even sudden death, was nothing new in a booming town like Helena. But death like this . . .

"Ripped from belly to brisket, he was. Throat cut so deep his head damn near fell off. And scalped, of course," the miner said yet again. Glancing toward a faraway spittoon, he swallowed his own spittle, apparently aware, for the first time, that there was a woman in the room.

"Cooley allus kept his 'baccy in a pouch made from an Indian woman's tit . . . begging your pardon, ma'am. Whosoever done him in cut off his . . . privates. Cut 'em off tidy as you please, tucked 'em into that there 'baccy pouch, an' the whole shebang was jammed into Cooley's mouth. Now don't that beat all?"

It certainly did, Rebecca thought, her gaze riveted across the table. Swallow's eyes were as expressionless as lake ice. While her coffee rose in her throat, he continued eating as calmly as if the miner had been commenting on the weather.

His Indian. *His* knife. There was no question about that, no doubt. She knew it and he knew it, despite the blandness of his expression. Despite the unruffled way in which he helped himself to fresh toast, then spread butter upon it with a lean, tanned, long-fingered hand that revealed none of the tension Rebecca was certain he had to be feeling.

Certain? She glanced down at her own congealing breakfast and swallowed an urge to fling herself up from the table and run. Run anywhere so long as it took her away from here, from this awful, stomach-wrenching exhibition of the callousness she so hated about the West. Then she reconsidered.

No, she decided, Swallow wasn't feeling any tension. He had expected this. He had known what that horrible, stinking old Indian would do with the knife he'd provided. Willingly provided. Known it and expected it and approved. He'd even told her as much.

And now look at him! Sitting there like a cat before the fire, his eyes cold and unfeeling, yet lazy, almost smug. It made her want to scream at him, to reach across the table and slap him, to throw her coffee at him. Anything to break that rigid discipline and arrogance he so easily displayed.

Damn, damn, damn, she thought, breaking her eye contact with him before she did throw something. Or throw up. The grizzled miner had finished his town crier's job here and was shouldering his way back outside to continue the task elsewhere. Cope and Sternberg were quietly discussing the news. But Swallow merely continued eating. Rebecca could see him in her peripheral vision, could feel his gaze upon her, a gaze she no longer dared meet.

"Right," said their employer, breaking the trance as he turned to include her in the conversation. "It is decided, then, that Charles and I shall take the coach to Fort Benton and organize the supplies we need, so as to be ready upon your arrival. Thee might consider coming with us, Miss Bennett, given this latest atrocity. Surely it would be safer for thee in company, and traveling by coach."

"I go with my stock and wagons," Rebecca replied almost without thinking. Then she couldn't help adding, "I'm sure I will be safe enough in Mr. Swallow's company. He *understands*

Indians, does he not?"

She shot a sideways glare at Swallow as she spoke, but there was no sign he recognized the underlying irony of her remark, for his eyes merely met her own with bland placidity.

At least, she thought, she would be granted the security of being able to drive one wagon while Swallow drove the other. She wouldn't have to be confined with him for the entire two-hundred-and-fifty-mile journey. Cope listened to her, but she noticed it was to Swallow he deferred before accepting the decision.

"I have found a family wishing company on the journey," Swallow said. "They are traveling light, they won't slow us up, and there are older children who can share the driving. Besides," he added, and this time there was a glimmer of that wolf's grin, "it will ensure the proprieties are met. I would wish Miss Bennett's reputation kept as safe as the rest of her."

Rebecca caught inflections that obviously sailed over the heads of Mr. Cope and his companion, but then, she thought, she was meant to. And when she met the family a few minutes later, she quickly decided there was something more than inflections involved. The family was clearly Métis, which bothered her not at all, and had hardly a word of English between them, which was only slightly more of a problem. But the "older children" Swallow had referred to included one of the most beautiful young women Rebecca had ever seen, and this, for reasons she didn't want to think about, bothered her very much indeed.

Rebecca's presence didn't seem to bother Lizette Berube one whit. The raven-haired, black-eyed maiden's attention was focused firmly upon Lucas Swallow, who was all too aware of the attention and in no way seemed to object. Neither did the girl's parents, who chattered like magpies in a French-Canadian *patois* Rebecca couldn't begin to understand.

The two Berube brothers, raven-haired, hawk-nosed, and with eyes as black as their sister's, sat their shaggy ponies like young centaurs, their buckskin clothing merging with the horses' coats. The brothers both carried rifles as if accustomed to it since birth.

The final child was a babe in the arms of a tiny woman so wrinkled and shrunken in her shapeless garments that Rebecca found it hard to comprehend that she was the mother of the baby and the beauteous Lizette, and not their aging grandmother.

As they departed Helena, Rebecca told herself that everything had worked out perfectly. Swallow was, as she had wished, not sharing her wagon. In fact, he was so busy entertaining his French-speaking companions he hardly seemed to notice her.

Of course, it was difficult to tell since her own wagon led and she was determined not to look back.

She had no interest in Swallow, except as a means to an end. She had no need to discuss anything with him, except for the necessary judgments that affected their journey. Furthermore, any decision would be hers to make. She was, after all, in charge. These were her wagons and her horses.

None of which explained why her first words to him when he unexpectedly rode up beside her on his great blue roan Appaloosa stallion were so hostile. "What do *you* want?" she snapped.

"You seem to be handling things fine," he said, slipping from his saddle to land cat-like beside her on the wagon seat. "No problems?"

"You mean apart from wondering how you so conveniently found company for our journey? To protect my reputation, I believe you told Mr. Cope. More to look after your creature comforts, it seems to me. And how do you propose to pay for all this? More knives? Or is it guns, this time?"

"My, aren't we cranky?" he responded, after a silence that

threatened to hang over the wagon like a visible, touchable cloud.

"*We* are not cranky. *I* am cranky. How could you sit there, calmly eating your damned breakfast, knowing all the while that you were responsible for that poor man's brutal death?"

"I didn't kill him."

"You might as well have. You're accountable. You gave that horrible old Indian the knife. And you knew when you did that he would cut off that man's . . . privates . . . and . . . and scalp him."

"All of which he deserved. The wolfer's tobacco pouch was made from the breast of Sleeping Fox's wife. And perhaps you've already forgotten how *that poor man* smashed a child's brains out."

"Against a lodge pole, you said. But surely those . . . those things are matters for the law. Justice isn't . . . isn't . . . blind."

"The law, at best, is justice's idiot cousin," Swallow retorted. "And not even that, if you're an Indian. Or of mixed blood. One of the reasons the Berubes chose to come with us is that with most white parties they'd have to guard their daughter. White men, especially here south of the line, think a Métis woman is fair game for anything. At least with us, they know she'll be safe."

"Safe? With you?"

"She's as safe with me as you are. Besides, her family would skin me alive if I so much as touched her. It would make what Sleeping Fox did look like a picnic."

"Wonderful. So who's going to protect me? I have no family." And that realization finally struck Rebecca so forcibly, tears blurred her vision. Her parents were dead, her sister as good as dead, and here she was in this bleak, unforgiving, violent wilderness with a man who helped others commit savage butchery.

"You have your sister and you have yourself. You're stronger than you think. I hope."

"You hope." The words emerged with all the bitterness she now felt, all the frustration, all the despair. "Because that's what matters out here, isn't it? Strength, violence, torture and killing. God, but I hate it here. It's a place for animals." She nodded towards those in the wagon behind her. "How can they manage? How can they even think to bring up a family where there's so much brutality?"

"They manage because they must, as we all must if we are to live here. And because this is the only life they know, although it's easier for them in their own country where the Métis are treated with less contempt. They are from the Red River country, far to the north and east. In Canada. There, the Métis are a respected people, even though they follow the ways of their Indian cousins in some things. And they will protect you as they do Lizette. They are people of great loyalty and you are helping them.

"But the way you talk worries me, Rebecca," he said, using her name for the first time and somehow giving it an unusual flavor because of that trace of accent in his voice. "You have embarked upon what can only be a very trying journey, yet you are terrified of the land, of the people here. I really do think it would be better for you to catch a downriver boat at Fort Benton and return to civilization. This is no country for you, and it's not forgiving. It will kill you, or worse, if you don't learn to live with it."

He whistled for his stallion and was in the saddle and gone before Rebecca could even think of what to say, or indeed if she wanted to say anything at all.

Three times the rifle barrel shifted, its foresight blotting out L'Hirondelle's head, but never quite long enough to assure accuracy, even if the rifleman had intended to fire.

111

Which he didn't. Luis Sebastian was merely playing mind games with himself and Dover Sugden, who viewed his subordinate with the caution one might reserve for a rattlesnake that was within striking distance.

"You shoot him without me telling you to, and it'll be the last bloody thing you do," Sugden snarled at the small *meztiso*. Sugden kept his voice low, even though they were too far away from L'Hirondelle and his party to be heard.

Sebastian didn't bother to reply, but in apparent deference to the command, he shifted his aim to the head of L'Hirondelle's horse. The man was too difficult a target. However, the smooth movement of the stallion made it a simple shot. Too simple, Sebastian thought, and besides, he had other plans for the horse. Plans that included a gelding knife and all the time in the world to use it.

"Bastard," he said, his voice sibilant with his hatred of the great Appaloosa that had nearly killed him.

"Kin I have that dark-haired girl when we take 'em?" The half-wit boy's voice was ragged, not with lust but with a disarmingly childish enthusiasm, as if he asked for another piece of pie. There was a lack of true humanity that, if Lizette Berube had been able to hear, might have frightened her more than the obvious intentions of the others.

"You'll have what I say you can have," Sugden muttered under his breath. Already he was quivering with the frustration of seeing his prey denied him by the sheer volume of traffic on the Helena–Fort Benton road. He had the men and weapons he needed to overcome the small group he watched, but not without a fight, and from his viewpoint high on the ridge overlooking the road, there were too many travelers who could intervene. Nobody in this country went unarmed, and even without the field glasses he'd stolen during a wartime raid, Sugden could tell that the redhead and her party were well-armed and ready for trouble.

"Are you sure that's L'Hirondelle?" he asked Sebastian for the fifth or sixth time, knowing the answer himself but unwilling to believe it. It was just too much of a coincidence. Otis Bennett, his almost-legendary gold, the girl, and now the arrival of another person somehow linked to it all. A man unknown to Sugden by sight, but whose name the dying old plainsman had screamed under torture.

"It is he," Sebastian replied. In truth, he did not *know* if the man they watched, the man he had trailed in Helena, was L'Hirondelle. And yet . . . he did.

"We could easy take 'em during the night," said the half-wit boy, a statement which provoked a growl from his leader.

"Too chancy," Sugden said. Lifting a bottle of whiskey to his lips, he drained its contents. "We'll wait for them to get past Benton. We know they're headed up into the Judith basin, where we won't have any goddamn interference."

"There will be two more then, at least," Sebastian said. "The bone-hunter and his assistant."

Sugden spit his disgust at the smaller man's concern, and a gob of tobacco hit the ground between them. "Maybe they'll lose the half-breeds in Benton, which wouldn't be a bad thing for us. That old man's tough. He's been over the mountain a time or two. And them boys. They're young, but I reckon they can shoot if they're pushed."

"If we lose 'em, I won't get me the dark girl," sniveled the half-wit boy, his whine emerging from a drooling smirk.

The smirk changed not a whit as a huge blow from Sugden's fist smashed him from the saddle to lie bewildered, but silent, on the ground beside his horse.

"Keep an eye on that fool, Luis," Sugden snarled. Turning his horse, he gestured for the others to follow. "We have a load of whiskey stashed up on the Teton, and a band of renegade

Flathead with gold to pay for it. I say we get that bit of business out of the way first, then worry about the Bennett girl. They're headed for country we know, and I've got good contacts among the Sioux."

Sebastian sheathed his carbine and turned away with only a single, obsidian glance at where Luc L'Hirondelle rode in one of the wagons below. Sebastian's slender fingers idly caressed the knife at his nape, and the taste of vengeance delayed was sour in his throat.

An uneven rumble of hoofbeats heralded the passage of a massed body of horsemen. They reined in as they approached Rebecca's wagon, their eyes divided between her own inquiring glance and some subtle change in the attitude of her companions.

The faces of the horsemen showed the effects of hard riding, and their horses were further evidence of it, blowing and wheezing, taking advantage of what was apparently their first chance to rest.

Before a word could be said, Swallow had drawn up beside her, and she could sense the intense awareness that existed between him and the posse. But it was the Berube boys who had drawn the posse's attention, she realized, as the leader spoke to Swallow, ignoring her.

"Them boys with you?"

The leader's voice was thick with dry dust and a dislike Rebecca could sense was aimed at the Berube family, who had prudently halted a short distance away.

"They are," Swallow replied in a voice so soft she barely heard him. But as he kneed his stallion another pace forward, in effect placing himself between her and the posse, she noticed how he cradled the rifle in his hands. Not threatening, but nonetheless evidence of an alertness even a tired posse could recognize.

"Breeds, are they?" asked the leader, not even trying to hide his contempt, mixing it with the antagonism of his attitude. Even at that distance, she could smell the whiskey on his breath, and several of his companions were noticeably drunk.

"Métis," Swallow said. His one-word statement wasn't strictly a contradiction, or even an argument, but could be taken so if the leader wished it—if he dared to wish it. The challenge was there, hanging between them like gunsmoke.

"Is there a problem?" Rebecca found herself asking, surprised at how her lighter voice seemed to cut through the tension. "These people are my . . . employees . . . and I can think of no reason why they should be of any concern to you."

Her intrusion surprised both men, but Swallow merely allowed his gaze to flicker briefly before he focused on the vigilantes again.

"Well, ma'am," the leader of the posse said, "we've been after the injun what butchered that poor wolfer back in Helena. 'Spect you heard about it."

"And since you obviously haven't caught him, you think to pass your anger on to an innocent family! Because they are Métis? Or have you a better reason?"

The leader stared at her in silence, but behind him she could hear mutters about "stinking Indians" and "all the same" and even a "like to get my hands on that gal of theirs."

The last remark brought the blood boiling to Rebecca's brain, and without thinking about possible consequences, she lifted her father's rifle from the wagon bed behind her and laid it conspicuously across her lap.

Her gesture was so unexpected, she had the hammer eared back before most of the posse realized what she was about. But when the click of Swallow's carbine being cocked echoed the sound, all eyes widened slightly and the tension became more solid.

"As I said, these people are my employees. They had nothing to do with the assault on that man in Helena." Rebecca tried to keep her voice as calm as she could, using Swallow's icy composure as her example. When the man who'd muttered the remark about Lizette nudged his horse a step forward, she idly let the muzzle of her rifle follow him.

"You have my assurance that these people are my responsibility," Rebecca continued. "But if you doubt it, may I suggest you consult Governor Potts upon your return? We are part of Mr. Edward Drinker Cope's expedition. I'm certain you've heard of him."

She couldn't determine which name had registered, but the posse began to fidget. The leader dipped his head and tipped his hat to her.

"Your pardon, ma'am," he said, then led his men past the Berube wagon without so much as a sideways glance.

Carbine still cocked, Swallow kneed his stallion and followed the posse.

Five pairs of black eyes swiveled from the posse and Lucas Swallow to Rebecca Susan Bennett.

10

Round black eyes, bright and shiny as chips of obsidian, stared up into Rebecca's face. The youngest Berube's gaze was as inscrutable as those of his . . . her? . . . centaur brothers.

The baby's stare was almost as disconcerting as had been the gesture of its mother bringing the child to Rebecca in the first place, lifting the infant from its cradle-board and handing him, or her, over as if he . . . or she, dammit . . . was a priceless gift.

"What am I supposed to do with this?" Rebecca couldn't help asking a clearly amused Lucas Swallow.

"First off, I suggest you don't drop it. It's a baby, not a rattlesnake. It isn't going to bite you."

"I'm more concerned about what damage I might do to him . . . her . . . it."

"One might think you'd never held a baby before." Reaching down, Swallow adjusted the infant's shawl.

"Well I haven't," Rebecca snapped, inordinately aware of the skill with which those long, slender fingers managed the simple task. She, on the other hand, felt as if she was all thumbs. She was certain the child would slip from her fingers at any moment, and this despite the fact that the baby never moved, never so much as squirmed. It just lay there, passively absorbed in its inspection of her.

"You should try it more often. I think it quite suits you."

Any possible reply, and she wasn't at all sure she could construct one, was forestalled by a pudgy little hand that reached out to grasp at a straying lock of Rebecca's hair. The child tugged, then gurgled with delight.

"You have good hands," Swallow said. "I've watched the way you handle the reins . . . and your father's revolver, of course."

Damn him! Why had he deliberately taken the compliment out of his remark by adding that? She found it impossible to understand the man. One minute he seemed almost civilized. Then he deliberately worked to remove any such indication as soon as it appeared. It was almost as if he didn't want her to like him.

The infant's mother was busy tending the campfire and preparing what Rebecca assumed was dinner. Their campsite had been located by the hard-riding Berube boys, on instructions from Swallow, and the entire party was now ensconced in a secluded glade well away from the wagon road.

Which suited an utterly exhausted Rebecca just fine. Ever since her confrontation with the posse, the tension had drained from her, taking her strength with it. However, she'd managed to hide from the others exactly how much her entire body had shaken with tremors of terror. Truth be told, after the danger had passed she'd come very close to flinging herself down from the wagon seat and emptying her stomach into the roadside shrubbery.

No one, not even Lucas Swallow, had said a single word to her immediately following the incident, although there had been a fair amount of discussion amongst the Métis family. But, Rebecca realized with some confusion, the Berubes had looked at her differently once they'd reached their campsite. In fact, they had been less speculative when she'd been introduced. Now, there was a strange manifestation in their eyes.

"Seems you've won yourself some admirers," Swallow said.

"Admirers?"

"You stood up for them, said they were your people. You and

I might know what you did with that vigilante bunch today wasn't as brave as it was foolish, or maybe just plain stubborn, but your heart was in the right place, and these folks recognize and appreciate that."

"Obviously more than you do," she couldn't help replying. The flash of lightning in his pale eyes was her reward, and she looked down to see if it was reflected in the baby's black eyes.

"I think you've got amazing instincts, Rebecca. And while it might have been foolish, you saved us a passel of trouble. Truth be told, I was as dumbfounded as those other fellows when you hefted your rifle." Retrieving the weapon from her wagon, he casually flicked the lever with his long fingers . . . once, then again and again. "Empty, just like I figured. Damned foolishness, but well meant."

To her surprise, he lifted the rifle over his head with both hands, repeated the levering gesture, and cried out a totally unintelligible stream of *patois* to the group around the fire.

The resounding cheer that followed an initial moment of wide-eyed silence needed no interpretation. The Berube family was now even *more* impressed! Rebecca was only more confused, a situation hardly improved when the elder Métis woman waddled over to exchange a cup of steaming coffee for her baby, shyly making some comment of approval as she did so. Then the father of the family lifted his coffee mug in an obvious salute and called out something which drew echoes from his family.

Une femme aux cheveux couleur du soleil couchant, qui vainct ses ennemis grâce à un fusil sans balles!

"Seems you've just got yourself a new name," Swallow said with a mischievous grin. "Remind me to tell you what it is, sometime."

Whereupon, despite her insistence upon being told immediately, he walked swiftly away to the wagon, sought out the boxed ammunition, and made a great show of loading Rebecca's rifle, pointing out with exaggerated significance that there was no cartridge under the hammer, then replacing the weapon where he'd originally found it. Throughout, his broad shoulders visibly shook with suppressed laughter. Rebecca wanted to throw something at him, but the coffee tasted too good to waste.

She glared at his back as he strode toward the fire. Yet she mentally determined to revert to what her father was . . . had been . . . prone to calling her "purdee cussedness." She would not, she told herself stubbornly, allow Lucas Swallow to torment her about this name business.

Which, in any event, didn't prove difficult. Dinner was a solemn, silent occasion during which almost nobody spoke. Rebecca barely had the meal inside her before exhaustion drew her into a lassitude that led straight to her blankets beneath the wagon, and she was asleep before the question of her new name could provoke further irritation.

It wasn't, Luc thought as he sprawled beside the fire with one of his cherished cheroots, a completely new name for Rebecca Susan Bennett. Sleeping Fox had used it, or at least part of it. Sunset Woman.

Even from where Luc lay, he could see the reflected firelight on Rebecca's distinctive mane of hair. Yes, the description was adequate . . . more than adequate.

Then he considered the entire name old Berube had bestowed upon Rebecca in that curious mixture of Cree and French-Canadian *patois*.

"Sunset-haired woman who defeats her enemies with an empty rifle" was the closest Luc could translate it into English, even with his powerful linguistic skills. Among his own people, it would probably have been shortened to something like "Wins Without Weapons." Or "Sunset Woman Warrior."

Neither would impress Rebecca all that much, he was certain.

She had clearly been terrified by the encounter, but had overcome her fear as the need demanded. Or she'd let her anger do it for her. Nonetheless, it had taken more courage than foolhardiness. He would have to tell her that. His concern for her had made him angry when he'd proven himself right about the empty gun.

Which was a concern. From the very beginning, Rebecca had been frighteningly unpredictable.

Luc pictured the red mare in his visions, the red mare with the dark violet eyes. It had to be Rebecca. Except, he thought wryly, she hated the West and was terrified of Indians.

Lord only knew how she really felt about the Métis family.

He should have told her that *he,* also, was Métis. Perhaps tomorrow morning. She was certain to insist he discuss this name business, and if things seemed right, felt right . . .

The problem nagged at him, returning as if by magic the instant the eldest Berube boy woke him for his shift on watch.

It was Luc who'd insisted on a night watch. They weren't that far away from their encounter with the vigilante posse, and in this country it was better to lose your sleep than your life.

Rebecca rode a nightmare out of her sleep, and surged upright so quickly she smacked her head against the undercarriage of the wagon.

She subsided with a moan that was well in keeping with the terror that had partially awakened her.

Blood. That was the overwhelming element. Blood and tortured, twisted limbs. And scalps and smoke and terror; the terror an Indian attack could provoke in the bravest of men. But the men in her nightmare weren't Indians. They were white and they were identifiable to her half-wakened mind. The slouching, fetid, cold-eyed men of the vigilante posse. And it

121

was she they wanted, not the black-eyed mixed-bloods she'd defended.

And she knew why they wanted her. Knew their intentions in a sort of detail her waking mind could not have comprehended. In the twilight between sleep and waking, cursing the pain in her head, she rolled from beneath the wagon and crept up the side of it, her fingers already searching for the rifle she had watched Swallow replace behind the seat.

As it came to her hand with a surprising familiarity, she quickly levered a shell into the chamber, eared back the hammer, and stepped out to swing the weapon across the sleeping camp.

Her half-awake mind counted the visible figures.

The Berubes, mother and father, the baby propped in its cradle-board beside them.

Lizette, safe within touching distance of her father.

Two blanket-wrapped figures on the other side of the young woman.

Which left . . .

A sound alerted her, and she swung about in time to halt the approaching figure in mid-stride.

"I'll shoot," she whispered, not knowing why she whispered, not even sure why she didn't just pull the trigger before the rifle in her shaky fingers went off by itself. "I will. Don't ever doubt it."

"Believe me, I don't," said the tall shadow in her sights. Slowly, cautiously, the man raised both hands level with his shoulders, open palms visible, empty. The voice was somehow familiar, and she shook her head because her dream state had made her eyes blurry.

"Are you all right, Rebecca?" the shadow asked anxiously.

She couldn't answer. All her energy was consumed in holding the rifle, in keeping at bay the swirling torment of her nightmare and the throb inside her head.

"Becky Sue?"

The use of her childhood pet name confused her. This wasn't her father. Her father was dead, tortured and dead and buried. Her father had died in her arms.

No, not her father. And yet, this wasn't one of the vigilante band, either. This figure smelled wrong, or right . . . had a sort of woodsmoke odor, not the rancid, animal rankness of those men who had eyed her so hungrily.

"Not another step!" she shouted, as she saw the figure move toward her. She raised the rifle muzzle, aware that she'd let it droop.

"I'll shoot, I swear I will!" she cried, then shut her mouth as confusion took over again.

Now there were two figures before her, one of them the tall slender man she'd halted with her rifle and someone else, a much smaller, more rounded figure, who seemed to waddle rather than walk.

"Dear God," Rebecca whispered. She was pointing a cocked and loaded rifle at a woman who carried a baby!

The plump Métis woman seemed oblivious to any danger. She moved forward, crooning a wordless, monotonous, almost hypnotic chant.

"Oh, dear God!"

Rebecca swung the muzzle away, then bent slightly to lay the rifle itself back into the wagon bed before turning to reach out for the child being offered her.

Rebecca's whole being focused on the baby. Then, without warning, the pain in her head surged into agony, smashing through her skull with a stunning intensity. She felt herself sagging and realized she was falling . . .

She woke to full daylight and the jarring motion of the wagon beneath her, each individual foot-fall of each individual horse hammering in her head as if the animals trod on it. The lurching wagon wheels felt as if they were rolling across the back of her neck, and the only solace was the caress of something delightfully cool and moist lying across her forehead. It felt so good, she just lay there, reveling in the sensation, until a portion of her memory returned with a fierce abruptness and she whipped away the compress to find the old Métis woman squatting cross-legged beside her, staring down through black eyes that clearly revealed the woman's distress.

"What happened?" Rebecca heard herself ask the question, but her voice seemed to come from a long way off, fighting through her pain.

Her companion apparently understood, but the woman's rapid-fire reply, accompanied by voluble gestures, was totally incomprehensible to Rebecca. They did serve, however, to shift her attention to the side, where Swallow sat tall upon his Appaloosa, his ice-pale eyes regarding her gravely.

"She says you had a nightmare. Reared up and smacked your head on the wagon bed, I reckon. Must have been a helluva smack. You went a bit loco for a time."

Memory seeped back slowly, but it was like trying to see her reflection in murky water. Some things were unclouded and others muddied so much she had to shake her head to try and see more clearly. That was a mistake! So was turning her head sufficiently to establish that one of the Berube boys was driving her wagon.

"I have a feeling I very nearly shot you," she said after a long moment in which she thought her head would fall off, almost wished it would, if that would remove her pain.

"You did consider it, Rebecca. I'm glad you tend to be hesitant about when to shoot."

His reply was followed by a great chattering and waving of arms from the woman beside her. Whatever was said, it seemed to amuse Swallow out of all proportion, and his unexpected guffaw of laughter rang in Rebecca's over-tender ears.

"She says I deserved shooting," he finally explained, if that could be considered any sort of explanation at all.

Rebecca fought down a growing sense of nausea to demand more. "*She* surely has a name, and even if we can't understand each other it would be nice if I knew it, seeing as how she appears to be nursing me. And what did you do to deserve being shot? Not that I dispute you probably did something."

This gained her a quizzical raising of one dark eyebrow, then a grin that warned her even before he spoke that she wasn't going to like his answer.

"She said if you'd been sharing my blankets like you ought to have been, you wouldn't have had nightmares. And her name is Monique, although she doesn't use it much, and her husband, whose name is Auguste, by the way, doesn't ever use it. Or at least not that I've noticed."

"I suppose there's as good a reason for that as there is for her to think I ought to be sleeping with you."

"Probably one and the same. They're both hopeless romantics, and when you mix that with the . . . earthiness, I guess you'd call it . . . of life out here, well . . ."

"Well, what? You've told me absolutely nothing. And I might just remind you that thus far you've made no sense at all. On the one hand you insist this family would protect their daughter—and me—to the death, and on the other you say they expect me to sleep with you. Why? Was I supposed to *know* I was going to have nightmares? Or is this just another example of life in this bloody, awful, godless country? Am I expected to sleep with you because you happen to be hand . . . handy?" She shook her head again at how close she'd just come to saying handsome. Another mistake. The shake almost took her head off.

"You're not *expected* to sleep with me at all," he snapped back, clearly annoyed by her verbal assault. "Even if you did, you'd be too damned busy arguing to enjoy it, I reckon. And if you always wake up this sore-toothed, you deserve to sleep alone.

"What I was trying to say," he continued with a stern glare that silenced her reply before it could escape her lips, "was that these two are so totally infatuated with each other, they think everyone else should enjoy the same sort of mindless obsession. She is his 'child bride' and his 'sleek young heifer,' among other things. And he, my dear Miss Bennett, is her 'mighty, rutting bull moose' when he isn't being her 'little bantam rooster.' Doubtless they have other, even more intimate pet names, but those are the only ones I've heard."

"Child bride?" She couldn't help but throw a sideways glance at the shapeless figure next to her. Whatever form the woman might have possessed was indiscernible beneath her dress.

After a quick mental calculation, Rebecca pegged the oldest of the Berube boys at no less than seventeen, but as usual Swallow was well ahead of her.

He threw a guttural question at Monique, who had been following their exchange with her snapping black eyes. She grinned, revealing several missing teeth in her round, pudgy face, before she replied.

"She has seen thirty-three winters, and given him eleven children," Swallow explained. Then he added soberly, "These four lived. It's tough being a woman out here, tougher yet if you're Indian or Métis. Many children don't survive."

"But . . . but that means . . ."

"She was most likely thirteen, fourteen, or fifteen when they wed. And they were properly married, priest and all, although it may not have happened until after they . . . got together. That, too, is not uncommon where there are few priests to be found.

126

And because they are so profoundly in love, they think everyone in the world should be in love. It doesn't make any sense to me, either, if that's any consolation, but then it doesn't have to, does it? Please don't go making judgments too quickly by standards that mean nothing out here. These are good, honest, religious people. Strong people. Very moral people. They don't come any better."

Before she could respond, he kneed his great stallion and was gone, leaving her to the tender mercies of a woman she couldn't understand, but whose gentleness and concern were obvious. Rebecca would have been happier if Swallow had given her the chance to say that to him.

She slumped back into her blankets and let Monique lay a freshly dampened cloth over her forehead. Good, honest, moral people, she thought, who'd decided she needed a man, and who had no scruples whatsoever about fostering a romantic union whether it was in the air or not. To cure her nightmares!

Moments later she was asleep again, and didn't come out of it this time until they'd reached their evening campsite.

That night produced no nightmares, possibly because of some herbal infusion Monique insisted Rebecca drink after a hearty dinner of stewed something-or-other. Nor did bad dreams awaken her during the following nights. Days, however, were a startling revelation as she came to know her "adopted" family better.

The "child bride" rode with Rebecca, even after she'd recovered sufficiently to drive her own team, and gradually each became proficient at a unique combination of words and gestures which allowed them a surprisingly effective communication. Sometimes Lizette, who spoke a smattering of English, would join them, and their passage along the road rang with their laughter.

Auguste Berube was rather less forthcoming, but his cheerful smile and expressive gestures also made him understandable, at least to some degree. It was a matter of shock and surprise to Rebecca when she found that he had been a lieutenant of Louis Riel. Indeed, one of the firing squad who had executed a white Canadian at Fort Battleford some years before. It seemed somehow . . . out of character.

She tried, with poor success, to imagine this pudgy, laughing little man, this romantic, as an executioner, as a killer of any kind. He seemed to regard *her* with some sort of awe, which was confusing, yet a pleasant change from the attitude Lucas Swallow showed.

He'd taken to avoiding her as much as possible. Monique managed through a series of ribald gestures to indicate that his manhood was affronted at having been almost shot off. Or at least that's what Rebecca thought Monique was trying to convey; she decided it best not to seek further clarification.

As for the boys, those black-eyed centaurs who seemed to spend more time away from the wagons than with them, Rebecca simply couldn't figure them out. They appeared to live on their horses and for them. She thought they were simply reticent about showing any emotion. Then, the day before their arrival at Fort Benton, the eldest arrived at the evening camp and shyly, silently, presented Rebecca with a bouquet of wildflowers.

The gesture was so unexpected, so completely out of character, she could only stare at the flowers and stammer a hasty *merci*, thankful to have learned at least that much French during the past few days.

Lucas Swallow, typically, was more voluble.

"I'd best warn that boy about your temper in the mornings," he said.

"You'd be better off getting him to teach *you* some social graces," she retorted, fighting an urge to leap up and fling the wildflowers in his face. "I think it was a lovely gesture, and if I could trust you to interpret, I'd get you to tell him so."

"You'll probably be able to tell him yourself by the time we get to the Judith."

That was a surprise. She had thought the family was only joining them as far as Fort Benton. But when she said so, Swallow seemed to regard the question as a waste of time.

"It's on their way home to the Red River country," he said.

"And, of course, you have organized this with Mr. Cope," she countered, knowing he hadn't, also knowing that what he predicted would be the way things would go.

"I expect he'll favor the idea," was Swallow's curt reply.

When they arrived at Fort Benton the next day and met their employer, the subject was not, to Rebecca's knowledge, even raised. Which wasn't surprising, given that Fort Benton had just received the news of General George Armstrong Custer's massacre at the Little Bighorn.

Fort Benton, a boomtown by comparison to Helena, was in uproar. Rumors abounded, some rational and others, even to Rebecca's ears, quite ridiculous. News of the massacre had generated a host of increasingly vivid reports regarding other atrocities, and she found herself instinctively worrying about her dark-skinned companions, the vigilante incident still fresh in her mind.

Sitting Bull, the majestic Sioux chief, was reported to be heading northwest into Canada, seeking refuge there from army units flocking to intercept him and obtain revenge for Custer's soldiers. Of the great General himself, public opinion was divided. Some said Custer was an arrogant fool who probably deserved his fate, while others thought him almost a god. But all agreed on one thing. Custer was white. Therefore, his assailants ought to be caught and strung up as quickly as possible, all five thousand, or ten thousand, or twenty thousand of them.

Most significant was that Sitting Bull was likely as not to

have chosen a route that would take him through the Judith basin, and if he wasn't enough of a problem, there were reportedly up to fifteen thousand Crow, Assiniboine and Blackfoot roaming the Missouri as far downstream as Fort Lincoln. It was said that they fired on steamboats and committed general mayhem. Obtaining men to accompany Cope was worse than impossible, and the Berubes' value became obvious as the rumors about Sitting Bull's retreat escalated.

Cope shrugged off the warnings. The next day they were trailing north toward the mouth of the Marias. Four and a half days later, they crossed to the mouth of the Judith and arrived at Fort Claggett, an insignificant trading post with prices even more outrageous than Fort Benton. And they saw not a single Indian on the way.

Claggett, however, was a different story. They had to move a few miles up the Judith just to find room to camp, and everywhere there were Indians. Various bands of Crow mingled with their traditional Blackfoot enemies. Some Gros Ventre were camped in another nearby valley. All of them knew about Custer, all of them were wild with anticipation at the possible arrival of Sitting Bull's Sioux . . . any Sioux! Some because the Sioux were their greatest enemy, others because . . .

"Because they hope Sitting Bull's war will lead to the removal of whites from the entire buffalo country," Swallow informed the Cope party in his usual laconic brevity. "And because they like to fight. An Indian without enemies to fight, horses to steal, coups to be won, honors to be gained . . . well, he isn't an Indian at all."

Rebecca was so overwhelmed by it all, so blatantly terrified, that nothing seemed to make sense anymore. She couldn't eat, could barely sleep. All those teepees! All those shaggy ponies whose painted riders seemed as much a part of them as their manes or tails! Her stomach churned and her mind numbed into uselessness.

Cope thought it was wonderful. He visited with Bear Wolf, the Crow chief, and listened to reports of the Crows stealing nine hundred Sioux horses and taking more than twenty scalps. How could he worry about the Sioux when he had the Crows to protect him, he was asked. A similar reception occurred when he and Lucas Swallow visited the Blackfoot, or so Cope told Rebecca on their return. Swallow, typically, said nothing.

Rebecca believed all of it and none of it, but when they moved on, following the mostly dry bed of Dog Creek up into the badlands, she never stopped looking over her shoulder, terrified she'd see a scalping party galloping up behind them. Assurances by the Berubes did nothing to ease her terror.

She took to carrying her father's rifle everywhere. It was beside her on the wagon seat, in her hands when she visited the bushes, beside her at meals, in her arms when she slept. Since Swallow and the Berube boys kept their weapons handy and ready, it seemed only logical for Rebecca to do the same. Logical, at least, to her.

"You're going to shoot one of us if you have another nightmare," Swallow commented, then withdrew, holding back whatever else he might have said in the face of her grim expression.

Monique Berube said nothing about the rifle, but hovered over Rebecca like a mother hen. Although they had come to a remarkably good understanding of each other through a weird combination of words and sign language, Rebecca could not explain her compulsive, perhaps unreasonable fears to Monique.

They *were* unreasonable. Rebecca herself conceded that. But there seemed nothing she could do about it, and Swallow's earlier claim about being able to detect those fears in her memories did little to ease her anxiety.

Nor did his change in attitude. He kept her at a distance. His remarks were brusque, as if he wished only to speak to her when it was absolutely necessary. He stayed away from the diminutive wagon train as much as possible, leaving the Berube boys to drive and help in camp while he, himself, did the scouting. And when Rebecca woke from an occasional nightmare—nightmares which, fortunately, did not cause her to shoot anyone—it seemed to her that it was inevitably Swallow who was on watch.

During their passage through the Indian camps at the Judith, he had disappeared entirely for most of one day, eventually riding back to act as Cope's translator; an appointment that had been predetermined. As they made their laborious way up the coulees and ravines into the badlands, he often disappeared for long periods, offering no explanation upon his return.

Their journey was laborious. Bad water was a major problem, what water they could find was alkaline, and the sheer difficulty of the country took a toll on the men, women, horses and, especially patience.

Then came the rains, and it got worse, not better. They were forced to the ridges, and while drinking water was no longer a problem, travel became something approaching a horrid dream. Wagons were no longer driven. Instead, they were winched up one precarious slope and down another. Every member of the party slaved from dawn to dusk in order to make any headway at all. The nights were too short by half, used only to bolt down a hurried meal and try to gain enough rest to sustain everyone for the next day's ordeal.

Yet, the ridges also brought benefits. It was in the sandstone of the ridges that Cope began to find the treasures he'd been seeking, days before they reached the area Swallow had known would contain them.

The whole party gained respite from arduous travel as Cope

and his assistant raced about, elated, speaking what sounded like a foreign language . . . *iguanodonts, adocus, trionyx.* They discovered the fossils of something Cope described as being a cross between a kangaroo and a crocodile, the gigantic *hadrosaurs.*

At one point, Cope claimed he'd been able to differentiate twenty-one separate species of dinosaur by their teeth. Often, an eruption of scientific words, understood by Charles Sternberg alone, emerged from Cope's mouth . . . with barely a pause for breath.

Vast quantities of bones accumulated in the wagons, many there only long enough to be discarded for bigger, better or different specimens. The pattern of their journey changed, slowing down to keep pace with Cope's explorations. There was less work, more time to think, and for Rebecca this was disastrous. Her paranoia increased, along with a new awareness of Lucas Swallow.

Lizette, needless to say, was entranced by the man, a situation neither encouraged nor discouraged by her parents. The Berube boys looked upon Swallow as someone just short of a god.

In Rebecca's eyes he was somewhere between a nuisance and downright tormentor, but even she couldn't deny his sheer masculinity, his easy, pantherish movements. Astride, he outshone even the boys, who only dismounted to eat and sleep. And despite the rigors of the journey, he always managed time to shave each morning, always looked, if not perfectly clean and tidy—impossible under the circumstances—at least presentable.

And now, it seemed, he hadn't been ignoring Rebecca's circumstances as much as she'd thought.

"If you're bound and determined to cart that rifle around, let's at least make sure you know what you're doing with it," he said on a morning that saw Cope and his assistant out fossicking without even waiting for their breakfast coffee.

"I know exactly what I'm doing!"

She found herself speaking to Swallow's back as he plucked the weapon from beside her, then strode over to her wagon and grabbed up a box of ammunition.

"We'll wander into the next coulee, no sense scaring the horses," he muttered, obviously assuming she'd follow without objection.

"I have other things to do today," she cried as she marched after him, almost running in order to keep pace with his long strides.

"So do I, Rebecca, but this is more important. You might not be having any more nightmares, but I am. I keep thinking of you lying there with this damned gun every night."

"Jealous of a rifle, Mr. Swallow?"

She should have saved her breath. His eyes flickered, but in the brilliant sunshine of this splendid autumn day she couldn't tell if he was angry or laughing at her. Or both.

"I believe you mentioned that your father once taught you to shoot," he said, slipping into that slightly lilting accent he sometimes revealed, an accent vaguely like the Berube family's, yet somehow different. "Let's see how good a job he did of it." Swallow gestured toward a small white rock about a hundred yards away, near the crest of the coulee. "Try that for a target."

Rebecca hefted the heavy rifle, levered in a shell, eared back the hammer, then squinted along the sights. Immediately, she became aware of how much the barrel seemed to sway, and how the sun's heat on the badlands seemed to create a mirage effect.

"No, no, no," Swallow said, reaching out to grasp the rifle and stop her. "First off, always take a rest if there's any chance at all to get one. Move over here and use this rock."

Rebecca thought he extended the rifle the same way Mo-

nique might extend her arms and offer Rebecca the Berube
baby.

"Cushion the barrel with your hand," he continued, "or
anything soft. Never lay the barrel down on something hard like
a rock or tree branch because it'll jump when you fire. Ease the
sights down from above. Start with the sight above the target,
and as the sight lowers onto it, squeeze the trigger. Squeeze . . .
not pull. Understand?"

She nodded, laid the barrel over her forearm, and tried to
sight into the growing swirls of the mirage. Then she squinted
harder, but that made things worse, so she opened her right eye
wide, only to gasp in astonishment, then sheer terror, at what
materialized from the mirage.

As if rising from water, she saw the heads of a horse and
rider, an Indian rider, then the rest of the horse and rider, rising
as if by magic until they paused, backlit by the sky. And, in an
instant of awareness, she saw the Indian's rifle, the intricate
design of the paint on his face, the strongly beaked nose and
muscular torso that gleamed with oil, or some kind of grease.
And the scalps—surely they could be nothing else—which fluttered from the rifle's muzzle in the prairie breeze. Fresh scalps,
and one of them, shorter than the others, was blond!

A malformation of the light seemed to make her eyes
telescopic. She could see every line on the rider's cruel face,
every line of muscle on his mostly naked body, the glare in eyes
that seemed to peer into her soul. As she watched, the light
behind him was washed with blood. She could smell it, even
taste it.

The light seemed to swarm around him, then swirl even more
as terror clawed its way up into her throat. She gagged, then
steadied her rifle as she saw the rider lift his own in what could
have been a salute. Or a threat.

Rebecca felt, rather than heard, Lucas Swallow's voice in her ear, but his words meant nothing. She was committed now.

Her finger tensed as she raised the sights to the rider's face and watched the muzzle drift down along the column of his throat.

Whereupon she pulled the trigger.

11

Hunkering by the fire, Luc contemplated his thumb. The goddamn hammer had smashed into it when he grabbed Rebecca's rifle to stop her from shooting Sleeping Fox, and he was less than amused.

"I think I'm crippled for life," he grumbled, his gaze flickering from the old Indian who squatted across from him to Rebecca, who seemed mesmerized by a pot of boiling coffee.

In truth, Rebecca was trying very hard *not* to look at Sleeping Fox. She still wasn't even sure it *was* Sleeping Fox. The barbaric, proud figure across the fire bore no resemblance to the ancient, blanket-wrapped drunk she remembered from Helena.

There was nothing pitiful about this man, nor was he as elderly as she'd thought. True, his face was lined beneath the paint, and there was a vestige of a paunch, but his arms and legs were roped with muscle, as was the chest on which she could see the ridged welts of almost identical scars in the flesh below his collarbones.

Only the voice was similar, or nearly so, as the Indian growled something at Lucas, followed it up with a flurry of sign language, then broke into a chuckle that sounded like a bull buffalo grunting.

Whatever he said, it must have been funny, because it drew a titter of laughter from Monique, who was stirring a pot of stew while Lizette minded the baby.

"He says he is glad you didn't shoot him, but your new name

will have to be changed because your rifle wasn't empty," Swallow translated, his own smile rueful at best.

"This, I assume, is the name you refused to tell me about." Rebecca couldn't see any humor in an anecdote she didn't understand, but was not averse to using the occasion to force information from Swallow. "Does this mean you're finally going to tell me my 'new' name, or do I get the 'new, new' version? Either will do, I assure you, since I already have a perfectly good name that I'm quite content with and have no intention of changing."

Swallow explained something to Sleeping Fox in both dialect and sign language. It was clear to Rebecca that Swallow's narrative involved her, a rifle, nightmares, and . . .

Her startled gasp at being able, inexplicably, to follow at least some of his sign language did not go unnoticed. Monique Berube tapped her on the shoulder and gesticulated, rounding out Swallow's recital of the incident in which Rebecca had nearly shot him. And to Rebecca's astonishment, she could pretty much follow Monique's gestures, too. Then she thought about what was being discussed and when both men chuckled, she turned on Swallow with a scowl.

"I don't think it's all that funny," she snapped.

"Ah, but you have no sense of humor."

"There's nothing humorous about shooting someone, Mr. Swallow, not even in this god-forsaken wilderness."

"We're not laughing at you shooting someone. How could we? You didn't. And I agree that there's nothing funny about shooting someone. It's the *almost* that's funny, especially to the old man. He thinks it's very funny, given that he thinks I was far luckier than he was, had you gone through with it."

"You're making no sense!"

"Sleeping Fox would rather be killed than have his manhood blown away. So would I, come to that."

Rebecca sighed. She was more or less accustomed to Monique's rather earthy approach when discussing things of a sexual nature, but that was between women.

"Personally, *come to that*," she said, keeping her voice as smooth as his, her expression just as bland, "I'd rather have nightmares."

"You're a hard woman, Miss Rebecca Susan Bennett."

Swallow relayed the conversation and joined in the gust of laughter it provoked from Monique and Sleeping Fox, who immediately began to reply in a mixture of guttural words and all-too-descriptive sign language. Swallow, damn him anyway, never so much as flinched before interpreting.

"He says if you don't fancy me, he has half a dozen ponies he, uhm, liberated from the Sioux. But since your father's . . . gone . . . he isn't sure who he should offer them to. And before you get all huffy, Rebecca, he says he realizes it's not enough of a bride price and he doesn't want to insult you, so he's prepared to go back and steal another dozen if that will make it better."

Rebecca didn't know whether to laugh or cry. She had only to look at the old man's glistening black eyes to see the mischief lurking there. He was teasing her exactly as he might tease a favorite daughter. "I cannot imagine anyone offering any number of horses for somebody named . . . what was it again?"

"Sunset-haired woman who defeats her enemies with an empty rifle. It's an honorable name. You should be proud of it, Rebecca. You earned it, which is the point, after all."

His comment took her mind back to the confrontation with the vigilantes, and she couldn't suppress a shudder. She watched as he translated his part of the conversation to their companions, which at least gave her time to think of something to reply, something that might change the subject at least temporarily.

"What about *your* name?" she finally asked, never doubting for an instant that he had a similar, Indian-derived name. "Did you earn it in the same way?"

The lightning flickered across his eyes so quickly, she would have missed it had she not been expecting, hoping, for some reaction. And it was vaguely comforting to find she'd struck a sensitive spot.

Swallow gazed at her for what seemed a very long time, then turned to translate her question before lapsing into immobility.

Dreaming up some plausible lie, she thought, only to have her thoughts interrupted by a gesture from Sleeping Fox.

Having captured her attention, he grinned at her, then began a lengthy, complicated, but unexpectedly easy to comprehend bout of sign language.

"Horses," Rebecca said to Swallow when it was done. "Something about . . . breaking horses . . . catching horses. You're a . . . what do they call it? A mustanger?"

"I have been. Properly, it translates as 'Tames the wildest of horses,' but whether that's totally accurate I couldn't say. You could ask my roan, I suppose. He's the wildest I ever went after, and he's the one that fulfilled the vision and provided my name."

"Vision? I don't understand." She glanced at the stallion, who stood calmly, watching them as if he did understand. Certainly he was the most magnificent horse Rebecca had ever seen, but the wildest?

"My stallion was born wild and grew up wilder. You can tell from his coloring there's some Nez Percé Appaloosa blood in him, but he was running way down south in the desert country, stealing mares where he could find them, fighting bears, cougars and other stallions to keep 'em. And winning! Took me nearly a month to walk him down. And longer than that to get him to where I could ride him. Now he's sort of like a one-man dog, if you take my meaning. Nobody else can handle him. He wouldn't tolerate it. And it's been tried. He's the finest war-horse and buffalo runner ever was."

All the while he talked, his fingers flew, translating. Rebecca was half certain he was deliberately distracting her, and was about to repeat her vision question when shouts announced the arrival of Cope, his assistant, and the Berube men, who regarded Sleeping Fox with evident suspicion until Swallow explained the Indian's presence. Without, Rebecca noted, mentioning the Helena incident.

Cope was visibly excited about more discoveries and clearly bent upon discussing them at length, dragging one bone after another from the wagon. Rebecca realized almost immediately she was going to learn no more on this morning about either Lucas Swallow's horse or his visions. Nor was he prepared to discuss it after lunch, when the others departed, returning to their bone hunt, and he insisted upon resuming their shooting lessons.

"No more storytelling," he said firmly. "Now we'll see about your shooting. That's more important. Besides, Sleeping Fox would probably like to hear it, too. I'm sure he knows some of it, but he's never heard it from me."

"Is he really the same drunken old Indian you gave your knife to?" Rebecca couldn't help asking. "I mean, I know he is, but he looks so different."

"Well, he is. The same . . . and different. He's a man again, I guess is the only way to explain it. He's got his vengeance, whether you agree with that or not. And from the look of those Sioux ponies and scalps, he's had himself a time since we saw him last. Have to get him to tell us about that, maybe after dinner tonight. It should be a story worth hearing."

"One of those scalps is no Sioux," she said, quite unnecessarily. Swallow wasn't blind. He knew as well as she that it was the scalp of the wolfer who'd been killed in Helena. Butchered in Helena. Left with his privates stuffed in his mouth . . . inside a tobacco pouch made from a woman's breast skin. Rebecca shuddered at the thought, then shook her head in a vain attempt to fling away the image.

Swallow made no attempt to diffuse the issue. "You can't judge an Indian's thinking by your standards," he said. "Can't be done, and you're wasting your time trying. Sleeping Fox is human, just like you, and he has feelings, just like you. But what he does about them is based on *his* culture, not yours. And his culture is something you probably couldn't understand if you lived to be a hundred, unless you lived those years with his people. And an open mind."

There was an undertone in those final words that told her he didn't think an open mind was possible in her case.

"What are those scars on his chest?" she asked, determined to persist, determined to understand at least something from all of this. "The similar ones . . . here." She drew her hands across her own collarbone.

Swallow's gaze followed her fingers, and lingered behind long after her hands had been removed. He seemed to caress the swell of her bosom with that gaze, a caress as tangible as if he'd reached out and touched her.

Her nipples thrust themselves out in response, welcoming his gaze. Her breasts seemed to swell beneath her shirt-waister. She could feel their weight increase, felt for an instant that the garment would be inadequate to hold her in.

Swallow's pale green eyes warmed, losing their usual coolness in favor of an intensity she could feel as much as see. Then the ice came down like a winter sleet storm.

"Sleeping Fox's scars are sundance scars," he said. "Now, let's get on with this shooting business before some other Indian comes riding over the hill and you have to start learning the hard way."

Rebecca ignored the jibe. Better to be scorned than have to deal with the feelings she'd just encountered within herself.

Never had her body so blatantly betrayed her.

Which did not improve her learning skills one bit. She began their lesson as a hopeless shot, and Swallow's need to touch her, to adjust an elbow, to fit her cheek to the stock of the heavy rifle, only served to confuse her further. When he stood close behind her, she could feel the heat of him through her dress, was all too aware of his touch, of his breath on her neck.

And the heavy rifle kicked! Snugging it tight against her shoulder did little to alleviate that problem. And when, at one point, Swallow laid those long, sensitive fingers on the growing sore spot and remarked, "You'll most likely have a bruise there, we keep this up," she knew the remark to be true, but half her mind was more attentive to his touch than his words.

"I've had bruises before, and will again," she said, levering another shell into the chamber and trying to focus, trying to will her bullet to shatter the innocent and pristine white rock that wavered in and out of her sights.

What had he said earlier? Put the sight above the target and let it drift down onto it? All right, she thought, and a moment later peered through the smoke to see that her target had miraculously vanished.

"There!" she cried with delight. "I did it!"

"Good thing it wasn't shooting back, although I suppose it might have run out of ammunition before you did."

Turning, he led the way over the ridge to camp. Rebecca scowled. If he hadn't taken the rifle with him, it might have been interesting to try one more shot, at very close range and with a moving target.

Dinner that evening was the quiet affair Rebecca had become used to. Antelope steaks, bannock, coffee, and an almost total lack of conversation. It wasn't until after the meal, when Swallow had lit one of his cheroots and Sleeping Fox his pipe, that Rebecca realized both men were gearing up for something that might prove interesting.

Sleeping Fox agreed to tell them of his horse-stealing adventure with the Sioux. Swallow translated.

"Now that I am no longer young, I do not sleep so well. I was camped in a coulee near the *Kiyaiyu-isisachta,* the Musselshell River, and the smell of smoke woke me up when it was still dark. That wolfer's horse was too fretful, so I left him at my camp and went on foot to see.

"I moved very slowly and with care, because I knew if anybody was there, it would be Sioux, because there were Sioux everywhere in that country. They are moving north to seek shelter in the land of the grandmother. Some are with Sitting Bull and others are following him. There are some Cheyenne moving north also, but they did not frighten me. Nor did the Sioux. They would run from one *Amskapi-pikunni* unless there were many Sioux, but I did not know how many there were, so I was cautious.

"In the next coulee I found the smoke, and there were three Sioux there and they were asleep. They must have made camp late, and because there were so many Sioux in that country, they must have felt safe, because it was almost a white man's fire, it was so large and made so much smoke. No Peigan would have done such a silly thing."

Swallow hardly needed to translate the next bits, in which the old man pantomimed creeping up on the camp, where each Sioux warrior slept with his personal mount tethered to himself, and the extra horses tied up nearby. The old Indian made it sound incredibly simple, his disdain for his traditional enemies coloring the story considerably.

"I could have killed them all, but that would have been too easy. And it is more important to count coup and shame them as they deserve, so that is what I did. I wove three little grass hoops as I studied the camp, and then I crept in and laid one on each sleeping Sioux. I was going to take all their horses, but the last Sioux was not sleeping too soundly, so I left some horses with the one tethered to him and stole the others, making sure the Sioux would wake up when I did so. Then I let them chase me for a while. It was much fun. They were still half asleep and I had three horses to ride and the wolfer's many-shoots gun."

As the tale continued, Rebecca could easily visualize the old man fleeing his enemies, but fleeing according to his own plan and tormenting them, insulting them as he did so.

"We rode the sun up into the sky, and then I circled back to near my own camp and the place I had already decided to ambush the Sioux." Sleeping Fox laughed, a chilling sound. "They were very foolish, even if they were warriors and had stolen horses and taken scalps. And only three. It was almost too easy."

Almost too easy to shoot down the three Sioux from ambush, then take their scalps, the rest of their horses, such of their weapons as he desired, and continue his journey as if nothing had happened. He hadn't bothered to return to their camp to see if there was anything worth stealing there, Sleeping Fox said. He had properly humiliated his traditional enemies, had counted coup, and if he was concerned about any of it, it was the fact it had been too easy and that he had no wounds to color his bragging when he returned to his people.

Rebecca couldn't disguise the revulsion she felt. She listened to the old man describe such atrocity as calmly as if he'd been telling them about an uneventful camping trip, and her stomach knotted. She stared across the fire at him, unable to assimilate the two sides of Sleeping Fox. The kindly, soft-eyed man who'd joked with her. Who had held the Berube baby in his lap and played with it, as if he'd been a caring, loving grandfather. Who had slain a man in Helena in the most brutal fashion. Who bragged about slaughtering three Sioux braves. Dear God, the braves hadn't bothered him, hadn't threatened him, wouldn't even have known he was there.

When she looked at her companions, she was equally shocked to find their attitudes not only accepting of the old man's story, but lauding it. Had they been in a theater back East, they would be clapping and hooting and . . .

"His people will give him much honor when he returns," Swallow said softly, as if reading her mind.

Which he'd most likely done; she had made no attempt to mask her feelings. But it was one thing to accept that violence was a way of life out here, another to have it treated so casually. And now to be told that such butchery would be honored?

Killing in self-defense, she might understand. But this? Rebecca couldn't answer Swallow, could only shudder and turn her face away as Sleeping Fox reached out to lift his rifle and display the grisly trophies that dangled from it.

Luc was troubled by the expression in Rebecca's eyes. They were so filled with disgust, they'd turned the color of a plum's skin. He had expected a harsh reaction, but not this harsh, and he now saw far more significant portents, at least from his own point of view.

He had noticed her reaction to Sleeping Fox holding the baby before dinner, had been pleased to see her grant the old Indian the gentleness and peace Luc knew the old man was feeling. Now, she stared at Sleeping Fox as if he were a creature without humanity, a demon fresh from her nightmares.

Damn! He must warn Sleeping Fox again about her nightmares. Given the chance, Luc would unload her rifle. She had that haunted, fey look about her now, eyes unnaturally wide. She hadn't experienced nightmares for some time, but tonight would be a worry.

That thought led to something else that had concerned him. The simple logic of Sleeping Fox being down on the Musselshell in the first place. It made no sense to Luc. The old man would have known that the country north of the Greasy Grass, where Custer had been wiped out, would be swarming with Sioux. The Musselshell was a damned dangerous place for any member of the Blackfoot confederacy, especially for one who wandered alone.

It was none of his business. The old man would have explained if it were. And yet . . .

Luc asked the question, throwing aside manners.

Sleeping Fox's reaction was a rumbling guffaw and a gesture that clearly indicated a stupid question was a stupid question in any language. "You gave me this knife so that I could regain my honor, so that I could become a man again," he said. "I give it back to you now, and thank you." He spun the throwing knife to land quivering in the dirt between Luc's feet.

Then his hands fluttered toward Rebecca. "You asked me if I knew of this sunset woman's sister. I thought it might be good for you to know, even though this one's sister is very bad, even worse than I had heard before. Evil. She is known as Blood Hand, and she is a sort of shaman with a small band of Minni-conjou. I think she is . . ." He made the gesture for crazy, so universal even Rebecca could understand. "But Blood Hand has much influence with these people. They are led by Bear's Blood, who is maybe as mad as she, and by now they should be where the Musselshell joins with the Missouri. Or maybe not that far."

Luc didn't dare look at Rebecca, didn't have to look to know that she had followed enough of the exchange to realize she was involved. Sleeping Fox's continual gestures in her direction would have ensured that. *Damn it, old man,* Luc chastised silently. *Couldn't you have chosen some other time to drop this little surprise?*

"I am grateful you have done this thing for me, grandfather," he said, still unable to look at Rebecca. Oblivious to everyone else around the campfire, he had stopped translating.

"You will have to be very careful when you seek this madwoman," the old man said. "I have dreamed of this, and it will be very dangerous, especially for the sunset woman." He smiled. "She is much woman, that one. I think she will cause you many problems."

"She already has," Luc replied without thinking. "But I would not take her with me. She is not of this land. She knows nothing of what would be involved in such a search."

"It is her right to go. She can have that wolfer's buckskin. This, too, I have seen in my dream. And you already have proper clothing for her, for the future, when she will need it."

Rebecca demanded to know what they were talking about. Luc waved at her in a brusque cut-off gesture, his mind whirling as he pondered how on God's green earth Sleeping Fox could know he had gone into the camps at the Judith and bargained for a complete outfit of doeskin clothing for Rebecca, clothing that, except for her hair and coloring, would turn her into a Peigan maiden. Doeskin dress and leggings and finely beaded moccasins, none of which she had seen, none of which anybody in the camp had seen, much less this old man who sat there, gravely regarding Luc through eyes as calm as black water and as knowing as eternity.

Then the impetus of the old man's words filtered into his mind and he cursed himself for a fool. What had he been using for brains? The logic of his purchases made no sense to him now. As if the smoke-tanned doeskins could disguise Rebecca's whiteness. As easy to disguise her femininity. She was what she was.

And Luc was everything she feared and hated. The stuff of her nightmares. He was Métis, but in his soul he was as Indian as Sleeping Fox.

"Don't you dare cut me off like that!"

Rebecca's voice shrilled in his ear as her small fingers slapped at his hands.

"Damn you, Lucas Swallow, you are talking about me! And about my sister! And don't try to lie your way out of it, either. What is this old man saying?"

Her eyes flashed fire as she switched her gaze between himself and Sleeping Fox. Lie his way out of it? *If only I could,* Luc thought.

"I would give many horses," Sleeping Fox grunted, his black eyes filled with amusement, "even more than I said before. But you can give her maturity as well as youth, Horse-tamer, and she is more of your blood. I think the taming of your stallion was only practice for the taming of your Sunset Woman."

Barely had Sleeping Fox shut his mouth than Rebecca was at it again, this time flinging herself in front of Luc, forcing him to meet her gaze, forcing him to either talk to her or talk through her.

"Will you please, *please* tell me what this is all about?"

Her eyes were wide with what could be either rage or panic. Or both. When she grabbed up the knife Sleeping Fox had returned and started waving it around, Luc decided that discretion was the better part of intrepidity.

He explained as briefly as he could, deliberately leaving out the part about Sleeping Fox's dream.

As well to chase the wind.

"How soon can we go?" she asked, her eyes aglow with excitement, her whole body aquiver with it.

Luc made one frantic stab at halting this conception before it got warm. "*We* are not going, Rebecca. I am going. There's no place for you, and it would be damned idiocy to even consider it. There are hundreds, maybe thousands of Sioux roaming around out there."

Her gaze flickered between Luc and Sleeping Fox. "Will you sell me . . . dammit, Swallow, can you ask him for me? I want to buy the saddle and bridle on his buckskin horse, the one he stole from the wolfer. In fact, I'll buy the horse, too. Mine aren't really riding stock, and Mr. Cope will need them."

Damn, damn, damn! Luc glared at Sleeping Fox, who seemed to understand every word of Rebecca's outburst. However, Luc's mental curses did nothing to help the situation. All the logic in the world wouldn't help. Rebecca wasn't going to be swayed by logic. She'd be off searching for her sister no matter what Luc said or did, her promise to her dying father stronger than her fears, stronger than her nightmares, stronger than her common sense. Assuming she had any. Assuming either of them did.

Surprisingly, it was Monique who provided the answer. Monique had been listening and thinking while he had been busy dreaming up arguments for the unarguable.

"Sunset Woman must go with you," she said in a voice that brooked no argument, punctuating her French *patois* with the descriptive sign language that was part of her heritage, and his. "You say but how, *non?* You do not think, you men. How can *you* go among the Sioux, Lucas Swallow, a white man in white man's clothes, when the Sioux are fleeing from the long-knives with the blood of Custer and his horse soldiers on their lances?"

She paused, the expression in her shrewd eyes demanding that Luc translate. Not necessary. His fingers were already doing it, and the English words flowed to his tongue without conscious thought.

"If you must do this thing, you must do it as a Métis," Monique continued. "Or better yet, as another who flees the long-knives. One with a white captive."

A flame flickered briefly in Rebecca's eyes, then surged into a full blaze of enlightenment. Even Sleeping Fox had a guttural grunt of approval for Monique's cunning. The deception would be dangerous, of course. Risky beyond all logic. But such a coup if it could work!

Only Cope and his assistant were less than enthusiastic, but their objections were too distant, too civilized, too . . . white. No one else around the fire expected them to understand, and no one was surprised when they didn't. Cope's objections were voiced, ignored, and dropped.

However, he was gracious in freeing Luc of his responsibilities so that he and Rebecca could take this idiotic chance at finding her sister. Swallow had done his job, Cope said, and the Berube family could help the expedition finish its work.

Sleeping Fox, somewhat surprisingly, refused to join the quest. "I am taking these horses and this wolfer's scalp and these Sioux scalps back West," he said. "Back to my people, to show that I have avenged my family. I give you the buckskin because I have dreamed I should do so. And," he added with a soft chuckle, "because I think it would not be wise for me to ride that horse anywhere near the settlements, where it might be recognized. If the sunset woman did not shoot me, there is no sense in offering my hair to the long-knives. Or to Sitting Bull's warriors."

Luc listened with disappointed understanding. It would have been good if the old man had accompanied him, and Rebecca might have preferred it, too. His gaze drifted toward the woman who, only moments before, had been consumed with excitement. Engrossed in the fulfillment of her dream, staring into the fire, she was with them but apart from them, lost in the pathways of her mind.

The reality would come later, when . . . if . . . this hastily contrived plan got them to where there was any chance at all of finding her captive sister. Blood Hand! And crazy, to boot! Even worse, a shaman of sorts. Truly the mad leading the mad.

By the time Luc rolled into his blankets, he wasn't sure Rebecca would have nightmares, but he felt more than half convinced he'd have some of his own.

12

Rebecca glared down at the thongs that bound her hands to the saddle horn and willed herself to believe they chafed her wrists, even if they didn't. Her bare thighs against the smooth leather of the buckskin's saddle were far more uncomfortable.

Lucas Swallow's thighs were just as naked against the saddle on his big blue roan Appaloosa. That was only too evident, as was the fact that he wasn't in the least discomforted. But then his thighs were sinewy with strength, ropy with muscle, and scarred . . . at least the left one, the one most visible to Rebecca.

"This is ridiculous," she muttered. "What if my horse stumbles or decides to stampede? How am I supposed to control him? What if he falls?"

"He might stumble. He won't fall, and he won't run away. How could he? I've got him on a long rein."

Swallow didn't even bother to turn and look at her. His eyes were too busy scrolling across the horizon, constantly checking for . . . what? There was nothing in any direction except the vast sea of grass and the looming bulk of the Bear Paws.

"Besides," he continued, "you could snap those thongs without the slightest difficulty."

"They're uncomfortable."

"They are not. They're soft as butter. But if you want to think so, that's fine. It'll fit in with the impression that you're a captive. Captives are seldom comfortable. Be glad you've got a saddle. You could be slung up in front of me."

How to argue that one? She was supposed to look like a captive, part of their plan. The problem was, even knowing she could break her wrist thongs, she *felt* like a captive, under control of a man who had so completely changed, she was no longer sure of anything, not herself, not the role they were playing, most certainly not him.

Especially not him, she thought, wishing she didn't have to trail along behind him, unable to keep herself from looking at the frightening figure he'd evolved into. She had almost quit before they'd left the Cope campsite, and the growing certainty that she should have quit plagued her throughout their steady journey up out of the Missouri breaks and into the ocean of grass. Grass that terrified her by its very vastness. No different, surely, than it had been during her childhood journey to and from the plains, but now . . . terrifying. Almost, but not quite, as much as Lucas Swallow now terrified her.

The first sight of him this morning ought to have warned her, *had* warned her, but her own stubbornness had been sufficient to carry her onward. He had been the stuff of her nightmares come to life in the shape of a man who somehow seemed more savage, more terrifying, more "Indian" even than Sleeping Fox.

Naked but for a breechcloth and moccasins, his dark hair braided and adorned with a single long feather, Lucas Swallow had risen like smoke from beside the campfire. Only his pale green eyes had revealed his true identity. Those damned eyes! They'd seen her inner surge of panic. Rebecca had felt both ashamed at and angered by her reaction, even though there was no reason for her to be. After all, this was the same man who claimed he could sense the fear in her memories.

The same, yet now so startlingly different! She had never quite come to terms with Sleeping Fox, not even when Monique Berube had placed her baby in the old man's arms and Rebecca had seen the tears that flowed down the rough contours of his face; tears of sorrow for his own children. She empathized with him, but still couldn't overcome her fear of him—that visceral, unthinking terror that would spasm out of her nightmares without warning, without any ability on her part to defeat them.

And now, riding along behind Swallow, she had to keep tempering those same fears. Because it seemed to her that with each pace of his big stallion he slid farther away from her, becoming more and more a part of the savagery this alien landscape seemed to create, even to encourage.

His skin was nowhere near as dark as the old man's, but his golden tan merged without the definitive markings that should have been evident where his shirt sleeves ended. In truth, his clothing should have created a difference between the tan of his face and the rest of him.

The rest . . . The rest was, she decided, almost too revealing, and yet somehow revealing so little. His scars, a sunburst pattern of markings that radiated up his back and over his left shoulder. Other scars that crept up his neck to be hidden beneath dark hair that revealed glints of auburn in the growing strength of the sun. The identical, puckered furrows below his collarbones, the ones he'd said were sundance scars on the old Indian. And the scars on Swallow's muscular thigh; deep furrowed marks, surrounding a puncture wound that must have gone right to the bone.

She wanted to ask him about those scars.

She wanted to turn her eyes away from the flowing, masculine strength of his body.

But she didn't . . . couldn't.

"What if we run into soldiers?" she asked, continuing her

verbal assault as if it could build up a confidence she didn't feel.

"If we run into soldiers, we ride like hell," he replied, still not turning to look at her. "Or at least I will. You might be safe enough, but they'd shoot or hang me quicker than talking about it, which, by the way, I wish you'd stop doing. I'm spooked enough without you messing up my concentration."

Secretly, Luc wished a squad of soldiers *would* appear. Under their protection, Rebecca would be out of harm's way while he went on—alone—to search for her sister.

"Concentrate on what?" she grumbled. "You can see fifty miles in any direction."

Luc gritted his teeth. They were only half a day's ride from Cope's encampment, and already many of his apprehensions had been realized. Rebecca was undeniably courageous, but her courage wasn't founded on any real knowledge.

"Listen," he said, this time turning to face her. "Half the Sioux nation could be within half a mile of us. Or closer. And, my dear Miss Bennett, we wouldn't even know it until we turned the corner of the next coulee and rode right into them."

"But . . ."

"But nothing. That country out there might look flat to you, but it's a labyrinth of coulees and gullies and ravines and low, rolling hills. You could hide an army in there, which, in fact, is exactly what Sitting Bull is doing. It's the only saving grace to this entire, rattle-brained scheme. If the Sioux are scared enough to be running for safety in Canada, they might . . . just might . . . be more concerned with their own survival than with collecting stray scalps along the way."

Controlling a shudder, at least on the outside, Rebecca averted her eyes until she was certain Swallow had returned his attention to the trail ahead. Not that *trail* was any description. Indeed, he seemed determined at any cost to avoid anything that even resembled a trail.

He moved them along steadily, but in no apparent hurry, always below the brow of an adjacent hill or ridge. Occasionally, he would urge his stallion up enough to give him a bird's-eye view of the vista around them, but never were they skylined.

As they gradually rode into rougher country, always traveling north and east to skirt the flanks of the Bear Paws, the journey became more and more difficult for Rebecca. Until she'd seen the way the Berube boys managed their shaggy ponies, she'd always considered herself a good, competent horsewoman. But now, watching the lean, muscular form of Swallow, a figure so fluid, so totally in unison with his mount, she realized there was a vast difference between her proficiency and his. If only they'd thought to bring a sidesaddle. She almost smiled. An Indian captive with her own sidesaddle? Not that they'd had one anyway.

"By tonight you'll be wishing we'd had a sidesaddle to use," Swallow said, and she wondered, not for the first time, if he was able to read her mind as well as smell her memories.

"I imagine there are lots of things we might wish we'd brought," she said, surprised that he would speak after having ordered her not to. That he understood her discomfort was an even greater surprise, for it was a matter of some pride that she hadn't *seriously* complained, even though her thighs were urging her to do so.

Why hadn't she purchased a proper riding costume in Helena?

Except a proper riding costume, without a damn sidesaddle, wouldn't relieve her anguish. How would the Sioux feel about a captive woman in trousers?

"We should have considered trousers for you," Swallow said, echoing her thoughts again. "But I've got some bear grease in my saddlebags. You can rub that on when we make camp."

Suddenly, his hand raised in an unmistakable gesture for

silence. He turned their horses downhill, onto a narrow, barely discernible game trail, and what had been an uncomfortable ride became a total nightmare. Prickly thickets slid past his naked body with hardly a whisper, but they seemed to leap out at Rebecca, first plucking her sunbonnet awry, then clawing at her clothes, then snagging at her hair with a million tiny claws.

Worse, she could do nothing about it without breaking the thongs which now did imprison her hands. She tried ducking her head, tried every feeble movement she could manage in the saddle, but it only seemed to make the surrounding brush more aggressive.

When they finally halted, again with an ominous gesture for silence from Swallow, insects stirred up by the horses' passage descended upon her with a savage and sadistic pleasure, biting, stinging, crawling all over her. She could have screamed, *would* have screamed, except she was more intimidated by Swallow's warning signal than by the insects' pervasive vengeance.

He had ridden throughout the morning with his revolver slung from his saddle horn. Now it was in his hand, and even as she watched, he slid like water from his huge stallion and paced back to close off her mount's nostrils with his free hand. He glanced at her only long enough to flash another command for silence with his eyes, then turned his attention to the hillside above them.

Rebecca sat there, immobile. With the greatest effort of her life, she endured the insects. Meanwhile, Swallow acted like a beast at bay, his nose drinking the wind, his eyes relentlessly searching. And she could almost swear she saw his ears twitch, as did those of his stallion, who watched and listened, too, its attitude more that of a dog than a horse.

For her part, there was nothing to see, nothing to hear. All she could do was close her eyes, clench her hands round the saddle horn, and suffer an assault by the midges and mosquitoes and, worst of all, the deer flies that chomped globules of flesh from her with each bite.

Clenching her teeth, she tried to force her mind onto something . . . anything . . . else. But her mind refused to co-operate. If she determined not to think about the insect plague, her mind focused on Swallow's revolver. She didn't know which was worse, although at least Swallow and his gun weren't feeding on her blood.

Luc stifled a sigh. Darting a glance toward Rebecca, he mentally cursed himself for bringing her along. He could actually *see* the welts growing as the insects feasted on her tender flesh.

Insects hardly bothered him at all. His blood didn't attract the myriads of insect life that plagued the sloughs and waterways of the prairies. But he knew all about them, had seen horses driven mad by the blackflies of the northern swamps and forests, had seen Indians and whites alike with eyes so swollen they'd lost all vision.

Damn, damn, damn. He should have abandoned Rebecca at the Cope campsite and gone on by himself.

Even then, it was a chancy business.

If the Indians holding Rebecca's sister were threatened, there was as much chance as not they'd simply kill their captive, although the fact she had been among Indians so long gave him hope that she must be valued.

Somebody's favorite wife? Perhaps. And yet this business of her having been traded to the Sioux was a mystery, defeating any logic. Hereditary enemies, as a rule, would not be trading captives, especially white, female captives. Although just who or what had been traded for Amy Bennett was an unknown in an already difficult equation. What had Sleeping Fox said? That the Bloods were glad to get rid of Amy? But why?

The stallion whuffled an impatient snort. Whatever had been

out there was gone. The Appaloosa no longer sensed any danger, and neither did Luc. Still, he waited another ten minutes or so before cautiously moving ahead through the bottomland thickets.

If memory served, there was a perfect campsite they might reach before evening. Assuming, of course, it wasn't already occupied by stray Sioux or wandering renegades.

When Swallow reached a secluded glade and thankfully halted for the night, Rebecca wasn't certain she could get off her horse without help. And she wasn't, she determined fiercely, going to ask for any.

Her thighs were locked in cramps, and her eyes were so puffy from midge bites she could hardly see. If she dared yank her hands free of the light buckskin tethers, she knew she'd scratch herself to ribbons, but that knowledge didn't help. Indeed, it only seemed to aggravate her compulsion.

Sliding from his stallion's back, Luc stepped over to help Rebecca dismount. The agony she must have endured, and the courage she had shown, shamed and angered him . . . although the anger was directed at himself, not Rebecca.

Reaching up, he plucked her from the saddle as if she were a child, ignoring her groan of protest. Then he carried her over to the edge of a small but mercifully insect-free pool, formed by a creek that trickled through the glade.

He wanted to murmur comforts to her, wanted to ease her pain, wanted, he realized with a sudden, wrenching clarity, to keep on holding her. But he didn't. Couldn't. Instead, he lowered her to the edge of the stream and began, with ruthless efficiency, to tug the boots from her swollen feet.

"Stop that!" Quelling another groan, Rebecca glared at Swallow through slitted eyes. What did he intend to do, for goodness' sake? Undress her?

"If you can manage for yourself, fine," he said. "But I want you in that pool and soaking while I get a camp together."

"The hell you do! If you think for one minute that I'm going to . . . going to . . . loll about . . . disrobed . . . exposed . . . in a pool of water hardly larger than a bathtub . . ."

"I won't look. You have my word on it. Difficult as it might be for you to imagine, I am a gentleman."

Gentleman! He stood there before her, the epitome of a half-naked savage, and had the audacity to say he was a gentleman! Rebecca could only shake her head.

"Into the water, lady. Now! You'll feel better after a bath. It will help soothe those bites."

Without another word, he strode away, then began leading both horses down the stream, assumedly to water them. Rebecca glared after him, but made no move to obey save to plunge her feet into the delicious coolness of the pool. Then she just sat there, not revived by the water, but lulled by it. Her eyes slowly closed as she slumped back on her outspread arms and felt the wondrous coolness work its way up her cramped legs.

It was, she thought, the next best thing to heaven, although throwing herself bodily into the pool held an even greater potential for luxuriant satisfaction. The insect bites made her itch all over, and she still had to restrain the urge to scratch until she bled.

Gradually, she let herself slide farther and farther along the bank. Soon, her knees and upper thighs were immersed. The balming effect of the water seemed to flow up her clothing. She never heard Swallow ease up behind her, never even realized he was there until strong arms slipped round her waist and she was lifted, then tossed into the pool, so swiftly and smoothly that even her gasp of alarm was stifled.

"I . . . you . . . you bastard," she sputtered as her head emerged and she found herself treading water, her hair a sodden mat that flowed over her face and eyes. Her clothing felt so heavy, she thought she might be dragged under again.

"Get yourself cooled off and clean, Rebecca!" Swallow turned abruptly on his heel and walked away, returning a few moments later with a skin bucket dangling from one huge hand and a rough scrap of blanket from the other.

"Catch," he said, dropping the blanket and throwing something she instinctively reached out to capture.

Soap? Yes, it was! Real soap!

"I need to get some cooking water before you lather up the entire pond," Swallow muttered, kneeling.

Rebecca thought he tried not to look at her, even though she was certain in her mind he could see the way her sodden clothing clung to her body. Whereupon, she became all too aware of her raised arms as she struggled to claw the hair away from her face, which only added to the denuding effect as her breasts strained against the wet material. And yet her throat was frighteningly exposed, as if to the fangs of a predator.

He was gone again before she could speak, moving like a wraith across the soft grasses beside the pond. Eventually he left her sight, allowing her the privacy he had promised. Assuming, of course, he'd stay away.

"Gentleman!" Rebecca sniffed her disdain, then maneuvered closer to shore, where she could find sure footing. The slight overhang of the bank offered even more protection from prying eyes. Suddenly, she dissolved into exhaustion. Reaching up to grip at a convenient clump of strong reeds, she let herself float.

The water soothed and rocked her weary, pain-wracked body, and it seemed like hours before she once again heard Swallow's voice, this time from a distance.

"I'm leaving fresh clothes," he said. "Then I'll have a scout around, so you can dry off and get yourself together."

"But I'm not even washed yet." She peered through puffy

eyes at the lump of soap she still held, unused, in her free hand.

"No rush," was his reply, this time closer.

Lifting herself up, ever so slightly above the overhang, she caught a glimpse of his shoulder as he knelt to deposit something on the grass. Then he walked away again, without looking at her.

Only when she was sure he was truly gone did Rebecca finally succumb to temptation. Slipping off her drenched dress and undergarments, she scrubbed herself quickly, as if every instant, every second, held her totally vulnerable.

And it felt good . . . so good. The insects in the coulee had, indeed, been gifted with a feast, but the worst of the itchiness was already dwindling and her most immediate sensation was one of relaxed pleasure, of drifting and flowing with the gentle current of the pond.

"Are you going to spend the night in there? Or do I have to drag you out before you shrivel up?"

Swallow's voice came from a distance, thank God. However, Rebecca wasn't at all prepared for the unexpected flush of sensation his suggestion caused. Half panic, half anticipation, and it was the latter which both startled and surprised her as she realized her mind had been seeing Lucas Swallow while her hands had been slowly, sensuously, caressing the soap across her insect-ravaged skin.

"Please g-go . . . stay away," she stammered. "I won't be long."

"Just as well." His reply seemed to be carried on the wings of a Peppergrass-scented breeze. "You're not the only one who needs a scrub. Or hadn't that occurred to you?"

It hadn't, of course. "I suppose you expect me to throw you in, as well?"

"You can try. But if you don't hurry, you'll be sharing that pool with me, so be warned."

Warned? Threatened was more like it, she thought, pitching the remains of the soap onto the bank and easing herself up to check on the exact whereabouts of Swallow, who was nowhere to be seen.

"I'm over here, sitting behind a bush with my back turned," said a disembodied voice. "There's clothing for you on the bank. Not what you'd prefer, I suspect, but it will have to do."

Rebecca grabbed up the scrap of blanket and hurriedly toweled herself dry, or at least as dry as she could manage. Only then did she look for the clothes, and she had to choke back her immediate cry of protest.

"Surely you can't expect me to wear this!" Swallow said it for her in a squeaky falsetto. "But I do, Miss Bennett," he continued in his own, far deeper voice. "Because there isn't anything else for you to wear, Miss Bennett. And you *will* wear it, Miss Bennett, because in about ten seconds I'm having my bath. So if you're not dressed by then, upon your own head be the consequences."

Despite his mocking tone, Rebecca thought he sounded somehow unsure. Almost . . . defensive . . . although she couldn't imagine why.

She shook her head, fairly certain she had imagined his subtle inflections, then forced herself to slip the soft, stunningly beaded doeskin smock over her shoulders. The dress had a vague, smoky aroma, and felt like velvet against her skin. It took her a moment to figure out the accompanying leggings, and she was slipping on the finely beaded moccasins when Swallow emerged from behind his bush and stalked toward her.

Dear God, but he moved splendidly. Like some great cat, not slinking but haughtily pacing, moving on feet that scarcely touched the ground. It was the walk of a predator, totally comfortable in its own pelt, totally in control of its life, of its entire world. Menacing, in a subtle way, and yet so . . . just so utterly complete.

He appraised her garments, raised one dark eyebrow, nodded, then said, "Won't be long," and without a pause dived cleanly past her, entering the glistening waters of the pool with the ease and assurance of an otter.

When he came up on the far side and looked in her direction, he gave her a genuine smile. "Good," he said, dipping once more beneath the surface. She could see his body flow through the water, and again she was struck by the elemental rightness of the way he seemed to be attuned to his environment.

She had barely made it back to the campsite when he reappeared, striding behind her in long paces that brought him to her side before she'd reached the neatly-arranged piles of their belongings. Water dripped from his loincloth and the ends of his braids, glistening in the late-afternoon sunlight.

This was the first time she and Swallow had camped alone . . . together . . . just the two of them. She felt less at ease than he apparently felt, and his near nakedness did little to improve things. But what she wanted—needed!—more than anything was access to her combs. Her waist-length hair was so matted, she knew if she didn't comb it before it dried she might as well hack it all off with a knife.

From the first tug of the comb, she realized there was an hour's work ahead of her. Even after washing, her hair contained bits of broken twig from their meanderings along the coulee, and the comb caught in her tangles so severely she grimaced with pain.

Swallow removed the comb from her fingers and led her over to where his saddle lay beside a large, fallen log. Placing his hands on her shoulders as he swung round behind her, he firmly but gently forced her to sit on the saddle with her back to him.

"Whatever are you doing?"

"I am going to fix your hair, Miss Bennett. And yes, I know you could do it yourself, and would prefer to, but since we can't eat until it's done, and since I am hungry enough to eat one of those horses raw, you are going to allow me the pleasure. Because I can do it faster and better than you can, Miss Bennett, and then we can both eat."

"I can comb my own damned hair!"

She started to get up, one hand reaching for the comb while the other reached out to steady herself.

Two large hands immediately locked upon her shoulders.

"We've already agreed that you can comb your own damn hair," he said calmly. "Sit down and keep still. Those knots are going to be difficult enough, and I don't need you squirming like a half-broke colt."

"Filly." The word slipped out with the speed of her thinking it, and she barely realized she had spoken aloud until Swallow's rich laughter rumbled in her ear.

"My apologies," he said. "Filly, indeed."

She might have continued her protest, except he'd already begun the task of unraveling the knots, and the touch of his fingers was so deft, so cunning, she was surprised into silence.

As he worked, he hummed. No. Chanted. There were words in the gentle, soothing cadence, not that she could understand them. They were clearly in some Indian language or another. But if she couldn't understand their meaning, their purpose, she could definitely understand and appreciate the dexterity with which this astonishing man handled her mane of tangled hair.

After only a few moments, she drifted into a half sleep, wallowing in the sheer luxury of it all. Then she had a mental image of Lucas Swallow—dressed formally, as when she'd first met him—in this ridiculous position of lady's handmaiden, and she giggled.

"You are finding this amusing?" His voice broke from his chant, then resumed it without waiting for a reply. It was some moments before he issued a whispered "Uhmmm," which could have meant anything. Or everything. Or nothing.

Rebecca suddenly became all too aware of how skillfully she was being manipulated. How she'd gradually sagged backward until she was propped tidily between lean, muscular legs. She could feel the warmth of his groin against her spine. She wriggled, halfheartedly attempting to remove herself, but those amazing fingers and that soothing chant drove off her best intentions.

Swallow was braiding her hair now. She could recognize the adroit orchestration of his long, strong fingers as they cleverly maneuvered her heavy ropes of damp hair. His voice chanted in a cadence that only enhanced the subtle, sensual indulgence.

Desire struck at Luc like a physical blow, prompted when his fingers neared the end of Rebecca's first plait. He had been paying no real attention, his own mind wandering in the pleasure he gained from weaving his fingers through her fine mane of hair. But eventually his gaze was drawn, as if by an arrow's flight, to the sagging neckline of her soft, doeskin gown. Then past that neckline to where one pale white breast seemed to lift, the slightly darker aureole almost screaming out to be touched, fondled, kissed.

Already warmed by the pressure of Rebecca's recumbent body, his manhood reared to attention with the vitality of a spirited stallion, and his chanting was broken by the harsh gasp of his desire.

She gave no indication she'd heard, made no movement, no gasp of alarm. Nor, he accepted with a mild taste of disappointment, did she reveal—by word, action, or even facial expression—any acceptance.

He looked to the heavens, seeking some sign to guide him,

then sighed heavily and forced himself motionless as he quickly grabbed up a strand of yarn from the parfleche at his saddlebow and whipped it round the end of her first braid.

Forcing his fingers to plait her other braid, he kept his eyes on the sky, letting his hands blindly guide themselves.

It worked, for a moment. But then his eyes were drawn downward, as the tempting globe of her other breast began peeping through the curtain of auburn. There was no reaction from his swollen groin now. It was fully occupied in straining against his willpower, pressing at her spine as if to reach through her to the delectable temptation of her bosom.

Luc swallowed a curse, muffling it within the cadence of his chant. What on earth was he doing? This was a respectable woman. A white woman! Among his own people, Indian, French or Métis, there was a strong earthiness, an awareness and a much broader acceptance of sexuality, but the way Rebecca Bennett had certainly been raised . . .

He must end this! Now! And yet even as his fingers tied off her second braid, his hands moved as if of their own volition to gently massage the doeskin-clad shoulders below her hair. Which caused a flicker of . . . what? Anticipation, he supposed, from his still-solid erection.

But not so much as a flicker of awareness from the slender form whose splendid shoulders he was manipulating. Was she asleep? He paused, and that was enough to finally draw a response from Rebecca. She moaned softly, thrusting back against him with the petulant willfulness of a child.

The braiding she had accepted under sufferance. Given no warning, the massage had lulled her into a sense of security so laughably false that Luc almost choked on his anger.

Damn the woman for her childish vulnerability! And damn her, equally, for being so totally desirable, for having emerged from the spirit-seeking of his youth to play havoc with his adult life. There was no sanity in trying to find her missing twin sister, even less in taking her with him on such a ludicrous quest. And a seduction, if that's what this was, would only . . .

The growl that emerged slew his chanting with the suddenness of a knife thrust. Luc's strong fingers quivered with tension as he pushed against Rebecca's shoulders, using the leverage to bring himself to his feet, using the anger to let him stride away without a word, without a backward glance.

Catching up his revolver in a gesture of innate caution, he moved purposefully across the meadow, pausing only long enough to lay the gun down as he plunged into the evening chill of the pond again, where the water shrank his passions to manageable proportions.

13

Sleeping Fox drifted into the deserted campsite like a wisp of wood smoke, his moccasins barely touching the ground, his movements so deliberate and controlled that he scarcely seemed to move at all.

He had left his ponies nearly half a mile away, and now he was glad. There would be less confusion in the tracking.

Obsidian eyes darted swiftly over the ground, reading the sign as easily as a white man might read a book. Within moments he knew how many people had used the site, who had sat where, who had ridden in on which horse, and . . . most important . . . simply *who!*

That knowledge brought a guttural snarl into his throat. Sleeping Fox had seen this one's spoor before. He had seen it in the dust of a Helena street, both with and without the accompanying sign of the harsh Spanish spur rowels behind the unusually small boot prints. This was the small man with the knives, the black weasel who had skulked along behind the moon-dreaming Métis who was Sleeping Fox's friend.

The aged Peigan snarled again, then spat as if to exorcise the evil he felt at the sight of Luis Sebastian's tracks, that same feeling of *unrightness* any wilderness hunter feels when confronted with the sign of the wolverine. And that one had been here, too . . . *Le Carcajou* . . . the man so aptly named for the vicious, always-dangerous scavenger of the forests. Dover Sugden.

So much evil, the old man thought. He expanded his prowling circuit of the campsite perimeter until he was morally certain, certain beyond any possibility of mistake, which direction the whiskey-trader and his band of cutthroats had taken.

Sleeping Fox was several days out from the Cope campsite near the base of the Bear Paws, heading north and west toward his people's country at the foot of the great shining mountains. Slow days. The Sioux ponies had been hard used when he'd taken them, and he wanted them fat and sassy and looking their best when he displayed them as evidence of his bravery and cunning.

This campsite was one he had thought would be unknown to anyone not of his people, and Sleeping Fox couldn't explain the unease that had trickled up his spine when he drew near the place. Indeed, he wouldn't even think to try and explain it. The feeling was there and he obeyed it, as any wise person should.

With good reason, he now saw.

Wherever *Le Carcajou's* band had been, it was now all too clear where they were headed. Due east, probably planning to skirt the northern edge of the Bear Paws. Nowhere near where the bone hunter was camped, but squarely on line to intersect the path his friend and the sunset woman had taken.

Sleeping Fox took a final prowl around the camp to ensure he'd missed nothing, then left to gather his ponies, his mind awhirl with unexpected concerns, surprising concerns. His friend the horse tamer was a man grown. Surely he could look after himself and the sunset woman. Except . . . Horse-tamer was smitten with the sunset woman, even if perhaps he did not realize it. She was much woman, but also much trouble. He, himself, had been half joking, half serious, when he'd offered many horses for her, and was just as happy no bargain had been struck.

Horse-tamer was a fool to try to go among the Sioux with this red-headed one. Her sister was known throughout the Sioux nation, and not with the best of acceptance outside the small band of Minniconjou she dominated. Also, it had to be considered that Horse-tamer could not know about *Le Carcajou* and his evil ones, and would not be watching for them. Watching out for the Sioux would take enough diligence.

"Waugh, this is not my business," he said, the words exploding in a guttural cough. "I have these horses to take west to where my people are. Horse-tamer rides the other way, towards the *Kiyaiyo-isisachta,* where I saw the Sioux with the sunset woman's sister."

Sleeping Fox checked his stolen ponies' rawhide halters, ensuring they were linked head-to-tail in proper fashion. His mind was already plotting how he could move slowly through the *Kutoyisiks,* the Sweetgrass Hills, fattening the ponies as he traveled westward, homeward.

A single grunt of satisfaction rode the wind as he examined his weapons and confirmed that his scant belongings were in order; the pigments he would use to paint himself for his victory entrance; the extra weapons he had stolen along with the ponies; the medicine bag that hung from his turkey-wattled throat.

As he leapt upon the lead pony with the agility of one half his age, his black eyes fixed upon the prairie to the west, the distant dark shadows of the Sweetgrass Hills and the more distant image of the great shining mountains that loomed over the foothills where he had been born and hoped, eventually, to die.

He kicked the pony in the ribs with one moccasin-clad toe, and his voice erupted in a huge, laughing curse as he turned the cavalcade eastward, instead, following the tracks of Dover Sugden and the deadly little Spaniard.

They were two days ahead at most, which should give him time to find them, overtake them . . . maybe even find Horse-tamer and his sunset woman.

Rebecca glared angrily at Lucas Swallow, her eyes flicking down at her thong-bound wrists, then up again in a futile attempt to dominate him by eye contact alone.

"This is damned foolishness, I tell you," she repeated for what seemed like the hundredth time, knowing he wouldn't even bother to answer, knowing that for some reason he was displeased with her, not knowing for the life of her why he should be.

He'd been . . . vexed . . . ever since the first night's camp; the night he'd given her Indian clothes and braided her hair with a care and attention she hadn't felt since childhood. Then he'd roughly pushed her away and left her half asleep . . .

And totally confused.

"You make too much noise," he now said, his own voice hardly above a whisper. "Do I have to gag you to make you understand this is a dangerous business? You may think finding your sister is worth dying for, but I've a hankering to live a fair bit longer."

"I don't know why you even bothered coming with me since you're afraid of every shadow," she muttered in reply, but this time kept her voice as low as his own. "And I simply cannot see how tying my hands is going to make 'living' any easier."

"Gagging you might make it a good deal easier for me! As for the rest, we've been over that ground, even you should understand. If . . . no, *when* . . . we meet Indians, it will be easier if they think you're my captive."

"Pooh! A captive on a horse with a rifle hanging at her fingertips and wrists tied with a cord so weak a child could break it! What an impression that's going to make!"

"It makes the impression I want it to make."

Rebecca shook her braids and stifled a sigh. Swallow's voice was almost too calm, too self-contained. The man had the uncanny ability to be both steadfast and argumentative at the same time.

She'd pegged him as an enigma the first time they'd met, and he hadn't changed one whit. He had thrust her away after plaiting her hair, and when he had returned some time later, dripping from his bath—why, for goodness' sake, a second bath?—he had virtually flung a skin bag of some foul-smelling grease at her and insisted she use it for her insect bites. Then he had positively glowered at her throughout a makeshift meal of pemmican and some roots he'd picked up near their camp, and he hadn't spoken a civil word to her since.

"It's not likely to be your wrists they'll be concentrating on, Rebecca, so stop complaining and try to keep up."

Whereupon, he increased his great stallion's pace. Silently, she stared at his magnificently muscled, strangely scarred back and the horse's equally muscular rump.

It was at least some consolation that Swallow no longer bothered to keep her horse on a long lead, not that she had any real control over the animal with her hands bound to the saddle horn. Even that scarcely mattered. The buckskin meekly followed step by step in the tracks of the much larger Appaloosa, and would have, she supposed, no matter what she might have been tempted to do about it.

Aware that Rebecca had . . . finally . . . hushed, Luc fought a losing battle with his own temper and judgment. Damn the woman! He didn't want her here, didn't want any part of this ridiculous escapade. What he wanted to do was turn the horses around, return to that first night's idyllic campsite, lift her down off her pony, and spend the next week or so teaching her about the dangers of arousing a man past all tolerable limits.

And I'd do it, too, if only I wasn't so damned sure she hasn't the faintest idea how tempting she is.

He tried to blot out an image of snowy breasts that fairly begged to be kissed, caressed, controlled by his lips and fingers. He had only to look at Rebecca to feel his body respond.

Unfortunately, neither of them had any place in the other's world, this current insanity aside, and even if they did manage to find and rescue her sister, she would return to her civilized, Eastern life.

Luc shook his head. Despite Monique's foxy scheme and Sleeping Fox's grunt of approval, he and Rebecca had as much chance of finding Amy Bennett as flying to the moon, and even less chance of rescuing her. Christ! Getting out alive would be tricky enough, assuming they stumbled onto the right band of Sioux.

Or any Sioux, for that matter.

They traveled most of the day in the silence Luc demanded, only to climb out of a coulee just before sundown and find that silence, alone, was nowhere near enough to guarantee safety.

Not a long shot's distance away was a band of Indians who clearly saw Luc as soon as he saw them. With nowhere to run, nowhere to hide, and everything to lose, he didn't so much as let his stallion break stride.

They were not Sioux, nor roving Crow, but Cheyenne. Seven horses, one dragging a travois. No war paint, but no women, either. Six riders, all of them men, warriors, all of them armed.

"Stay well back and for God's sake keep your head down and your mouth shut," Luc warned Rebecca, just before he booted his stallion and let his fingers idly, almost casually stray to the rifle at his saddlebow. Whereupon, he surreptitiously cocked the weapon.

Sliding easily into the guttural formal dialect of the Northern Cheyenne, Luc kept his free hand lifted in the peace signal, but never once took his eyes from the slitted gaze of the Cheyenne warrior who faced him.

"Red Calf, I greet you," Luc said. "You are far from home."

For an instant, Luc was certain he and Rebecca had no chance at all. He knew Red Calf, knew him only too well. The Cheyenne sat quietly for what seemed an eternity, his black eyes flickering back and forth between Luc and Rebecca. A trade musket, stock shiny with brass tacks, dangled from his hand, and the beads on his buckskin medicine shirt flashed in the sun. But no paint adorned his face, and his glossy black scalp lock was not braided for war.

Finally, the Cheyenne said, "And you, Horse-tamer, you, too, are far from the place I saw you last. Is this your new woman? Who did you steal this woman from? Some white-eyes with a broken leg or two?"

Red Calf made no attempt to hide the scorn in his deep, rasping voice, and the hard-flung gesture of his head was not lost upon Luc, who cursed inwardly at the elderly warrior's desire to resurrect the past. Obviously, Red Calf's old hatred still smoldered.

"She is nothing," Luc said with caution. "But she might be of some value to the people of Sitting Bull, if I can find him. And if I can get her there without her falling off her horse. She does not ride well."

Red Calf scowled. But the mention of Sitting Bull drew a cry of interest from the prone figure on the travois.

"Who is on the travois?" Luc said. "If he is injured, perhaps I can help. You know I have some skills in that way."

For whatever reason, Red Calf's antagonism lessened. He appeared to ponder the question for a long time before answering, but the easing of tension was almost palpable.

"It is Medicine Horse on the travois, Horse-tamer, but you cannot help him. We are taking him home to die, I think. Ever since we began to follow Sitting Bull toward the land of the Grandmother, devils have been eating at his stomach. He is an

176

old man, as you know. He cannot fight the devils much longer. He has decided that he wants to die in the land of his own people, so we will take him there. I am not certain it can be done. He is already dying, and in great pain."

"I knew him long ago," Luc said. "Medicine Horse is a great man and I am saddened by his sickness. Could I speak with him, do you think? I must try to find Sitting Bull, or at least some of those who are with him. Medicine Horse was once my friend. I would not harm him."

"You *could* not harm him," the scowling warrior amended. Then he laughed, but it was a sound devoid of any humor. "Go ahead, Horse-tamer. This is not the time for you and me. The old man wishes to go home in peace and to die in peace, and I will not go against his wishes."

With a quick glance toward Rebecca, a glance he hoped would tell her to stay motionless but alert, Luc reined the big roan stallion widely around the other Cheyenne until he came up behind the travois. That way, he could look down at the aged, seamed face of its occupant without losing sight of the others.

"Greetings, grandfather," Luc said politely, his voice low but clear enough to bring a grunt of surprise and pleasure from the shrunken body on the litter.

"Is it you, Horse-tamer? I thought I heard your voice." The old man's inflections were ragged yet strong. "My eyes are no longer so good. I think they already go ahead of me to look at death."

"Yes, grandfather, it is Horse-tamer. I am sorry to see you are not well," Lucas said soberly, and truthfully. He had always liked the old man, one of the first of the Cheyenne to consider peace with the whites as a viable option, a man respected throughout the plains.

"Red Calf says you have been with Sitting Bull," Luc

continued. "Were your eyes there? Or had they gone on ahead of you even then?"

Medicine Horse shifted slightly on the travois. "Until a few days ago, my eyes were as good as yours. What is it you wish to know? I believe you would not disturb an old man on his final journey without some good reason."

"I seek a white woman captive, the sister to the one who is with me." Luc nodded toward Rebecca. "The captive would be with a band of Minniconjou, I think. Though she was once known as Amy Bennett, I have been told she is now known as . . ."

"Blood Hand!" The old warrior spat the words out like rotten meat. He gasped with the effort, then seemed to find new strength as his dark eyes peered up at Luc.

"We have been friends, Horse-tamer, you and I," he said. "Enemies, too, of course, but always friends in spirit." His gaze encompassed the warriors he could see, as if to impress upon them the seriousness of his words.

"Hear me, Horse-tamer, because now I speak only as a friend. And as one who is going to die and should never, therefore, lie. Not even to one who is not totally of the people, but has white blood in him as well.

"If this woman with you is like her sister, do not go further toward Sitting Bull. Go instead into the nearest coulee and shoot the bitch as you would a wolf with the foaming-mouth sickness."

The vehemence in the remark was so vivid, Luc glanced around in order to ascertain that none of the braves had decided to take Medicine Horse's words upon themselves.

"They are identical, grandfather, but only on the outside," Luc said. "There is no evil in the one who travels with me."

Once again, Luc's finger drifted toward the trigger of his rifle. This situation was obviously heading in directions he didn't, and couldn't, understand.

He never saw the gesture that began it, and had no chance to parry before one of the Cheyenne grabbed up Rebecca's halter and dragged her hesitant buckskin over to Medicine Horse. A knife flashed. The thongs that held Rebecca's wrists to the saddle horn parted, and she was kicked unceremoniously from her mount to land sprawling at the base of the travois.

Wide-eyed with terror, she pawed with still-bound hands at the dust on her face. Then she turned to Medicine Horse as if she had understood the command he growled at her. However, she was trembling, clearly terrified, as one of the old man's hands reached out to grasp a braid and pull her face close to his. For an instant Luc was terrified, as well. He could do nothing, say nothing. Any move by him could too easily be misinterpreted.

The dying warrior glared into Rebecca's eyes for a long time, and Luc watched with surprise as her fear diminished. Her shoulders relaxed and her head lifted imperceptibly so that she could meet the old man's eyes more directly.

Medicine Horse muttered some words.

"What does he want?" Rebecca said. "I can see he wants to know something important, but I don't understand." Never for an instant did she attempt to break her eye contact with the old man. In fact, she and Medicine Horse seemed linked by an almost visible chain.

"He wants to know if you are evil." Luc translated the guttural command as best he could. It didn't really mean that, but there were no words to accurately depict the question.

"Evil?" She shook her head ever so slightly, could hardly have done more, given the old man's hold on her braid. "No, I am not evil. And certainly not in the sense I think he means."

She hadn't been able to understand Medicine Horse's words, but his attitude was clear enough, and Luc marveled at her perceptiveness.

"He is dying, isn't he?" she continued. Not expecting—or maybe not wanting—an answer, she reached out with her bound hands to touch gently at the old man's brow. Then she removed his grasp on her braid with equal gentleness. "Is there nothing that can be done for him?"

"Nothing I can do, probably nothing anyone could do," Luc said, wanting to sag with relief but forcing himself to remain upright in the saddle as the tension left his body.

"Well, somebody should do something!"

There was a curious mix of helpless anger and compassion in her tone, but she didn't turn away to look at Luc. Her attention was totally focused on the sick man before her.

Medicine Horse's eyes suddenly flared into life. His fragile, wrinkled fingers also found new life as they moved with astonishing agility to strip the thongs from Rebecca's wrists. Then he rubbed them gently, as if to restore circulation. She didn't flinch, Luc noted with an unexpected surge of pride.

"This one is no sister to the one called Blood Hand!" The old man's voice cut through the eerie silence like a shout, although in truth he hardly spoke loudly at all. "Listen to me, Horse-tamer. Do not risk this woman in a search for one who is . . ."

The words he used could not be translated. They didn't mean crazy woman, nor evil witch, nor anything the English language could perceive. But the meaning was there; even Rebecca understood it; Luc could tell by the sudden shift of her head.

"Take this woman into the land of the Grandmother if you wish," the old man continued. "But take her west, not east. Take her to the land of your own people and breed strong sons from her if you are man enough to handle her. But do not go into the country around Wood Mountain, where Sitting Bull is headed.

You will only get her killed if you do. I, Medicine Horse, tell you this."

"You tell me, grandfather, but I do not understand."

"I do not know how I can explain it to you," the old warrior said, visibly sinking away from the strength that had briefly sustained him. "But I *know*. That is all I can say. The woman they call Blood Hand is the captive wife of the renegade Minniconjou called Bear's Blood. You have maybe not heard of him, I think. A man of great evil. If it were not for the latest war with the long-knives, his own people would have driven him out. They almost did for the way he behaved in the battle at the Greasy Grass, the place your people call the Little Big Horn. But they did not. And now he travels ahead of Sitting Bull, who should also have driven Bear's Blood out, because he is an evil man, one not worthy to be called even Sioux."

Medicine Horse leaned his aged head over the side of the travois and spat his distaste upon the ground.

"This I tell you, Horse-tamer. The evil of Bear's Blood is nothing . . . nothing! . . . compared to the evil that lives in the white-eyes woman you say is this one's sister."

The old eyes gazed at Rebecca and visibly softened, the almost toothless mouth twisting into something akin to a smile as he stroked her now-freed wrists.

"That Blood Hand . . ." He paused to gasp as pain visibly charged through his body. "She is one reason I am going south to die."

The old man's voice waned, and Luc bent down to hear the final gasping words. "I did not want her to drink my blood . . ." The voice tapered off into nothingness as weakness captured it. But even as his eyes faded with his voice, the old warrior waved his hands in the fluttering sign language for respect and peaceful departure. Then he gently pushed Rebecca from him and nodded to his own warriors.

181

Luc returned the gesture, but watched as the Cheyenne began their departure, his rifle still cocked across his saddlebow, his eyes wary. Especially when Red Calf spurred his own mount to rear in a halt so close to Luc, the two men could have touched.

"It has been good to see you again, Horse-tamer," he growled. Though many years Luc's elder, an almost youthful hostility was evident in his voice and gestures. "When I have taken the old man home, I shall remember this place. Maybe I will come back and kill you." Red Calf spat, kicked his pony's flanks, then galloped away to join the other Cheyenne.

Luc waited until the ponies and travois were beyond gun range before he dismounted. Rebecca's mouth looked like a small volcanic aperture, from which molten words and steam would soon emerge. He could almost *see* the questions that formed on her pale lips.

"Later," he said, tossing her into her saddle, then leaping into his own saddle. "Now . . . we ride!"

It was all Rebecca could do to keep up, even with her hands free, as Swallow drove his blue roan stallion on a course that first followed the Cheyenne travois tracks backward, then jinked from one rocky patch to the next, from one scrap of cover to the next, putting as much ground as possible between her buckskin, his blue roan, and the supposedly peaceful Cheyenne. At the same time, he tried to disguise both their direction and every indication of their passage.

They rode into the twilight, rode on into the descending darkness, until Rebecca couldn't imagine how Swallow managed to find his way, much less disguise their trail. But eventually, as her night vision kicked in, she realized he knew exactly where he was going, and that nothing she could say or do would slow him down.

Finally, he entered a tiny, brush-choked gully, and dismounted to lead the horses through a trail that wasn't a trail, merely a series of interlocking tunnels through thick brush. Even the horses had to duck, and Rebecca lay flat against her mount's mane to keep from being wiped off its back.

"No fire . . . no noise," Swallow whispered, appearing beside her as if from nowhere and lifting strong, sure hands to hoist her down from the saddle. He led her through yet another brushy tunnel, saddlebags in his free hand, then guided her toward what seemed no more than a shadowy space beneath a spreading cottonwood.

"There's water in here, and pemmican," he said, handing her the saddlebags. "I want you to eat, drink, try to rest. Stay quiet. I'll wipe out our trail, if I can. Mightn't be necessary. I'm half ready to believe Red Calf . . . the Cheyenne who threatened me . . . won't follow."

His fingers brushed gently against her cheek in a gesture so tender Rebecca thought she might have imagined it, and then he was gone, a shadow amid shadows, a whisper amongst the other whispers of the night wind.

Rebecca was sound asleep when Luc returned. He spread a blanket over her and tried to fall asleep himself, a difficult task. She had understood more of the sign language than he would have expected, and he anticipated her questions.

What answers could he give?

How to explain the hostility of Red Calf?

Luc had wintered with the Cheyenne of Medicine Horse two seasons after avenging his father's murder. And it was that winter when he found his true manhood, despite his medicine dreams, despite having, long before, undergone the ritual self-torture of the Blackfoot sundance ceremony. The agonizing dance around the medicine pole, his flesh riven by the thorns through his breast muscles, had—to Blackfoot eyes—made him a warrior, and he had left his boyhood behind forever, there on the Kootenay Plains, high on the headwaters of the Saskatchewan.

But his manhood in the eyes of the Indian women—the soft black eyes of the young Blackfoot, Cree, Cheyenne and even Crow maidens whose robes he'd shared during his years as a horse tamer—had come from a different kind of ceremony, a ritual begun at the hands of Red Calf's youngest and most expensive wife.

Red Calf had broken a leg earlier in the winter, a bad break made worse by a kick from the wild horse he'd been trying to ride. He had been confined to his lodge with his three older wives, and spent most of the winter drunk, paying little attention to his youngest wife.

Deepwater was among the loveliest of Cheyenne maidens when sold to Red Calf at the age of fifteen. The already aging warrior had been able to guarantee possession of the girl by outbidding his younger rivals, and while it had cost him seventeen horses and several trade blankets heaped with trinkets, he had considered the deal a bargain.

But for a girl who had long been the favorite, much courted and much admired, even seventeen horses couldn't compensate for the trivial status of being fourth wife to an aging and none-too-kind warrior. With Red Calf drunk most of the time and asleep the rest, the mastery of the wild horse by the visiting stranger with his pale eyes and young, vigorous body was only a natural first step for what eventually followed. A grateful, incautious Luc had never been sure which was the most grievous sin—cuckolding a Cheyenne war chief or causing Red Calf's loss of face by taming the horse that had trampled him—but one whispered word of warning from Deepwater and Luc was miles from the Cheyenne camp before it saw the next day's sunrise.

"Try explaining all that to Miss Rebecca Susan Bennett," he

muttered, just before he drifted into a restless sleep, punctuated by periods of wakefulness as his mind tried to envision what questions the morning would bring.

That turned out to be a wasted effort.

As dawn began to penetrate their brush-tunnel retreat, the very first question Rebecca asked was one Luc hadn't even considered.

14

"What did the old man mean about children . . . sons? And please don't lie to me."

Lie? Luc wished it could be that easy. But he was so surprised by her question, he had no time to conjure up even the flimsiest of lies. Nor was he in any mood to prevaricate. His eyes felt gritty, as if he hadn't slept at all, and he wanted nothing more than to pour a bucket of cold water over his head. Or Rebecca's head.

"Old Medicine Horse said I should forget about the Sioux and take you west. He said I should take you to the Peigan country, over that way, under the shadow of the mountains. He said I should breed strong sons with you." Luc decided not to include the part about being man enough to handle her. Instead, he added, "If I could only shut you up long enough to try."

"Shut me up? Breed strong sons? Medicine Horse must have been a good deal sicker than I thought, although I do realize he's dying."

Her voice was calm and controlled, and Luc almost looked round to see if someone else had spoken.

"The old man wasn't so sick that he couldn't make the effort to save you from getting killed, Rebecca. And if we're damned lucky, Red Calf might not sneak off after us and try to kill *me*."

"I liked Medicine Horse," she said, ignoring Luc's words. "He had an amazing . . . dignity, I guess you'd call it."

"He's been one of the most influential Cheyenne chiefs, over the years. One of the first to realize that his people could only lose if they continued to fight the incursion of the whites."

"And yet he obviously met up with Sitting Bull. Does that mean he was there? At the Custer massacre?"

"I expect so," Luc replied, once again surprised by her question. Rebecca might have forestalled her fear of Indians long enough to find compassion and respect for Medicine Horse, but apparently she hadn't noticed the scalps that decorated the lances of his warriors. Scalps that were blond, brown, copper, ginger, saffron, and all colors in between.

"I couldn't swear that Medicine Horse was involved with the actual fighting, Rebecca, although if he was there I'd be surprised if he didn't join in. But he's a peace chief, so I suppose . . ." Luc paused, aware that this time he *was* prevaricating. "The others were in the thick of it, for sure. Red Calf has been a war chief of that band since I can remember. He wouldn't have missed a chance at Custer."

"Or a chance at you. What did you do to him? There were moments when I thought we might be in very deep water."

After spending half the night pondering the answer to a question he knew she'd ask, Luc simply muttered, "It was a long time ago," and turned away to assemble their gear.

To his surprise, his third surprise of the morning, she didn't pester him for details. Nor did she question him further. She merely helped him stow the gear, then followed in his footsteps as he worked their horses out of the labyrinth of brushy tunnels. And before he could even think to offer assistance, she was mounted on her buckskin—whom she'd named Governor Potts because he stumbled drunkenly when she least expected it— and was gazing down at him with the most curious expression on her face.

"We *will* continue our search for Amy," she said firmly, leaving no room for discussion or argument. "I can accept that

Medicine Horse thought it right to warn you, Lucas, but I'm afraid his proposed alternative is not viable from my point of view."

Surprised for the fourth . . . or was it the fifth? . . . time that day, Luc realized that this was the *first time* Rebecca had ever used his given name.

Whatever was going on beneath those auburn braids, it was beyond his capacity to comprehend it, and if he had learned one thing about women since his encounter with Red Calf's wife, it was that there were times when saying nothing was not merely the safest option, but the only option.

He halted mid-mount, his leg suspended over his saddle. "How much of what Medicine Horse said did you understand, Rebecca?"

"I understood the part about my sister, if that's what's bothering you. The old man sounded like . . . like thunder, muttering . . . but his hand movements were mostly clear enough."

Which did nothing to ease Luc's mind as he carefully made his way out of the thickets and began moving steadily, if warily, north and east toward where he thought he'd pick up sign of the Sioux passage.

His stallion obeyed, even though it could sense that Luc wanted to ride in the other direction. Any other direction.

At first, Rebecca kept glancing up at the sun. But once she'd determined that Lucas was headed in the right direction, she let her mind turn in upon itself as Governor Potts plodded along.

She *had* been able to follow the old man's conversation to a remarkable degree. Even . . . especially . . . the part about her becoming some sort of brood mare. That hadn't been very difficult to confirm. Dark golden skin or no, Lucas had blushed! And the quick look he'd flashed in her direction had spoken volumes.

I should be blushing for the pleasure such a thought gives me, she told herself.

Still, she couldn't stop watching the way his muscular body moved, a component of the horse he rode. A centaur, just like the Berube boys, only this centaur was no smooth-cheeked lad who'd grown up atop a horse. Lucas Swallow had an elemental, mature masculinity that even his current Indian dress—or to be perfectly accurate, undress—enhanced.

With a bold, candid enjoyment, Rebecca gazed at his broad back and shoulders, and she couldn't help but remember his occasional moments of tenderness. What a contrast to the savage barbarity he displayed here, in what seemed to be his natural environment.

No. Barbarity was the wrong word. Although he often looked as if he wanted to pour a bucket of cold water over her head, Lucas wasn't rude, vulgar, or cruel.

Lucas Swallow hadn't killed the Helena wolfer. And, despite her abhorrence to violence of any kind, Rebecca was beginning to accept the fact that Sleeping Fox's motives were pure . . . justified, even.

How would she feel if she found the men who had tortured her father, then discovered that her father's skin had been turned into a tobacco pouch? Could she kill with a clear conscience? Or would she turn the men over to the law?

Laws grind the poor, and rich men rule the law. Where had she read that? Oliver Goldsmith: *The Traveler.*

A verse about lawyers, written by Samuel Coleridge, always made her smile. "He saw a lawyer killing a viper," Mr. Coleridge had written, "on a dunghill hard by his own stable; and the devil smiled, for it put him to mind, of Cain and his brother Abel."

Lord, she had almost forgotten that, not so very long ago, she'd been a teacher! So much had changed.

Rebecca surreptitiously stroked her soft doeskin smock as she brought her attention back to Swallow. It was nice having him off balance for a change. He didn't know that her reactions the evening before had been unnatural. Everything had happened so quickly, she'd never found time to be frightened. Not until it was all over, and by then she'd been too damn tired.

Despite her initial panic, despite having been unceremoniously kicked off her horse, she'd been both soothed and mesmerized by the old Indian's touch. She'd felt an emotive empathy with him, which had made it easy to follow his fluttering hands. Hands!

"At least Medicine Horse understood how stupid it was to keep my hands tied," she muttered, not realizing she'd spoken aloud until Swallow turned to glance back at her.

"What did you say?" Luc asked, startled at hearing Rebecca speak after a morning's worth of silence.

She simply waved her hands and he decided he wouldn't pursue the subject. With a shrug, he returned his attention to the rolling prairies ahead.

Knowing where they had met Medicine Horse and Red Calf was one thing. Figuring out the route taken by the homeward-bound Cheyenne without actually tracking them was another. And Luc had no intention of tracking them. The easy route taken by such a party—with a travois to drag—was all too likely to be the course traveled by others, who might be much more unfriendly.

Riding the day away, they crossed the Milk River, then cut the big loop of that river north of the Larb Hills, moving as much as possible in a northeasterly direction. Sooner or later they'd have to come upon the sign of the main Sioux bands. Indians in such number could *not* travel without leaving abundant proof of their passage.

He and Rebecca were not far off, either. Throughout the past days Luc had noticed less evidence of wildlife along their path. Buffalo, especially, were absent from a range that should have been black with them. And yet . . . Had he swung too far north?

Two people on good horses could cover a lot of ground, even if they were cautious. Sitting Bull would have a slower time of it, with women and children and travois dragging behind him.

Luc had a vague memory of Sleeping Fox saying the Minniconjou were ahead of the great chief. Maybe they hadn't traveled this far north yet. Damn! He cursed himself for not having questioned the Cheyenne more carefully. They might not have come from the north at all, but from a more easterly direction. They could have been swinging south to avoid extra crossings at the Milk River.

He desperately wanted to ride up out of the coulees and seek the high ground, giving him the ability to see for long distances. But it was far too dangerous. If he could see, he could be seen. And to be seen, now that he knew the Sioux had to be relatively close, might lead to his, and especially Rebecca's, death.

They camped fireless again that night, and were on their horses with the dawn, moving slowly but steadily northeast, holding to cover wherever possible. Luc had awakened with a growing sense of unease. By mid-afternoon he was riding with his rifle cocked, the hair at his nape fairly prickling with apprehension.

Rebecca sighed. Her brief exuberance had been worn down by exhaustion and hunger. Now she merely slumped on Governor Potts as he shadowed Swallow's stallion. Binding her wrists had become even more absurd, since it would be obvious to anyone, anyone who cared, that she couldn't possibly escape. It took every bit of her strength just to hold onto the saddle horn.

Tired as she was, she couldn't miss the way Swallow kept switching his route back and forth, causing them to travel three miles to make one, often losing as much ground as they gained.

At first she thought maybe he was as exhausted as she, but gradually she came to realize that he was following some sort of plan . . . even if she couldn't understand it.

Luc's grunt of pleasure brought Rebecca's weary head upright, but he either didn't notice or didn't care. Instead, dropping back to where he could grasp her buckskin's mane, he spoke without looking at her, his eyes probing the thickets beyond a dead cottonwood.

"There's a safe camp here, if memory serves. Or at least a camp that can be made safe . . . if we're very careful and if I'm right. It's been years since I was down this way, Rebecca. Anyway, we'll see. Try to keep your horse directly behind mine. Try not to break any branches. Just . . . well, ride as quietly as possible."

She could only nod and follow his instructions. It wasn't all that difficult, although the way he threaded his stallion and Governor Potts through the thickets she couldn't avoid the branches that reached out to clutch at her. Perhaps she could occupy her mind and control her growing panic by conjuring up a poem about trees.

Under the greenwood tree . . . who loves to lie with me . . . here he shall see no enemy . . . hah! Obviously, Mr. Shakespeare had never stalked Indians!

Abruptly, Governor Potts halted as the roan halted. Swallow began pawing through his saddlebags, muttering to himself under his breath as he did so, and Rebecca sat there, unsure whether to climb down or not, almost too exhausted to care.

Until he stalked over to her after a particularly explosive curse and said in a voice that brooked no argument, "There's nothing else for it. Take off your leggings."

"I will do no such thing!" Was he mad? Riding astride forced the doeskin tunic high onto her thighs. Without the leggings she would be . . . well, indecent wasn't a sufficient word.

"I've seen legs before, Rebecca. What I *don't* want to see is your lovely red hair on some Sioux lance. Take the leggings off and be quick about it. We haven't a lot of time."

Nor did he wait for her to reply. Already he was slashing at one of their blankets with his knife, crudely carving it into four equal portions. She hadn't even started to remove her leggings when he was beside her again, knife flickering in the sparse sunlight as he trimmed entire sections of the fringe along her legging seam.

"Get them off, Rebecca! Unless you want me to use the other blanket as well. Damn it, I need something to put over these horses' hooves, and I need it right away! Decide pretty damned quick if you want to have your legs covered or sleep cold tonight, and every night from now on, because either the leggings get used or your blanket does. Is that clear?"

It was. But the decision was less so. She was still pondering the choice when he ducked under Governor Potts' neck and began slashing the fringe off her other legging. Rebecca fought for some sort of sanity. She could use her saddle blanket to sleep under, sweaty and filthy as it might be, but she had no other protection for her legs, and if Swallow insisted upon leading her through every thicket he could find . . .

"Use the blanket," she said, her mind made up. "And since you've already cut off the fringes, please try and leave my leggings intact."

Eyes like pale green ice studied her for an instant, then his mouth split in a wry grin. "Okay, Miss Bennett," he said. "I just hope you still think your choice is a good one if there's frost on the pumpkin tomorrow morning."

"I'd rather be cold than have to ride half naked all the way to Canada," she retorted.

Which brought her another smile, before he bent and lashed

the provisional coverings up over their horses' hooves.

"This is a makeshift ruse at the best of times," he said, smile gone, his expression solemn, "but with luck, it might work. There should be no reason for any roving Sioux to be down here in the thickets, unless they're chasing game. But if we make no tracks, we leave no tracks. No noise, either, please. Do you suppose you can manage that?"

A reply formed on the tip of her tongue, but she bit it back. Silence was a better answer.

Whereupon, Luc insisted upon retracing their steps, using the blanket-clad feet of the horses to dissemble what tracks they might already have made. Occasionally, he dismounted to destroy their spoor. Then it was back into the thickets, where he led a twisting, turning course that soon had Rebecca totally confused.

Finally, they reached a tiny island in a sea of brush, a clearing mostly overhung with brambles and tall shrubbery laden with purple berries. At the end was a minuscule cave, merely a shadow under an overhang, really, but shelter. A trickle of moisture emerged from the bank beside the cave. The "spring"— man-made, Rebecca decided—flowed only a few feet before disappearing again into the sandy soil.

Swiftly unloading the horses, Luc removed the now-tattered blanket pieces from around their feet, tethered them at the far end of the tiny glade, then turned to find Rebecca already slumped beside the discarded saddles, clearly at the edge of exhaustion.

She was a tough woman, tougher than she gave herself credit for, but the rough travel she'd endured thus far was nothing compared to what lay ahead, and Luc had to wonder if she'd be tough enough.

He looked around the tiny campsite, momentarily pleased with himself for having been able to find it again. It had been years, and he'd only stumbled across it the first time because he'd been tracking a wounded doe.

For his and Rebecca's purposes, the hidden glen was splendid. Not as idyllic as their earlier camp by the pond, but far safer. There was no reason for any Indian to try and get near the place. What hunting the Sioux must do to feed their numbers would be aimed at the buffalo, in the open prairies to the north and east. Or so Luc hoped. As for him and Rebecca, the lack of buffalo was no great hardship. Smaller game would easily sustain them. And would have to, because they were running short of pemmican.

"Rebecca." He whispered her name and was pleased to see that she responded not with alarm but with a cautious alertness. "I'm going to make sure our tracks are wiped out and see if there is any meat about. We might be here quite a while and I expect you could do with a decent meal."

"Sleep," she replied. "I need sleep more than food."

"You need both, but sleep for now if you like. I'll be gone a fair bit, since I want to make a thorough scout."

"Fine," she said wearily.

Luc wanted nothing more than to re-plait her tangled auburn hair and massage her slender shoulders. Damn! He was loco to even contemplate such a thing. Sleeping Fox would say . . . well, there was really no English translation for what Sleeping Fox would say!

Loco or not, Luc's impetuous . . . contrivance? . . . desire? . . . didn't matter. His mouth turned up in a wry smile as he realized that Rebecca couldn't stay awake long enough to watch him unwrap a short but powerful buffalo bow and a quiver of arrows.

He was able to walk quickly through the tangled network of brush, his memory fully returned, the layout of the land around him clear in his mind. It took hardly any time to complete the erasure of their few remaining tracks. Then he navigated the northeastern edge of the ravine, where the brush thinned out as the land raised up to meet the open prairie. Here, on his first visit to the region, he had shot the deer which had led him to the hidden vale in the thickets, and here again luck intervened to provide another deer.

An arrow from his powerful bow caught the dry doe so precisely that she fell without taking a single step. Almost immediately, Luc hunkered down beside the animal, his knife easing its death struggles with a single slash across its throat.

He offered his thanks to the deer for giving up its life to feed them, then quickly dressed out the animal's hindquarters, rolling them into the hide along with the heart, liver and tenderloin. There was enough good meat to keep him and Rebecca going for several days, and he was beginning to think they might need that long . . . and more.

Moving well away from the carcass, Luc stowed his bundle of choice meat high in a tree, then continued his search for evidence that he had not come too far north to be behind the Sioux, but might actually be ahead of them. Or else that the main Sioux bands were even farther east than he'd anticipated.

He recalled that there was a natural and easy passage through the labyrinth of ravines and thickets at the prairie's edge. Although it offered good water nearby and several excellent campsites, it was too exposed for his own furtive purposes. That, of course, would be no impediment to the northbound Sioux. With any luck, Luc might learn whether or not the Sioux had traveled this far. He had several hours of tracking light left, and there was no question Rebecca could use the opportunity to rest.

He, too, was tired, so tired that he almost blundered into an open crossing before he realized where he was. Only his instincts, far more reliable than his exhausted brain, gave him warning enough to heed a sound he hadn't consciously registered—the tiny ping of a shod hoof striking rock.

Luc dropped to his belly and wriggled off to one side, just in case he'd been seen. After several minutes, he risked moving toward a tiny hollow, not far off the main trail, yet effectively hidden.

Whereupon, his ears and nose revealed what his eyes couldn't see.

Horses. Not Indian horses. And not Indians, either. There was no taint of bear grease or deer fat, and the scent from the horses told him the animals had been ridden hard and were poorly cared for.

As Luc crept closer, the loud crackle of a blazing fire confirmed his suspicions. No Indian party would light such a large fire.

Using every patch of cover, he finally came to where he could actually see the camp, and he felt his eyes widen with a mixture of surprise, shock and disgust as he heard the voices and figured out what was being said.

"*Merde!* I do not like this. We should have found their trail yesterday. Me, I think the Cheyenne did not tell us all they knew."

"Easy, Luis," said a tall, lanky fellow, whose deference to the small man in black was clearly tinged with caution. "Why in hell would the Cheyenne lie? That Red Cow, or Red Bull, or whatever his damn name was, didn't like L'Hirondelle. Red Cow woulda' come with us and helped us kill L'Hirondelle, if the sick chief had let 'im."

"That is true. I know Red *Calf* from the old days, when Sugden and I ran whiskey to the Cheyenne. Red Calf would not lie about such a thing . . . not to Luis Sebastian! Besides, I know also the story of why L'Hirondelle is so hated by Red Calf. The Cheyenne, they are funny people. They might give you a woman, or even let you borrow her, for enough whiskey. Or because they feel like it. But to take a woman without permission . . . no, Red Calf would never forgive L'Hirondelle for that. He was lucky to escape with his hide."

"More than luck, I reckon. How the hell did he escape this time? That's what I want to know. There were enough of them Cheyenne bucks to deal with him, even hauling their chief on them pole things. If we hadn't been lucky enough to get the drop on 'em, I guess they'd have had our hides, sure enough."

Sebastian used one of his razor-edged throwing knives to slit the end from a thin, black cigar. "Us, they would kill simply because we are white. But L'Hirondelle is a half-breed. He has lived with the Cheyenne and hunted with them. The old man on the travois was Medicine Horse. He would have nothing against L'Hirondelle, and without his word, none of the others would bother L'Hirondelle. I'm thinking Red Calf decided it was more important to get the old chief home to die. Red Calf would not want to challenge L'Hirondelle alone, and maybe die himself."

Rasping a match on the sole of a spur-shod, tiny boot, Sebastian lit his cigar. Then, without turning his back on his companion, he sank to his spread-out bedroll.

"Forget about the Cheyenne," he continued. "We will scout again in the morning, and if we find no sign, we will join Sugden at the Minniconjou camp and let him decide what to do. If we find L'Hirondelle, Luis Sebastian does not need the help of a Cheyenne to deal with him. Besides, Williams, I want L'Hirondelle for myself."

"You're welcome to him, Luis. He's either a helluva good man at hiding his tracks or he's had the devil's own luck. And that's the problem. He's sure as hell had all the breaks in this game, right from the start. First the old man dies without telling us anything worth knowing. Then we miss out on getting the girl in Helena. Then she gets hooked up with L'Hirondelle and that goddamn bone hunter before we get another chance at her. And now . . . well, how the hell can a man just drop out of sight? I tell you, Luis, it worries me. It ain't natural."

Sebastian licked at the corners of his tiny, neat mustache, and even from a distance Luc could see the Spaniard's dark eyes flare with contempt.

"Williams, you always were a superstitious fool. It has nothing to do with luck. It has to do with this L'Hirondelle, this half-breed the Indians name as the finest horse tamer who ever rode. He is good. Very good! And for reasons I do not understand, Sugden is afraid of this L'Hirondelle."

One hand flashed to his boot-top and Luc caught the gleam of a flying blade as it flashed across the campsite to chunk into a log only inches from the tall, lanky man.

"But I am Luis Sebastian! And I am not afraid of anyone!"

Luc shuddered at the laugh that followed, hardly even human.

Sebastian leapt to his feet, retrieved his knife from the log, and sneered at his companion's instinctive flinch.

"I will find this L'Hirondelle, this tamer of horses, and he will learn that my knife is a tamer of men!"

Sebastian caressed his knife's blade as if it were some living, sentient thing, and in those fingers, Luc thought it might well be.

So this was the man who had trailed him while he moongazed in Helena, the man who would have delighted in slicing Luc up, had his stallion not intervened. It was sobering to see how deadly quick the small man was with his knives.

Luc himself was a tough, hard man in a land where toughness was a prerequisite to survival, but by his standards anyone who deliberately sought trouble the way Sebastian did was either a fool or mad . . . or both. Sebastian's attitude was not that of the Indians, where bravery was recognized and honored, even if it led to foolishness.

This small weasel of a man, with his cruel spurs and ready knives, was as out of place here as he would be anywhere. Except here in the wilderness he could indulge himself and, at the same time, not concern himself with consequences.

Worse, he was clearly a careful, thoughtful man. If Sebastian's tracking skills matched his skill with knives, Luc and Rebecca were essentially imprisoned. To move was to leave sign, and to leave sign might mean capture, even death.

Returning to where he'd cached the deer meat, Luc was extremely circumspect, knowing full well he could leave no sign of his passage.

There were, however, advantages to being vigilant. On his way back he spotted a young bear, and Luc gifted the animal with the remains of the doe. It took two trips to complete his mission, but the bear would make short work of the carcass, and in doing so would destroy—or at least confuse—any signs that might link the kill to a human.

Then Luc returned to his own camp with the beginnings of a plan in mind, and the first part of the plan meant the one thing he'd rather avoid; a fire on which to cook the deer meat. He had oft eaten raw meat and would have done so this night, although not by preference. But to expect Rebecca . . . no.

At least the wind would carry the unavoidable odor in a direction that was far away from Sebastian's camp. Hopefully, the wind would lose the smell in the thickets, and the thickets would be devoured by frost before the sun rose.

That is, if he and Rebecca were lucky. And after listening to the conversation between Sebastian and his partner, Luc knew that he and Rebecca had already used up an awful lot of luck.

Once again, he wondered how Sugden and his crew could possibly believe the tale about Otis Bennett's "Spanish" gold?

And where exactly did Rebecca and Amy Bennett fit into Sugden's scheme?

If the outlaws were with the Minniconjou, they had access to one sister. If they managed to capture Rebecca, they would have both sisters. The reality of the legendary gold wouldn't protect either. Sugden and Sebastian would torture the women for the sheer joy of it, gold or no gold.

And Sugden's presence among the Minniconjou could only make Luc's problems ten times larger and twenty times more dangerous.

Everything he had heard so far indicated that Amy Bennett was mad, hopelessly insane, and evil in the bargain. Rescuing her was a fool's errand, but Luc's honor demanded no less than a try at it.

As for the gold, he had yet to crack another nut. How could he tell Rebecca that her father's gold no longer existed?

15

"Suppose we found your sister tomorrow, Rebecca? What would you do?"

"I don't know."

"That's no answer," Luc said softly, tossing a few more sticks into the fire.

The damn fire was a risk, but one he deemed necessary. Rebecca desperately needed solid food and there were dark smudges beneath her violet eyes.

Eyes to drown in, he thought, and almost flinched at the sudden rush of heat to his loins. She was only a few feet away, and yet as distant as a dream . . . as *the* dream . . . for surely she embodied the red mare of his boyhood vision. He had never caught that mare, never even attempted it. Now, ironically, his vision-mare had captured *him*.

He saw Rebecca looking down, practically batting her thick lashes. Her whole demeanor fairly shouted: demure maiden. Despite the seriousness of the moment, Luc couldn't quite repress a chuckle.

"You find me amusing, Mr. Swallow?"

"Only when you attempt to be what you are not," he replied, searching his mind for the right words, wanting to draw her out, to understand her.

"I didn't think I was attempting anything."

"You are attempting to be shy and demure, which is about as believable as Julia Grant playing the coquette."

"Why can't our president's wife play the coquette?"

"Well, for one thing, she's cross-eyed."

Rebecca's mouth twisted in a wry grin that evolved into a brilliant smile. "I was taught to be demure," she said. "However, it was one of many lessons in my life that didn't take too well."

The opening was there and Luc lunged as deftly as a swordsman.

"You weren't taught to lie. Or else that lesson didn't take too well, either. 'Fess up, Rebecca. 'I don't know' is not an answer, and you must have considered the problem."

"What problem?"

"We've been informed by two trustworthy men that your sister is mad. She probably has no idea she might be rescued, likely wouldn't even *want* to be rescued, and may prove impossible to rescue. So what are we going to do if that turns out to be the situation?"

Having sat in the same position so long, Rebecca felt as if pins and needles pierced her legs. She staggered to her feet and told Swallow she had to use the necessary. He was correct; she hadn't been taught to lie. But at least this fib was plausible, and it gave her time to think.

She leaned against the portly tree she'd chosen as her water closet door. Of course she had considered the . . . problem . . . and yet she couldn't put into words her only solution. She knew she'd come face to face with her sister soon, perhaps very soon, but she simply could *not* tell Lucas Swallow that she was prepared to keep her promise to her father and kill Amy rather than see her remain in Indian hands.

The real question was whether or not Rebecca Susan Bennett, "demure" schoolteacher, could carry out such a drastic, merciful plan.

"Sugden would kill for your father's gold," Luc said on Rebecca's return. "In fact, he'd do a lot worse even without the gold. You're an attractive young woman in a country where any sort of woman is rare . . ." Luc paused. Nothing he could say, or would say, could adequately portray the horrors Sugden and his men would inflict on Rebecca.

He was only too aware that "attractive" didn't begin to describe the woman who sat across the fire from him. She had been striking in her ball gown, when he'd first met her. Now she was trail weary, dressed in doeskin, her hair braided into a parody of a Blackfoot maiden's coiffure, and yet she was breathtakingly beautiful.

"I have to try and save my sister, Lucas. I promised my father. But even if I hadn't, I would still have to try. You, of all people, should understand that."

"Why, Rebecca?"

"Because you understand . . . honor."

Luc thought about his debt to her father, and his breath caught in his throat. "What do you mean?"

"Sleeping Fox. What you said . . . how you explained . . ." She waved her fingers around as if she could pluck words from the air. "Killing that horrible man who massacred his family was . . . honorable. You made me see that. You are very close to the Indian culture, Lucas. One might even think you had Indian blood, and I reckon, to use your expression, there are lots of things you haven't told me."

"What things?"

"I know you've hunted with Indians, but I think . . . I reckon . . . there's been some sort of ceremony, a blood ceremony, that made you a member of a tribe. Or tribes. That's true, isn't it? I guessed right, didn't I?"

"Yes." Luc thought about his sundance scars. Close enough.

"At first I believed you . . . barbaric." She blushed. "But I was mistaken. Because now I can see how much the Indian culture has influenced you. In fact . . ." she blushed again ". . .

sometimes you seem more Indian than white."

Luc's mind raced. No, he decided, now was not the time to confess his dual identity. He had other things to sort out first. "Would you give up your father's gold to save your sister, Rebecca?"

She nodded. "I'm beginning to think the gold is covered in blood, and I'm no longer certain I want anything more than to rescue Amy." She took a deep breath, then let it out slowly. "I know it isn't going to be that easy, Lucas. The gold will haunt us, Amy and me, just as it did my father. Assuming, of course, it existed in the first place."

"Does it?" He dared not let her know he knew the answer to his question, much less that he knew the answer even better than she did, and that it wasn't hunger for the almost-done venison that caused his gut to knot like a hangman's noose.

"I believe it does. I have to believe it does. Otherwise, my father died for naught. If the gold was a figment of my father's imagination, I have nothing else to live on, except for my wagons and horses. And if I . . . if Amy and I . . . don't get back by the time Mr. Cope is ready to move out, I don't know what will happen to my stock."

"I suggested that Cope let the Berubes take your horses north. It seemed easier than Cope toting them back to Fort Benton. He'll probably pick up a downstream steamboat at Cow Island, or even Claggett. The Berubes will be heading up north, into the Cypress Hills, where they have relatives, before they travel east to the Red River settlement."

"Oh, I'm glad. The Berubes will take good care of my horses. And wagons."

"That doesn't solve your long-term problem, Rebecca. What will you do after you redeem Amy?"

He had deliberately used the word redeem rather than rescue, but Rebecca didn't wince. Nor did she frown. Was she too

G. K. Aalborg

exhausted? Or did she believe, as Luc did, that redemption would be in the cards?

"Until recently, I taught school," she said.

"Well, there you are. There's always work for a schoolmarm, especially out here."

"So I've heard. Out . . . here."

Luc kept his face expressionless. Was Rebecca so totally set against ever coming to terms with this country? His country?

"You could always marry," he said then, and wanted to kick himself. But the words were out even as he thought them, although thankfully without any sign of his own too-personal interest in her answer.

"If I do marry, it won't be for financial security."

Luc raised one eyebrow. "Is that your way of saying you'll marry for true love or not at all?"

"It's my way of saying that I will *not* marry for money. I could have done so, back East, had that been my desire."

"I imagine you amassed quite a few serious suitors."

"No." She smiled. "I've always been too 'serious.' There was one gentleman who quite liked my sobriety, but his financial assets could never make up for his lack of deportment. My goodness, Sleeping Fox and Medicine Horse have more breeding, more refinement, more common sense . . ."

She paused to take a deep breath, and Luc wondered what her ill-mannered "gentleman" had done to her? If he'd lied, or simply tried to evade the truth, Luc was in the same boat. And sinking fast.

Retrieving some meat from the flames, he passed Rebecca her share. Then he scooped dirt over most of the fire, leaving their tiny camp even gloomier than before.

"I'll cook the rest of the meat slowly," he said, "and as soon as we're fed, that fire's going out. It was a risk having it at all, but I reckoned we both needed a decent feed. However, the last

206

thing we do need is a meat scent, or even the smell of a fire. Sugden's men will be on the prowl early, and we don't know for sure which way the wind will blow."

"What shall we be doing tomorrow morning?" she asked around a mouthful of tenderloin.

"*You* will be staying right here, keeping out of sight and very quiet. From what Sugden's men said, the camp where I think your sister is being held . . ." Luc paused to consider his words. Rebecca's sister was not, to his knowledge, being *held* at all. "Once I've figured out a way to find the place without Sugden's men finding me, I'll sneak over and have a look."

"You won't take me with you."

It wasn't a question, although Luc suspected she wouldn't meekly accept his plan. He tried to elaborate without getting her dander up. "The idea is to find your sister and get her out of there, Rebecca, not wind up with both of you in the Sioux camp."

"What if you end up getting caught?"

"If I'm not back in three days, you mount that crowbait pony you've named for a goddamn governor and ride like hell back to where we started. You'll be safe enough if you can reach Cope. The other alternative is to head northwest and cross the line into the Cypress Hills, where there's a mounted police post. Either way, the risks are enormous. Make no mistake about that."

"I won't."

"If we had any real sense, we'd both get out of this as fast as we could. The deck's stacked against us now, with Sugden involved, and since he's after your sister, too . . . that's it, isn't it? I forgot that part of the story because it isn't always told. Something about you two sharing some sort of map. You mentioned something about it, if memory serves."

Swallow's gaze seemed to bore into her very soul, but Rebecca forced herself to meet his eyes. He deserved no less than the entire truth.

"Amy and I were each given half the map to memorize, when we were quite small. Too small, actually, to appreciate the seriousness of it, and too young to recognize my father's acute . . . mistrust . . . of society. I never really believed his story about the gold until . . . until I tended him while he was . . . was dying."

"You and your sister never compared notes or traded secrets? Seems mighty strange to me. Most kids would've . . ."

"Amy and I were never close, not even as children."

Rebecca lapsed into silence, unable to continue, unable to explain that Amy had always hated her. Suddenly, with hindsight, she realized that Amy had never been totally sane, that insanity fed on hatred, and that envy was the daughter of dementia.

Luc let the silence build on itself as he chewed his venison. He didn't look into the dying fire lest he risk his night vision, and he could no longer look at Rebecca, whose inner pain was obvious.

His own problems were only intensified by her revelations. She wanted to rescue her sister to satisfy a promise to her dying father, or a promise to herself, and the fact that she needed her sister to find the missing gold was, he honestly believed, secondary.

Could this be the right time to blurt out his true identity? To admit that he was Luc L'Hirondelle, the only other person besides her sister who could conceivably help her find Otis Bennett's gold?

In truth, it didn't matter *when* Luc made that admission.

The damage would be immediate, the destruction of her dreams devastating.

Because there was no gold.

Not anymore.

Luc didn't want to tell her that, although he knew the time would come when he'd have no choice.

Nor did he want to reveal his identity yet, even though that, too, would eventually have to be done.

His eyes touched upon the half-reclining figure across the fire, and he relished the sight. The loose-fitting doeskin tunic couldn't hide Rebecca's breast and hip. So lovely, he thought. She was so lovely and intelligent and courageous.

Together, they could breed strong children.

If only she weren't white or he was not Métis.

No, he thought . . . no! His feelings for Rebecca must not be allowed to develop. Loving her would be—*was*—an exercise in futility.

It was one thing for an Indian or mixed-blood woman to marry, or even live with, a white man. Marriage *à la façon du pays*—after the fashion of the country—was not only traditional in the history of his people, it *was* their history! *His* history!

For generations, the men of the fur trading companies and the explorers, most of them French and Scottish, but white, had taken Indian or mixed-blood wives without benefit of clergy. Clergymen of any description had been as rare as eligible white women. In the early days of the fur trade, there were no other women but those of the various tribes, and that was still true in some of the remotest areas of both Canada and the American West.

Nonetheless, the practice was dying out. And being driven out by the arrival of white women in places they had never traveled before. In any case, Luc thought, his problem was not the same and could never be.

It was one thing for a white man to take a native woman to his bed. It might be frowned upon and his half-breed children might be scorned, especially south of the medicine line, but such scorn was nothing compared to what awaited a white woman who allowed herself to become involved with a man of Indian blood.

Even in his own country the long-held respect for the Métis was dwindling as white settlers encroached, moving farther into areas formerly considered Indian territory.

In most regions the Métis tended to live their lives the same way their Indian cousins did. Though most, like the Berubes, were staunch French Catholics, and many preferred settlements to a nomadic life, most worshipped the freedom to roam as they wished and run the buffalo. Many were farmers, and good farmers, but their attitude was too earthy for some of their white neighbors to comprehend, much less accept.

As Luc looked at Rebecca, his mind looked into the future. How could he even consider that someone of her genteel background might welcome the life he was bound to by blood? He had spent time in Montreal as a student, had seen other cities, and was not ignorant of the way settlers were moving westward. He knew from his father's words and his own observations that the Indians' way of life was threatened with extinction, perhaps even in his own lifetime. And with that extinction, Métis tradition also might be destroyed.

But for him, for the life he envisaged, change and adaptation would be a gradual thing, a controlled thing. He could no more live in a city than he could live in a jail. To be without space, without freedom, would suffocate him.

And if there was a chance, a prayer, to keep Rebecca in his life, how could he explain that her father's gold had already been found, by him; had already been spent, by him; to purchase the foundation for a future she'd never contemplate?

He looked at her more closely. Poor girl. She wasn't merely reclining; her entire body sagged as she drifted toward an exhausted slumber. She twitched slightly as he gently covered her with both the saddle blankets, but didn't wake.

He made a last-minute check on the horses, cached the cooked meat, smothered the fire, then rolled up in the dry leaves that carpeted their small dell. The leaves provided enough warmth, and he managed to sleep well enough.

Until the first scream brought him instantly awake.

He palmed his hand over Rebecca's mouth to stifle her second scream.

Her nightmare had returned, and with it the danger of drawing an even worse nightmare should roving Indians or Sugden's men hear her.

Rebecca's nightmare was a curious mixture of past and present.

Indians, their lances strewn with scalps. Fire raging as if fueled by screams. Terror evident in the shrieks of the men, women and children. And blood. The blood on her father's body as she tried to remove his buckskin clothing. The memory of his bleeding head after the raid in which Amy had been stolen.

And faces . . . worst of all, the faces. The cruel face of the posse leader. The lust she had seen and felt from so many of his vigilante companions. The bitter hatred on Red Calf's face as he glared at Lucas. The fierce pleasure of the man who had kicked her off her pony to land sprawling at the feet of Medicine Horse . . .

Rebecca wallowed in her nightmare, unable to find purchase, unable to find a footing from which to escape. And then, as she screamed her torment, a hand pressed against her mouth, preventing even that escape, immobilizing her, confirming her worst fears.

"Easy . . . easy . . . you're all right. It's only a dream . . . a dream."

The words swirled around in her mind, but the hand across her mouth was more immediate, more real. She tried to bite it, writhed and twisted and thrust with all her strength to escape, to breathe, to scream again. But she was held down by a strong body, and powerful legs fought to keep her own from kicking.

"Becky Sue, it's all right. You're dreaming. There's no danger. You're safe."

The voice began to penetrate her dream, but didn't stop it. She heard her father's pet name for her. It sounded different, sounded right and wrong, but it had to be an hallucination because her father was dead.

Raising her heavy lashes, she saw the moon first, very bright, well-nigh as bright as daylight. Then she found herself pinned by a gaze; eyes like green ice, so pale a green as to be almost translucent.

"It's a dream . . . only a dream."

The hands holding her and the body smothering her were warm, but she was cold, so cold. She had removed her leggings and tried to cleanse them. The chill, however, was inside her body. Her bones felt brittle. If she moved her toes or fingers, they'd snap like twigs.

"Easy . . . easy, now."

The voice slid into a crooning, hypnotic chant, toneless and tuneless but soothing, bringing to her tormented mind the safety she so desperately craved.

"You're dreaming, only dreaming. It's all right, now."

"But . . ."

"A nightmare, that's all. Gone now."

The icy eyes weren't icy after all, but soft and warm and gentle and caring. Against her breasts, the muscular warmth of Lucas Swallow's chest, against her bare legs, the strength of his legs, around her, the strength of his arms. And against her cheek, the warmth of his breath, the softness of his crooning voice.

His hand no longer clamped her mouth shut. Instead, it stroked her shoulder in tender, hypnotic movements, as if she possessed ruffled kitten fur, while his other arm kept her motionless against the healthy warmth of him.

Rebecca sighed heavily, trying with a conscious effort to still the trembling that seemed to have its foundation deep inside her, that seemed to radiate out through her body, through her skin, until it positively vibrated.

"Easy . . . easy . . ."

His voice, like muted, distant thunder, rumbled in her ear, radiating even more heat. Meeting his eyes again, she suddenly became aware of his warmth in a new way, and she began to twist and turn slowly, seductively, acknowledging the closeness of their bodies and their intertwined legs. She felt him respond, could feel the sudden surge of desire that brought him erect against her.

The touch of his hand took on a different cadence, its movement not merely on her shoulder, but roving down her arm to drift across her hip, down the long length of her thigh to where the doeskin dress ricked up. His fingers were sparks of fire along her bare skin, and when he shifted his weight to bring both of them into more intimate contact, she neither thought about it nor objected.

Her sigh had become a gasp. His tuneless, toneless crooning had muted to a guttural groan of wanting, of needing, and she could feel their hearts thundering in unison, a tempo that rose with every caress, every touch.

His avid gaze trailed an almost tactile handprint along her cheek and her throat. His lips followed, their touch so light, so fragile, she had to hold her breath to be sure she felt them at all. His throat was within reach, and she found herself drawn to touch the straining cords of muscle with her own lips, to reach out with her free hand and tug at the nape of his neck, pulling him closer.

Beneath the doeskin frock her stomach writhed in an eddy of

giddiness and her nipples throbbed as her breasts seemed to push against him, seeking the hardness of his muscles. She shivered, but there was no fear in it now.

When his hand progressed to the inside of her thighs, gliding, caressing, arousing, she shifted ever so slightly to ease his hand's passage. His fingers traced delicate paths along her skin, moving ever upward, and she reflexively thrust her own hand down. To stall his advance . . . aid it . . . she didn't know, didn't care.

And it didn't matter, because her fingers missed his hand entirely, finding instead the now-gaping breechclout, the swollen, straining essence of him. Her second gasp resounded in her own ears as her fingers clutched at him, drawing a strangled moan from lips that immediately sought her own, from a mouth that captured her lips without any feeling of restraint, but somehow managed to touch her, exploring, arousing. Their tongues met, danced briefly together, parted. The very taste of him seemed to fill her mouth. The touch of him certainly filled her hand, and more.

Some tiny semblance of sanity shouted at her to let go, to free herself, even to flee this torrent of emotion, but it was too weak. Her grip eased, but only so she could move her fingers slowly, stroking him, learning him. The moan that fled his mouth to fill her own was half persuasive, half denying: "My . . . God."

He shuddered within her grasp, his entire body trembling as his tongue plunged to capture her own, his hand like sheet lightning upon her thighs, in a soft touch, so deft, and yet so totally overwhelming, she writhed against it, wanting more, wanting his fingers to move higher, closer to their target.

"No," he whispered.

But his voice and his body said he didn't mean it.

"No!"

She didn't want him to stop, didn't want herself to stop.

Couldn't stop.

But *he* could.

Ruthlessly, he pushed her from him, then yanked at her doeskin dress until it lowered to cover what it could.

"Mon dieu!"

He was on his feet, reeling as if drunk or wounded, his eyes raised to the night sky, his head and body turned away from her in a rejection so obvious it was like a blow.

All she could do was lie there, her lips swollen from his kisses, her body quivering with need, the taste of him in her mouth, the feel of him on her hands, branded into her fingertips. She saw his body tremble as if consumed by rage, but she wasn't frightened.

"Lucas, I . . ."

"Say nothing. Please, Rebecca . . . say nothing."

His words came in ragged gasps, audible despite the fact he faced away from her.

"But I . . ."

"Must try and forgive me, even though I don't deserve it. What just happened was not planned, believe me. But it shouldn't have happened, and I apologize."

Apologize? For what? Did he think her a child? It took two people to create what had just happened . . . almost happened.

"There is nothing to apologize for," she said, her voice straining to convey a conviction she didn't feel.

She had been taught to be demure, obviously a wasted effort, but she had also been taught not to lie. So had the *honorable* Lucas Swallow, one would assume. His body shouted his desire loud and clear, and only a blind, deaf fool could miss it. But he had rejected her . . .

Luc spent the night waiting for the dawn. There was no pool of water here. He couldn't plunge his fever-ridden body into icy water, couldn't cool his inner flames . . . or ease his conscience.

Rebecca had curled up in the horse blankets again, and she slept, if fitfully. Luc didn't even consider sleep. Instead, he paced the tiny glade like a caged beast, berating himself mentally for having let the situation get out of hand. At the same time, his physical being complained that it hadn't gotten far enough out of hand.

God, but he wanted this woman!

She had wanted him, no doubt about that. But had she *known* what she wanted? There had been an almost childlike sense of trust in her reaction to him, a trust he had very nearly betrayed.

And still wanted to betray. Because, if he chose, he could steal over and crawl beneath her blankets and pick up where they'd left off. He cursed himself for thinking it, but the sensitive throbbing beneath his breechclout cursed him for a liar.

Granted, she was innocent, a virgin. Granted, she could never come to terms with this country, his country. Granted, she was white and he was Métis. All that aside, he had a debt of honor, and while that debt existed he could not—dared not!—let his personal feelings interfere. Because her life, perhaps both their lives, lay at stake.

There was, as he had expected, frost on the ground as dawn drew nigh, but to Luc the weather was nowhere near cold enough to calm the hot storm of blood that continued to rage through his body. At least his memory had returned, telling him where he would most logically expect to find the Sioux encampment, *and* a route to it that would allow him to avoid Sugden's men. It was risky, just as leaving Rebecca alone was risky, but he could see no other way. He couldn't take her with him, not with Luis Sebastian on the prowl. Rebecca, he knew, simply couldn't be trusted to stay quiet with either her mouth or her feet. He'd be better off with Governor Potts and his drunken, noisy stumbling.

"No fire, no noise, and stay damned close to camp," he said, after gently waking her. "I'm leaving you this rifle, which with any luck you won't need, and you should have no problem handling the buckskin. I doubt I'll be gone more than today, maybe tonight as well, so don't worry, don't even *begin* to worry, until three days are up. Then, get on your damned pony and head southwest as cautiously and quickly as you can. Cope should still be in the badlands. Please remember to be careful, Rebecca, very careful. I think all the Sioux are east of us, but I could be wrong."

Luc realized he was running off at the mouth. Damn, but she looked vulnerable. Momentarily, he considered putting Rebecca atop the buckskin and hightailing it back to where he could keep her safe.

But he knew, without a single doubt, that unless he used force, she'd never let him. Because something had happened to her last night, something other than their near descent into the abyss of physical gratification. Her evasive mood had changed, albeit subtly, after his first question about her sister, then her visit to the necessary. Trust? Acceptance?

"No fire, no noise, stay close to camp," she repeated.

There was nothing in her expression to suggest she humored him, just a bland acceptance, and Luc wondered what lay behind her easy acquiescence. Should he repeat his admonitions? No. She'd heard him and she wasn't stupid. Instead, he wrapped the tattered blanket pieces over his blue roan's hooves and checked his weapons.

He wanted to kiss Rebecca good-bye, or at least shout a farewell.

Ignoring both impulses, he swung up onto his saddle.

He was Horse-tamer, a horseman to his very soul, and the sound of a steady *clip-clop* had always soothed him. But today his great stallion's tread was muffled by the blankets and the predawn stillness.

16

The bear was as surprised as Rebecca, and considerably smaller.

Rebecca had been picking ripe serviceberries when she saw the black bear rear up on the other side of the thicket, a hundred yards from camp. She might have seen it sooner had she not been lost in thought.

She could still feel Lucas Swallow's lips on her breasts, his feathery caress between her thighs. She could still smell him, taste him, and her fingers seemed etched with the touch of his body. The rich purple berries tasted like his breath, and she hardly noticed the morning chill or the brilliance of the sky or her leggings drying on the brushwood or the scuffle of dying leaves beneath her feet.

Then the black bear reared up in front of her with a startled *whoof* that ripped a scream of terror from her own throat.

One scream. Before she could even imagine a second, she was running for her life, diving behind the log where Swallow's spare rifle lay, where Rebecca herself then lay, the rifle in her hands, her gaze locked on her back trail.

The carelessness that created the name *Sunset-haired Woman Who Defeats Her Enemies With An Empty Rifle* no longer existed. The wilderness had stripped that away just as it had stripped away her "demure" education and her sunbonnet.

This time her rifle's hammer was eared back and there was a cartridge in its chamber.

Except . . . there was no enemy to shoot at.

Rebecca couldn't know that the bear had run, too, but in the opposite direction. By the time she lay shivering in wait, with death in her hands, the bear was half a mile away and still running.

Sun Eagle's medicine was good. It was a known fact among his people. Although he did not have the standing of his chief, Bear's Blood, Sun Eagle was nonetheless a respected Sioux warrior with a following of his own.

Moreover, he had learned early in life a virtue few of the plains Sioux had ever truly mastered. He was patient almost to a fault. That attribute had, on more than one occasion, saved his own life and those of his followers. Sun Eagle never had a problem raising company for any expedition because he always brought his raiding bands home alive, not tied up on their ponies' backs.

Immobile atop his big, piebald war horse, the faint memory of the scream echoed in his mind. As he cast his deepset eyes back and forth across the landscape, he tried to pinpoint the direction of the scream and the distance involved.

Behind him, his companions sat equally still, equally silent. Some had heard the scream while others had not, but he was their leader and must make the decision. Which he did, but not for many minutes, and not without much thought about potential risks and possible dangers.

When he moved, it was slowly, with caution.

And with an impressive efficiency.

Silently obeying Sun Eagle's brusque hand signals, the small Sioux band fanned out and prowled with the fierce determination of hunting wolves. Occasionally, tiny glimpses of evidence were found, examined, then carried to Sun Eagle for judgment.

It took the Sioux until noon to gather at the fallen cottonwood.

The youngest stayed with the horses; it was his role and he accepted it without rancor. The others waited while their leader moved aside to squat in silent prayer. Then they followed him into the pathways of the thickets.

They watched the red-haired woman for half an hour, a testimony to Sun Eagle's own patience and the quality of his leadership. Others would have rushed into the camp and captured her within minutes, but Sun Eagle was more prudent, more assiduous. He also believed that anticipation was the best part of victory.

Defeat never entered his mind.

Having recovered from the black bear incident and sworn she'd be more cautious, Rebecca saw—too late—an Indian step from the thicket, a knife in his fingers, a delighted but savage grin on his face.

Her buckskin horse whickered an alarm as brown fingers grasped at his picket rope.

Too late, Rebecca thought, strangely calm. *Too late!* The rifle lay just beyond her reach.

Even as she determined to make a try for it, a blow from the Indian's callused hand sent her flying in the other direction.

She had hardly struck the ground before her wrists were grasped and rawhide thongs strapped around them. Not the butter-soft leather Lucas had used; these lacings were stiff, brittle, but pliable enough to snare her wrists and chew into her flesh. She bit her lower lip to stop her instinctive shriek of pain.

A show of weakness wouldn't help her situation, so she resorted to her mind's book of quotes. "When sorrows come, they come not single spies," she said under her breath. "But in battalions."

This time Mr. Shakespeare was spot-on!

The tiny clearing was suddenly awash with Indians, whooping like a pack of children at a birthday party as they displayed the variety of treasure they found, and Rebecca realized that while quotes might rescue her mind, her mortal body was thoroughly trapped.

Sun Eagle felt a smile stretch his face. He'd never minimize his capture of the white-eyes woman. But even more significant was the many-shoots gun, which he brandished with exuberance as he ordered his followers to rekindle the cooking fire. They would eat, he said, while he determined what to do next on this auspicious day.

Rebecca was not fed. Indeed, she was essentially ignored as the Indians plundered the camp, filling their mouths with enormous bites of the cooked venison, even scoffing down the scanty remains of the pemmican. She lay there, hands bound in front of her, eyes still blurry from the force of the leader's blow, and listened as the Indians growled at each other in guttural mouthings she couldn't understand.

Their gestures, however, were easily understood, especially once the feasting was over and their attention turned again to the spoils of their successful raid. Her insides shriveled at the brutal directness of what they seemed to be planning for dessert.

She tried to dissolve herself into the ground, but the hard-featured face of the leader loomed above her, his fingers yanking at her chin to force her head up. Behind him, one of the younger braves tugged his swollen organ from beneath a filthy breechclout. At the same time, he mouthed what could only be obscenities.

The leader didn't even bother to look around. Without any warning, he turned and smashed his huge fist into the younger man's jaw, driving him into the dirt, then kicking him viciously in the face.

Dragged upright by her braids, Rebecca couldn't control her

squeal of pain. Or her shrill screech of terror.

The leader pointed toward her face, his voice rising in what could have been impatience, anger, or both.

But when he pointed again, first at her and then vigorously at his own grease-stained chest, the message became all too clear. She was *his* captive, and any arguments would be met with sudden and direct action. And yet . . . there was something more. She could sense it, even if his words were incomprehensible. She was being compared with something, or exhibited as an example of something.

Could these savages be part of the Minniconjou band that held Amy captive? Lucas had said the Sioux band was nearby.

Rebecca's gaze flickered across the faces, seeking a semblance of reason. If her mind hadn't been so blurred by fear and pain and useless quotes, she would have remembered immediately that she and Amy were identical twins. That, and that alone, might have saved her from a quick death, or, at the very least, a brutal molestation, for she could see no compassion in the Sioux leader's expression. Pride, yes. Contempt, yes. And yet . . . every once in a while, he looked . . . baffled.

Minutes later she was astride her buckskin, her swelling fingers lashed tightly to the saddle horn, her doeskin shift ricked far too high along her naked thighs for any sort of comfort. The chastened young Indian kept looking at her, his tongue licking at the blood which oozed from his bruised lips.

The leader led them out of the tangled thicket to where the Indian ponies waited, then gathered up her buckskin's reins and brought her horse into line with his own.

An hour or so later they halted. Chattering like schoolboys at recess, the Indians cleansed themselves.

Rebecca stayed atop her horse as the men stripped and washed in a small stream. She wanted to close her eyes, but was inexplicably afraid she'd never open them again. Thus, she watched as they painted their faces and naked bodies in vivid, intricate patterns, before donning finely beaded clothing.

Under different circumstances, it would have generated a bubble of laughter. The Indians looked for all the world like a group of young ladies primping for a ball. Except that young ladies would not have spent half the effort on their own hair that these savages spent combing and oiling the scalps that decorated their lances, bridles, even their horses' manes.

Rebecca was painted, too. After a good deal of consideration, her captor carefully drew a scarlet dot within a scarlet circle upon her dirt-stained forehead and her buckskin's quivering flank.

Her forehead seemed to burn, as if she'd been branded.

Dover Sugden was beginning to believe that it might have been a mistake to try and buy Amy Bennett from the Minniconjou.

Staring at the arrogant face of Bear's Blood, Sugden decided it was an even bigger mistake to have offered whiskey, the most logical currency. Half drunk, the huge chieftain was more than half belligerent, and his demands for more whiskey—and guns, damn it!—made Sugden's gut twist.

No amount of foot or buttock shifting could alter his uncomfortable squat as he glanced uneasily around the smoky lodge. Everything had gone wrong from the start. First, he'd begun negotiations for the Bennett girl without seeing her, a bad decision. Very bad! Because now that he'd seen Amy Bennett, he wished he hadn't. And he was increasingly certain she wasn't worth one small cup of trade whiskey.

The girl was as mad as a cut snake. As for any value as a woman . . .

I wouldn't screw it with somebody else's pecker, Sugden thought, trying to keep his gaze away from the filthy, wild-eyed apparition who sat across the fire from him.

He remembered his first look at Rebecca Bennett, a vision of clean-limbed, auburn-haired loveliness. The repulsiveness of her sister made Sugden shudder inside. But he deliberately withheld any evidence of his feelings from the ugly war chief, who leered with satisfaction as the madwoman's fingers toyed beneath his clout.

Amy's other hand absently pawed beneath her foul, grease-stained dress, but whether she played with herself or simply chased vermin, Sugden didn't know and didn't care. There was nothing lascivious about her motion. The absence of reason behind her mad eyes made it simply the preoccupation of a somewhat retarded and definitely evil child.

That, he decided, was the worst of it—the evilness that seemed to emanate from the woman as clearly as her fetid smell. There might be no sanity in her bleary violet eyes, but there was evil. And Sugden, to whom evil was as common as ditchwater, felt himself outmatched.

"Whiskey . . . want more whiskey. And guns."

Bear's Blood kept repeating himself, but to ignore him would be a dangerous and possibly fatal mistake. While the Sioux leader might be drunk as an owl, he was perfectly capable of using violence to get what he wanted. Leaning forward, Sugden began the complicated effort of communicating with words and hand signals.

"Map," he said, enunciating clearly.

He had no real expectation that the word *map* would sink into the Sioux's besotted mind or the faded intelligence of Amy Bennett. So far, she'd shown no sign she understood the language she'd been raised with, and her only "white" word usage had been a meaningless chant which, eerily, had sounded like deformed nursery rhymes.

"Ask her to draw me a map," Sugden insisted, forcing himself to meet the chief's bloodshot eyes.

"Whiskey . . . want more." Bear's Blood was tenacious, despite the half-full jug that dangled from his fingers, threatening to spill.

"Map!" Sugden gestured toward Amy Bennett, who regarded him with vacant eyes while she continued her genital stroking. Again, he was struck by the differences between the twins. If Amy's hair had ever been the same red as her sister's, he was fairly certain it hadn't been washed since her capture all those years ago.

Shit! Maybe he should just get up and get out of this camp!

Purchasing Amy Bennett made no sense. She couldn't, or wouldn't, communicate . . . hell, she didn't even seem to know what a map *was*, much less anything about *the* map.

The smoky air within the lodge was suddenly pierced by hoots and cries of . . .

Elation!

Victory!

Bear's Blood reared upright, then staggered into the eye-shattering daylight to view the arrival of Sun Eagle and his raiding party.

Sugden exited the lodge on the chief's heels, and had to choke back his own elation when Rebecca Bennett, kicked from her horse's saddle, landed at his feet.

Sleeping Fox laughed. A Peigan child of five winters would have noticed the whiskey from five pony-lengths away, and if it had been hidden to save it from the Minniconjou . . . well, even a useless Sioux would have found it eventually.

Deep, distinct tracks fairly shouted: *Le Carcajou*. The outlaw's whiskey had been inexpertly secreted in a windfall of downed timber. Sleeping Fox had spent an hour stalking the dozen small oaken kegs before he allowed himself to approach. And now . . .

Now it might be best to liberate the whiskey and get *it* and himself well away from this place. Because Sugden and his men would surely be back for it, and only a fool would stay to see that happened.

It took him little time to load the kegs onto his Sioux ponies, using the whiskey trader's own ropes, and although the ponies hadn't been trained as packhorses and didn't much like the weight, they endured it well enough. Before the sun had moved above him, Sleeping Fox was miles from the site.

He was Peigan, therefore more than a match for the impotent trail craft of any Sioux. Yet he tried, the best he could, to conceal all sign of his passage through the ravines and coulees that led to the little box canyon he remembered from an earlier visit.

No hint of an afternoon breeze. The high sun held unusual warmth for the lateness of the season, and by the time he had unloaded all the whiskey kegs, then watered and pegged out his ponies, he felt more tired than he would have expected.

Sleeping Fox stared at the whiskey. Surely it must be tested, just to see if it was the usual rotgut trade whiskey distributed by someone of Sugden's stripe. Or maybe decent whiskey, tasty and fit for a warrior. He had a minor twinge of conscience, a small one. But he had turned away from his triumphant return to his own people in order to follow these evil men, and he deserved a taste!

Broaching the nearest of the casks, he filled a tin cup from his saddlebag and leaned back against a fallen log to let the warmth of the sun play upon his naked torso. His aged eyes closed in weary appreciation, then opened wide as the first bite of whiskey flowed down his wrinkled throat.

"Pah," he grunted, and spat out the foul-tasting fluid. This had to be the *worst* trade whiskey he'd ever tasted, and he was a connoisseur of bad whiskey. Or had been . . . here, in the wide emptiness of his native prairie, the liquid tasted worse than usual, and the memories it prompted were just far enough away to protect him.

With another growl of distaste, he flung away the tin cup, then kicked over the whiskey keg for good measure. He stubbed a toe in the process, but the pain was cleaner than the pain of a hangover.

Before Rebecca could gasp back her breath, a white man knelt and spoke to her in a low tone that hardly carried past her ears.

"I can get you out of this, missy," he said. "But it won't be easy and it may not be quick, so try to keep your head. And for Christ's sake keep quiet. There's nothing you can say that will help, and if you get these heathens stirred up any more than they already are, it will make it harder for me to deal with them."

She could only nod.

Rising, the white man turned toward her abductor, still atop his war horse.

"I will give much whiskey for this one," he said through the greasy beard that encompassed his mouth. "*Much* whiskey! But I must have her now!"

Sun Eagle pondered this unexpected development, even though he knew that his habitual, serious deliberation was perhaps the reason Bear's Blood ruled the Minniconjou.

By all other standards, he was a more powerful leader. But his slow, deliberate way of thinking was inadequate to deal with what passed for politics amongst the Sioux. Bear's Blood had always talked his way around any disagreement, and that skill was duly appreciated by a people who loved oratory for its own sake.

Sun Eagle had not been slow to recognize that his white captive was a sister, perhaps even a twin sister, to the raddled hag who seemed to enhance the power of Bear's Blood. And while Sun Eagle had not yet worked out how the sunset-haired woman could give him a superior advantage, he was certain such an advantage existed and equally determined to find it.

But now . . .

"No!" he shouted.

Sun Eagle didn't trust the whiskey trader. And even though *much* crazy water for one useless white woman would be equitable, he wanted time to think.

"Five kegs of whiskey," Sugden said, splaying his huge, fat fingers in a gesture aimed at emphasizing the amount.

As well talk to the moon! Sun Eagle sat his horse and stared down at the Bennett girl, his black eyes hooded.

"Six! All right?"

Sugden snapped out the question, his own impatience surging up within him, fueled by his sense of danger. The camp already reeked of whiskey. Bear's Blood was a mean drunk and it would take little to provoke him into violence.

Shit! Sugden could probably buy half the camp and the whole horse herd for six kegs, if these damned savages would just get on with it!

The Bennett girl began to crawl away. Sugden assumed she could understand none of the Sioux and only part of the sign language, but she'd feel the growing tension and all her instincts would tell her to hide somewhere . . . anywhere.

He stretched out one huge, booted foot, placed it deliberately on her ankle, then listened to the growl of disapproval from Sun Eagle.

With a ferocious snarl, Bear's Blood shouldered his way into the dispute, pushing Sugden from the girl.

To Rebecca, the three men looked like starving wolves fighting over a fresh kill. She took the opportunity to crawl away again, this time between them.

Around her, others of the band gathered to watch. She

couldn't understand the guttural Sioux language, but she managed to follow at least some of the sign language.

Holding her breath, she made it through the forest of legs. Then, backed up against the skin wall of a lodge, she huddled, her entire body trembling, her mind almost blanked by fear.

She heard a cry of rage. Then another, distorted by emotion. The white man's voice roared, more distinct because at least some of the words made sense to her.

Then, another sound, this one totally at odds with the primitive aura of barbarity and violence.

Whistling?

As the muted mutter of the crowd stilled, Rebecca heard it again, this time more clearly.

Whistling!

Luc was no Peigan lad of five winters and he was well beyond five pony-lengths when he spotted the site of the disturbed cache.

Dismounting, he approached on foot, ensuring his own movements did nothing to displace the sign until he'd read it.

A surge of excitement faded to deep concern when he recognized the various tracks of Sugden's party, not least the tiny footprints of Luis Sebastian.

Luc stared at the more recent sign, such as it was. This visitor had not only stolen what most assuredly had been Sugden's whiskey, but he'd gone to tremendous extremes in order to disguise his visit.

The vague, nearly indecipherable hoof marks that led away from the site included several ponies, and Luc remounted, then nudged his roan forward to follow them. After following the fresh tracks for a while, he paused to consider. He could almost swear he'd seen the spoor of at least one pony before, but he knew he must shove his curiosity to the back of his mind.

It would come to him, in its own good time. If he'd seen the tracks before, sooner or later he'd remember the horse. He had never forgotten a horse track in his life.

He forced himself to focus on more immediate issues, made less difficult by the easily followed spoor of Sugden's party. Luc paralleled it, keeping to cover, and he wasn't the least bit surprised when he found himself within rifle range of the Minniconjou camp.

Leaving his stallion in a well-secluded glade, he continued his approach on foot, making a wide circle so he could come at the camp from a less-traveled direction.

Armed with his pistol, slinking like a shadow through the trees on the edge of the coulee, he arrived in time to watch Sun Eagle's party ride in, whooping their victory. Painted and oiled bodies gleamed. Carefully combed scalps fluttered like cavalry pennants.

Only marginally surprised to see Dover Sugden in the camp, Luc's breath caught in his throat as the doeskin-clad bundle that was Rebecca Susan Bennett tumbled from her pony's back to land sprawling at the outlaw's feet.

Dear God! Luc hadn't noticed her in the plunging melee of the raiding party.

Sudden anger clouded his vision.

What could she have done to bring the Sioux upon her?

He looked down to see his hand filled with the dark menace of his gun. Filled, but shaking.

Using his free hand to steady the pistol-filled one, he closed his eyes. Panic, not his brief burst of anger, had obscured every perspective of his vision . . . and his thinking.

If he fired his gun, Rebecca could be a victim of the retaliation sure to follow. If he didn't . . .

Opening his eyes, he watched Sugden and the two warrior

chiefs shift into aggressive positions, like dogs about to fight over a bone.

"Five kegs of whiskey!"

The outlaw leader's words floated up from the camp and into Luc's brain, where they swelled and bubbled and frothed with the potency of rotgut. And from that came the idea . . .

As he carefully returned to his blue roan stallion, Luc thought it might just be the stupidest, most inane idea he'd ever had.

It would take all the nerve in the world, all the luck in the universe.

He reached the outskirts of the camp unseen, the squabble between Sugden and the two chiefs having captured every Sioux's attention.

Luc licked his dry lips. Then he chewed his cheeks, praying he'd get a semblance of moisture from his equally dry mouth.

And then he began to whistle.

17

Dover Sugden's eyes were very small. In fact, they'd once been described as "tiny compasses on shoestrings." Now, Sugden felt them bulge to at least twice their size. He had never, in all his years as a trader, heard an Indian whistle, much less whistle "Across the Wide Missouri."

Then he saw the well-oiled pistol hanging from the Indian's saddle horn, the saddle itself, and finally the horse.

A tall, fiercely prancing blue roan Appaloosa!

Sugden cussed silently as recognition dawned. L'Hirondelle! It could be no one else!

Bear's Blood and Sun Eagle stared at the newcomer with open astonishment. Who in his right mind would ride into a village of Minniconjou with such arrogance, such utter insolence?

Sun Eagle's hooded eyes narrowed. Did the stranger who blew music from his lips have something to do with the female captive?

A gentle, welcoming whicker from the girl's horse confirmed his suspicions. As the splendid Appaloosa danced closer, Sun Eagle reached down to loosen the knife at his breechclout. Carefully, the warrior ensured his war bow and quiver were in place, his tomahawk at his saddlebow.

Luc saw the hand movements but kept his own hands empty. He removed his gaze from that of the hard-featured warrior. To stare would spawn problems—one stray dog eyeing another.

Instead, Luc focused on Rebecca, huddled against the edge of the lodge. He noted the bindings at her wrists, and her quivering terror.

Be still . . . be quiet . . . be invisible. He relayed the message to her without words, over and over, praying she'd understand. Then he scrutinized the assembled Sioux, hoping against hope there'd be an old acquaintance here, someone who could speak up for him.

Nobody looked familiar, nobody stepped forward. Luc wasn't all that surprised. He'd traveled among the Sioux, the Hunkpapa, but he'd never encountered any Minniconjou. Still, there couldn't be a significant difference regarding language or custom.

"I am the one known as *Tamer-of-horses,*" he said, fluttering his hands in the universal sign language of the plains tribes. "I have come to thank the Sioux, the Minniconjou, for rescuing my woman and my buckskin pony, and perhaps to reward whoever did this favor, for surely he has saved me much trouble."

Sun Eagle bit back a reply as his obsidian eyes met the stranger's ice-green eyes in silent challenge. He had not *rescued* the woman. He had *captured* her. She was his! He ran his gaze over the horse tamer's lean figure and snorted his contempt.

Having verified Rebecca's captor, Luc shifted his focus to Bear's Blood, the chief old Medicine Horse had described in detail and talked about with such disdain.

Wearing off a drunk, Luc thought, despair battling optimism.

Optimism won the skirmish, if not the war. Luc's memory kicked in and the Sioux words came back to him, words he hadn't used in years, locked in the vault of his mind.

"It would seem that perhaps a gift of the buckskin pony and the many-shoots gun would be enough to pay for this favor," he said. "Truly, my woman will not need the pony because after I have beaten her she will walk many days tied to the tail of my warhorse, although the many-shoots gun is a high price to pay for such a useless woman."

"I am Sun Eagle," said the hard-faced brave atop the piebald.

He might have said more, had Luc not interjected. "I have heard the name Sun Eagle," he lied. "I have heard that Sun Eagle is a fearless warrior and a fair man. I now realize I have not offered enough for my useless woman and will include my saddle."

Before any response could be uttered, Luc continued, "I suppose she was trying to gather berries." He threw an angry glare at Rebecca. "She is very foolish, this one. I told her there could be bears, that she should stay hidden in the camp and try to improve her skills at dressing hides. Did she do anything at all with the skin of the deer I left with her? I don't suppose she bothered to feed you from the deer, which was young and fat."

Horse-tamer's words were so nonthreatening, Sun Eagle almost said that he and his men had done their own cooking. But even as the words crept toward his lips, his stolid mind rejected them. The sunset-haired woman was *his*, no matter what this ugly, music-lipped stranger might say.

Luc saw the impasse, and sought more words. New words. Any words . . .

The whiskey trader saved him the trouble.

Sugden had watched L'Hirondelle with amazement, and once again felt outmatched. "Are you going to listen to this rubbish?" he demanded, turning toward Bear's Blood. "Look, I've offered good whiskey for this woman. And for the other woman. *Much* whiskey."

"Quiet!"

The Minniconjou chief whirled toward him, waving a war club in one huge fist. Sugden cringed.

"You have whiskey?"

The question wasn't directed at Sugden, but at the lounging figure on the blue roan stallion. A figure who shrugged, not at all concerned by the chief's belligerence. Again, Sugden cringed.

"I have offered the buckskin and the many-shoots gun and my saddle," Luc said calmly. "What has this useless woman done that makes such a high price not high enough? Surely she has not offended the great one who rescued her, and if she has, all that is required is for that warrior to have his own women beat her a little."

Baffled, Bear's Blood lowered his club. What to say that would not tell this stranger more than he should know? Obviously, he did not truly understand the high value the ugly whiskey trader had already placed on Sun Eagle's captive.

Luc saw the chief's confusion, but he held his tongue and let his other senses roam the camp.

Momentarily, Sugden would be no real problem. He and Luc were both, for all purposes, guests of the Sioux and therefore safe from each other. Luc would worry about Sugden later, but where the hell were his men? They had to be near the encampment, and Luc would rather have them where he could see them.

"Whiskey."

Bear's Blood said the word sullenly. The whiskey trader had *much* crazy water, and he wanted it now. Horse-tamer's bravery . . . riding openly into the Sioux village . . . meant he should receive the traditional hospitality . . . but only when, and if, Bear's Blood deemed it worthwhile.

Luc realized he could deny the existence of any whiskey, knowing as he did that Sugden's cache had been violated. But what if *Le Carcajou* had brought a keg or two along with him? What if his men guarded such kegs, waiting for a signal?

A gunshot? Not likely! An owl's hoot? Possible.

If Luc could approach the camp unseen, so could Luis Sebastian!

Luc had lied when he'd flattered Sun Eagle. He had lied about beating Rebecca. But lying about the availability of Sugden's whiskey could too easily seal his fate. And Rebecca's.

Again, he glanced toward her. She looked less befuddled and seemed to be watching alertly as his hands and those of the Indians flew like soaring birds.

In one fluid motion, he slid down his stallion's side and walked quickly toward her. His skinning knife severed the thongs at her wrists, but before the Sioux could feel threatened, he'd sheathed the knife.

"Get over to your pony, stay there, and stay quiet," he said. Not in English, which Sugden would have understood. And certainly not in Sioux, which Rebecca couldn't understand. But in the French *patois* she had absorbed along the trail, thanks to Monique Berube.

She squealed with indignation when he swatted her soundly across the rump, then scurried toward her pony. Before she'd even reached the buckskin, Luc turned away, ignoring her. If he wanted to play this dangerous game, he'd have to play by Sioux rules.

He returned to Sun Eagle, who still looked as if he was mentally plodding toward a confrontation.

Staring up into the warrior's face, Luc said, "If the buckskin pony and the many-shoots gun and the saddle are not sufficient in my new friend's eyes, then perhaps he could tell me what he thinks is a fair gift for keeping this useless woman safe for me."

Sun Eagle didn't reply, and Luc saw that the other Sioux didn't expect an immediate answer. First, Sun Eagle would have to split the question into a dozen pieces, like a hammer pounding at a walnut. The ponderous deliberations gave Luc time to think, too. Welcome time, if only he could use it wisely enough.

His simple act of riding openly into the camp should have certified his safety, but one glance around this shoddy Minniconjou band and Luc understood that normality might not apply here. He had never seen a worse lot of Indians. Most were filthy. Their clothing showed a lack of standards. And the camp, cluttered and dirty, would be considered a pestilent hole by Luc's Peigan relatives.

The disorderly filth had to be the fault of the half-drunk chief, who swayed back and forth while Sun Eagle pondered Luc's question.

Sun Eagle would definitely be a problem! Luc could almost see the thoughts churning in the warrior's head. Rebecca was his captive, therefore not worthy of gifts, but of ransom . . . much ransom . . . and Sugden could only make things worse if he kept offering his rotgut whiskey.

A stick of half-lit dynamite, Bear's Blood might detonate at any moment. Once he did, all hell would break loose, the last thing Luc needed or wanted.

At least he'd accomplished something. Rebecca, her hands free, stood silently beside her buckskin, her fingers not too far from the much-coveted many-shoots rifle that rested in her saddle's scabbard. If she had to use it, could she? And even more important, would she? Everything might depend on her courage, her ability to back him up without hesitation.

Suddenly, a far worse problem erupted onto the scene and Luc's throat constricted.

Walking fearlessly between Sun Eagle and Bear's Blood, a vaguely female figure crouched and stared up at his face. He saw the gleam in muddy but distinctly violet eyes, and felt himself shiver inwardly at the realization.

This . . . *creature* . . . was Amy Bennett!

Matted hair, so filthy there was no longer any sign of auburn, hung in dank tangles around a face so covered in grease and soot, she looked as if she'd been rooting in the dirt like a hog. As she rose to her feet, Luc couldn't read her expression.

A hand dark with—blood?—reached out to first stroke his cheek, then run like vermin down along the taut muscles of his chest to the flatness of his stomach. He wanted to recoil, wanted to slap away the horrific touch, but forced himself to remain motionless, his jaw clenched as his mind whirled with implications.

It was out of character for Sioux warriors to allow such a display. And yet every single person watched Amy drool out indecipherable comments so shockingly clear that words were not required . . . and no one, except Sugden, even flinched.

Luc knew the Sioux, along with most Indians, believed mad people were special in the eyes of their gods, but this acceptance of such an evil presence went beyond that belief. Tribes had their own concept of morality, some cherishing it, others making little of the sanctity of their women, but this . . .

He met the girl's gaze, forcing himself to endure for the moment. However, the moment was short-lived.

"Amy?"

The question emerged from Rebecca's mouth as a tentative plea, but it was enough to make the creature turn its muddy eyes in her direction. Luc stifled a groan. Despite the remnants of her terror, despite her instinctive repulsion at the barely human thing that stared at her, Rebecca stepped forward, arms outstretched.

"Amy? Amy . . . it . . . it *is* you," she cried.

"Becky Sue."

The words emerged clearly enough, though Amy's voice didn't reveal any enthusiasm, excitement, or pleasure.

"Bad! Becky Sue . . . *baaaad!*"

Amy's hand swung out to smash into her sister's face, driving Rebecca backward. Then Amy struck again, this time driving Rebecca to her knees. Amy's voice issued forth maniacal shrieks as she struck out with her fists and filthy, moccasin-clad feet in a frenzied attack so quick, so fierce, Luc had no time to intervene.

Had he dared! One look at the impassive face of Bear's Blood, and Luc realized that any intervention would only make it worse for Rebecca. Fortunately, Amy's attack was largely ineffectual, a buffeting whirlwind of blows that could do no real damage.

Luc held his ground, steeling his nerve for the dash he might yet have to make. Surely the Sioux would expect him to defend his woman. He'd made it perfectly clear that Rebecca was his, a valuable possession. Or had he overplayed the useless, worthless part?

The chief's shout of rage stopped Amy, who turned abruptly away from the assault on her sister as if Rebecca had disappeared, didn't exist.

Rebecca lay there, all in a heap, dazed. Luc wanted to run to her, comfort her, yet he knew he'd upset the precarious balance between himself, Bear's Blood, and Sun Eagle. Damn! He felt as if he walked a tightrope, stretched over a deep canyon.

Bear's Blood chewed his lower lip as he returned his attention to the problem of Horse-tamer. It was not, he decided, the right time to deal with this. He was tired and hungry. And thirsty. And although he'd never admit it to anyone, he didn't know what to do.

"Late," he said, glaring around as if his words could emphasize the obvious fact that the sun had faded and the autumn air grew cooler.

He pointed at a lodge. "You go there, Horse-tamer. Take your woman. Sleep tonight. Tomorrow we talk."

Sugden began to protest, but Bear's Blood cut him off. "You find your own people. Stay there. Tomorrow you go get whiskey. Maybe then we talk."

With an effort, Sugden kept his mouth shut. To argue could mean his life. His piggy eyes narrowed to mere slits, but he held his ground long enough to show spirit, then turned and shouldered his way through the dispersing Sioux.

Luc headed as quickly as he could for Rebecca, but was blocked by Sun Eagle's warhorse.

Using unmistakably clear sign language, the warrior gestured that he would consider trading Rebecca for the many-shoots gun, the buckskin, the saddle, *and* Luc's Appaloosa stallion.

Luc had no choice but to show interest in the offer. If push came to shove, he'd accept the trade. In truth, he'd accept any swap that would guarantee Rebecca's safety. But this solution created more problems than it might solve.

"My stallion would kill you, or try," he said. "It would not be a fair thing to do to someone who has saved my woman for me."

Which gained him a scornful snort from Sun Eagle. The warrior kicked his piebald's flanks and rode toward the blue roan Appaloosa, only to retreat when the great stallion reared up and lunged, baring huge, fierce teeth. The slashing hooves were aimed at Sun Eagle, not the piebald.

Luc stood silently, holding in the chuckle that would mean a swift death should it slip between his lips. Bear's Blood, thankfully, didn't laugh, either. Instead, he brandished his war club toward Sun Eagle and shouted at him to do what he'd been told. Luc surmised that a lifetime of obedience to authority, rather than the club, kept Sun Eagle from arguing further. The warrior turned and rode away, then glared back over his shoulder, and once again Luc could almost hear the thoughts

grinding inside the warrior's head. How could he have captured a woman, a horse, a gun and a saddle, then lost them all within the same half a day?

How in the name of everything holy are we going to escape with our own lives, much less try and rescue a clearly deranged Amy Bennett?

With that thought, Luc glanced around the lodge. His gear had been carefully stowed, well away from any part of the perimeter that seemed vulnerable to a visit from sticky Indian fingers. Rebecca kneeled beside her buckskin's saddle, her head down, as if she were praying.

Luc wanted to put his arms around her, but dared not. Logic said they would be brought some sort of food soon, and it might be important for Rebecca to appear appropriately chastised rather than cherished and comforted.

Assuming he could provide comfort. He wondered how the attack by the hag-ridden creature she'd recognized as her sister would affect her rescue plan?

"We're not going to be able to rescue her, are we?"

For an instant Luc felt certain he'd uttered his thoughts aloud. Rebecca had answered his unspoken question without looking up. Her arms were crossed tightly against her bosom, her hands no longer in a prayer wedge, and he saw that tears threatened to spill from the corners of her eyes.

"We'll be damned lucky to rescue ourselves," he replied, his voice very soft. He ached to lift her into the safety of his arms and console her, but he still didn't dare.

"The . . . the man with the beard. He said he could help."

"That man is Dover Sugden, *Le Carcajou,* the whiskey trader and leader of the gang that tortured and killed your father."

Rebecca lifted her lashes. Her eyes, plum-black and bleary from strain, revealed comprehension rather than astonishment.

"I didn't take to him," she said. "Now I know why. He wants

to buy Amy, too, doesn't he?"

"That's his plan, I believe."

"The chief would sell his own mother for whiskey. Which only makes our situation worse, Lucas, because we have nothing to trade."

"Neither does Sugden."

Luc told her about Sugden's cache having been raided.

"Trouble is, when he finds out he'll try to blame me, and it wouldn't surprise me one bit if the Sioux accepted his arguments. Frankly, I wish it *had* been me. At least we'd have something to bargain with, Rebecca, and a helluva lot better chance to leave alive and save our hair."

Luc could have kicked himself when he saw the way his words slammed into her like physical blows.

"It could be a lot worse and it might get better," he said. "We do have *some* bargaining power, although I'd hate to end up walking out of here with no horse or gun between us, especially with Sugden nearby." The question that had been on the tip of his tongue since entering the lodge finally escaped. "Rebecca . . . did your sister hurt you?"

"Yes. But not physically. A few bruises. They'll go away."

"And did you understand my . . . ploy? The Sioux must believe you're my *property*, nothing more."

"Your smack on my behind was quite emphatic, Lucas, but yes, I understood. Is . . . is Amy the chief's . . . property?"

"Seems to me it's the other way 'round. Sleeping Fox said your sister sort of rules this band, and Bear's Blood as well."

"And knowing all that, you still came for me. Why?"

Because I owed a debt to your father, because even then I had begun to love you. "Because you were determined to try a rescue come hell or high water, and you couldn't go alone."

"In other words, I'm your responsibility rather than your property?"

"I guess the Sioux aren't going to feed us," he said, sidestepping her question by retrieving some pemmican and a canteen of water from his saddlebags. "So this dried meat will have to do. When we get out of here, I'll cook us the biggest steak you can imagine. Buffalo, deer, your choice."

"*If* we get out of here," she whispered.

He finally put his arms around her. "Let's get a good night's sleep, Rebecca, or at least try, because tomorrow will be a difficult day no matter what the hell happens."

Sleeping Fox eased his way backwards, losing sight of the Sioux encampment, and his efforts to hold in his laughter did nothing but provoke more chuckles to hide.

Truly, he thought, these Sioux were children. He had much to ponder before he let loose his Peigan wrath upon them, which was why he had not ridden into their camp this very evening, numbing them with his war cries and counting coup many times.

"Strangers in their camp and they do not even set out sentries," he muttered to himself, shaking his graying head at the folly of such a thing; carelessness beyond belief.

They would pay for it tomorrow. Tonight he would speak to his gods, seeking advice and assistance. Someone had to take control, and clearly it would not be his friend Horse-tamer, who had ridden into the Sioux camp with great bravery but little common sense.

"It is the sunset woman who has done this to him," the old man told his pony, and smiled as the words brought to him memories long buried. Memories of his youth. Memories of a certain doe-eyed Peigan maiden who had provoked a similar recklessness.

He reached his camp in fine mettle. His contempt for the Sioux allowed him to risk a small fire upon which he could roast the fat young jackrabbit he had killed. As he ate, he pondered how best to invoke the spirits and plan the rescue of his friend and his friend's sunset woman.

Once fed, he lit his pipe. Offering the pipe to the four sacred directions, as well as the sky and the mother earth, he puffed gently on it, and pondered his options.

The spirits would come to him. *Good* spirits—not those from the whiskey barrel. He was content.

Sun Eagle sprawled against the willow backrest in his lodge, his belly full, his youngest wife massaging his feet. Sleep should have been next, but he couldn't even contemplate sleep.

Too many problems crowded his brain, leaving little room for peaceful rest, much less a satisfying slumber.

First, the white-eyes woman and her buckskin pony were Sun Eagle's captives and Bear's Blood should not have interfered.

Second, Sun Eagle felt deep humiliation over Horse-tamer's blue roan stallion. Revenge could wait, however, since dealing with the Appaloosa would be easy enough. A bullet in its head would suffice, if nothing else could be done.

Third, and most important, Bear's Blood . . .

Various members of the Minniconjou band had been after Sun Eagle for months now to depose their brutal leader, a man who struck fear into his followers because of his whiskey temper. And because of his white captive, the madwoman known as Blood Hand. The witch, the sorceress, the evil one.

Under her influence, things had happened in the band which all good Sioux knew to be wrong and improper. But Bear's Blood seemed impervious to complaints. The woman had him enthralled with her ruttish, animal-like sexuality. She seemed to have drawn him into her own circle of madness, and it was making the other Minniconjou more and more nervous.

Then there had been their leader's actions during the battle against the yellow-haired Custer. Had it not been for the intervention of the great chief Sitting Bull, the honor of all Sioux would have been tarnished forever, in their own eyes and the eyes of all people.

Perhaps the time had come to defy Bear's Blood. Sun Eagle had the support of many warriors, and surely the spirits were with him. Witness his fine luck in capturing the white-eyes woman and returning with the plunder of her camp. He was known to be lucky, known to be prudent, careful of his followers' lives.

Bear's Blood was no longer a proper leader. It was that simple. No proper leader would take fairly won booty from a follower without so much as a reason.

Tomorrow morning Sun Eagle would assert himself. He would, if necessary, fight Bear's Blood. Sun Eagle was younger and at least as great a warrior. *And he was lucky.*

In his opinion, the chief's luck had run out.

Follows-the-Badger had never been lucky. Throughout his young life—only fifteen winters—everything great he had ever tried to accomplish had gone wrong.

The first horse he had attempted to steal had kicked him, nearly breaking his leg and stirring up its Crow owner so quickly that Follows-the-Badger had nearly been caught. The first buffalo he had shot had reared out of *certain death* to graze him with a mighty thrust of its horn, almost disemboweling him.

But now, with the predawn darkness thick about him, the young Minniconjou felt more confident than he'd ever felt before. Judging from their snores, the whiskey trader and his companions slept soundly. And their status as visitors had changed; the chief's attitude toward their leader had made that clear enough.

Best of all, the little man who dressed in black and carried the beautiful throwing knives had left one knife in his saddlebags.

Follows-the-Badger could see the sleeping men clearly, his young eyes fully adapted to the darkness. He squatted near their lodge, his breath controlled, his body immobile, undetectable . . . the body of a warrior!

A shadow within a shadow, he crept toward the saddlebags heaped at the entrance to the lodge. Thin, deft fingers plucked open the lacings, reached inside, and foraged among the contents, seeking only the wonderful knife, ignoring all else.

Follows-the-Badger smiled, his luck confirmed. He had found the weapon he craved.

A throwing knife left the fingers of Luis Sebastian, who'd been roused by a whisper of instinct, and it sped to merge with the shadow that hovered over the saddlebags. The shadow stiffened, half erect with shock, then died screaming, and the small *mestizo* could have sworn the shadow's voice linked frustration with disappointment and pain.

Sebastian condemned his throw as a poor performance. He had aimed for the shadow's upper arm. Miscalculating by a whisker, he had caught the thief high in the rib cage, the knife snicking between a couple of ribs to puncture a lung and sever major blood vessels.

Follows-the-Badger's cry of anguish had been very loud.

Before Sebastian could recover his knives, he found himself surrounded by sleepy-eyed but surly Sioux warriors.

18

When Lucas Swallow awakened with his pistol in hand, it seemed to Rebecca that he *flowed* from the immobility of sleep into the startled alertness of a prowling wolf.

Outside their lodge, the din of shrieking Sioux rang in her ears. She struggled to get herself upright, into some sense of reality, after a night in which sleep had been fitful and broken, at best.

Lucas pulled aside the entrance flaps and slid through, his free hand waving in a gesture that demanded she stay put.

She hadn't even begun to conquer her confusion when he returned, shaking his head in what could have been astonishment or concern. Or both.

"There'll be hell to pay now," he said, unbuckling his gun belt. "Hitch up your dress, Rebecca."

"What . . ."

"Do it!"

She'd only meant to ask him what kind of trouble brewed outside, but apparently he thought she'd questioned his demand. Impatient hands pushed her own aside and the next thing she knew her doeskin frock was bunched up above her waist and Lucas had buckled the gun belt around her. Then he yanked the dress down, turned her to one side, and drew his razor-sharp skinning knife.

"Hold perfectly still," he said, as he snicked with his knife's point at a side seam, opening a long section where the bulk of his holster strained at her frock's side.

Once he had completed his assault on her dress, he stepped back and regarded her with wary eyes.

"Now that you've played deranged couturier," she said, "won't you please tell me what's going on?"

"A member of Sugden's gang, Luis Sebastian, has killed a young Sioux. Which is nothing to us, assuming the Sioux confine their anger to him, or to Sugden's band of bloody cutthroats. But if the Minniconjou are bent on revenge, and if they get it into their heads that *any* white blood will do, we could be in worse trouble than we already are."

His words were prophetic. The lodge entrance flaps suddenly opened and several Indians surged inside. Their arms waved like agitated seagulls and their voices shrilled like seagulls, too. An almost inhuman fury distorted their words, and Rebecca felt her blood turn to ice. Then she squared her shoulders and stiffened her chin, whose color she presumed now matched her eyes . . . thanks to Amy.

"Here's a sigh to those who love me, and a smile to those who hate," she said to Lucas. "And, whatever sky's above me, here's a heart for any fate."

"Lord Byron."

It hadn't been a question but she said, "Yes. My head is full of such useless quotes."

"That one isn't useless, and neither are you."

Warmed by his compliment, Rebecca lifted her bruised chin higher. Crowded, rather than escorted from the lodge, she glanced around. It seemed to her that every Indian stood there, the whole camp, sharing the faint light of early dawn. Lucas kept one hand on her arm, drawing her along with him in an attitude that clearly stated: *This is mine!*

Nobody objected, not even her captor, seated motionless upon his horse as if an artist had painted him there, his tinted background the amethyst-streaked sky. And even though, in her opinion, at least some woman should have noticed the revolver-like bulge at her hip, nobody gesticulated. In fact, Rebecca had a feeling she and Lucas were merely spectators, a couple of Romans watching Dover Sugden and Luis Sebastian toe the mark against a multitude of hungry lions.

The aura of excitement grew, hanging over Rebecca's head like a tangible cloud, as she and Lucas were shoved to the front of the keening assemblage.

"I'm truly sorry," Luc murmured in Rebecca's ear. "I wish I could have spared you this. It is liable to be . . . messy."

His own insides trembled. Several Sioux held Luis Sebastian immobile over the body of the boy he'd killed, and the expressions on the Minniconjou faces told Luc all he needed to know. Sebastian appeared less upset than anyone else. He stared implacably at Bear's Blood, who raged before him, questioning Sebastian in strident Sioux, barely intelligible English, and wild hand gestures.

The other Indians jostled like wolves around a fresh kill, none quite brave enough to snatch the first bite but all ready to charge in for the second. Then, to Luc's surprise, a fidgety Sugden stepped forward and confronted Bear's Blood.

"The boy was trying to steal from my companion, right here in this camp," Sugden said, his hands flying in a vain attempt to support his poorly spoken Sioux. "Is this how your people treat their friends? By stealing from them?"

But no assuredness colored Sugden's voice, and his face revealed his own personal fears. Sebastian knew it, too. Luc saw the small killer stare at Sugden without any expression of hope.

"Not that I approve, you understand," the outlaw leader continued, managing the about-face without turning a hair. "Nothing could be further from the truth, I swear. My people would place this man in front of a firing squad.

"I have always worried about this one's tendency to kill without thought." For the first time Sugden sounded sincere. "And that he would do a thing in the camp of our friends, the Sioux . . ." Sugden shook his head. "Rather than a firing squad, this man must submit to the justice of Bear's Blood and his people. I would never have allowed such a man to come with me, amongst you, had I realized he was without . . ."

Sugden mangled the next word. Translating for Rebecca, Luc whispered, "I'm sure he meant principle, but it came out principality."

"What a yellow-bellied coward he is," she whispered back. "Luis Sebastian deserves everything he gets, but for his own leader to turn on him like that . . . why, it's like . . . like a spider eating its young."

Deserves everything he gets? Luc blinked. Ordinarily, he'd expect Rebecca to spout some nonsense about an arrest and trial.

Bear's Blood still raged. The dead youth was, he said, only a boy. He might have fancied the small man's knife, but could this be a good reason to *kill* him? What sort of man would kill a mere child for something as petty as a knife?

"A bad man," Sugden said. "A depraved man who should now face Sioux justice, not only for killing a Sioux, but for betraying his own company by doing such an awful thing."

Luc nearly choked at the blatant way in which Sugden condemned his companion to a certain and painful death. Sebastian, however, didn't seem the least bit shocked. He glared at Sugden, but remained silent, merely spitting his disgust in a stream that splashed on the outlaw leader's rundown boots.

The snarling Indian pack howled acceptance at the whiskey trader's words and gestures, but something seemed wrong. Their reaction was discrepant, Luc thought. Normal outrage had been verbally expressed, and yet they all lacked physical assertion. It took Luc a moment to recognize what bothered him, and with that comprehension came a sudden spurt of fear that transmitted itself down his arm to the hand which still held Rebecca's wrist.

Rebecca's sister, who could only with the greatest leap of imagination be the twin of the woman he so desperately loved, had evolved into some sort of shamanic, evil force that permeated the entire Sioux band. Not even the mother of the slain youth, with her blackened face and slashes of self-mutilation along her arms, seemed ready to deal with her son's killer.

Only one person could confront Sebastian, it seemed . . . Amy Bennett.

Even as Luc realized this potential for corruption, the source of his thoughts shoved through the gathered throng that surrounded Sebastian and the body of his victim.

There was no hesitation in Amy, none of the subdued violence so obvious among the other women. She approached the small *mestizo* directly, boldly, her power so great, so assured, that nothing dared threaten her.

Generated and upheld by her madness, by the inherent evil which the superstitious Sioux could recognize but not oppose, Amy's authority was absolute. Bear's Blood accepted it, and approved, because Amy's omnipotence could only enhance his own.

Luc also understood that Bear's Blood had been playing with Sugden all along. No amount of whiskey could ever pry this woman loose from the chief. Medicine Horse and Sleeping Fox had been all too right. Amy, not Bear's Blood, ruled this band.

Sebastian twitched slightly, but didn't struggle as Amy stalked up to stare into his eyes. Held upright by warriors on both sides, Sebastian was defenseless . . . and knew it.

Amy stared for what seemed like many minutes, then spun away and began to gesticulate wildly, her voice keening in a banshee sound that rent the solemn atmosphere. She paced over to the body of the young Sioux. A grimy finger reached out to touch the dead face in a caress that was both gentle and obscene. Especially when her hand moved downward and her fingers began to puddle in the dark red evidence of the boy's fatal wound.

Luc felt Rebecca move imperceptibly closer. He knew she didn't want to see what would happen next, but had willed herself to watch, hoping she could make sense of the travesty that had once been her sister.

The banshee wails continued. Amy's hand puddled in the spilt blood. Her howls rose in volume as she spun upright, whirled toward Sebastian, and with a single final shriek, planted her palm squarely on his forehead. Only after she'd removed her palm did the assembled Sioux take part in the proceedings.

"Blood Hand!"

The cry came first from Amy Bennett's twisted lips. Soon it was caught and thrown high into the dawn sky, caught and lifted and carried by a growing number of voices. The filthy shaman shambled in a clumsy circle, her bloodied hand pointing to the body, the prisoner, the sky.

"Blood Hand! Blood Hand! Blood Hand!"

The obscene mantra rose and fell and rose again, taken up by ensuing voices, until it seemed as though Luc and Rebecca must be the only ones who did not chant the litany of repressed rage that echoed throughout the valley of the Minniconjou camp.

They could only look at each other, mute in their disbelief. Then they were shouldered along with the crowd as the prisoner, dragged to the edge of the camp and stripped, was backed up against a cottonwood stump and bound tightly, his wrists behind the tree.

"Blood Hand! Blood Hand!"

The chant continued, but diminished slightly when Bear's Blood strode forward and began to harangue his people, his huge hands gesturing at the prisoner and the shambling female shaman who lurched before him in a parody of dance.

Luc placed his mouth near Rebecca's ear and interpreted Bear's Blood's remarks. First, the boy's body must be prepared as custom dictated so that he would face his trip to join the ancestors properly cleansed and clothed, his weapons gathered, his spirit in readiness. Then and only then would this slayer of an innocent Sioux youth pay the ultimate penalty for his act.

Bear's Blood's porcine eyes flickered across the dispersing crowd until he pinpointed Sugden. "You . . . stay!" Then he gestured toward Sugden's three followers, huddled in obvious distress. "You . . . get whiskey!"

Although the chief's next words left little room for doubt or misunderstanding, Luc continued to translate for Rebecca. Bear's Blood wanted the whiskey he knew Sugden had, *all* the whiskey, and he wanted it here, in this camp, by the time the sun was at its highest point. Fail, and their leader would join the small man in the tortures to come. Fail, and the Minniconjou would hunt Sugden's followers down like the white-skinned dogs they were, subjecting them to even harsher penalties.

Luc wasn't surprised by what he saw on the three white faces. Clearly, the half-wit boy didn't comprehend much, or reveal it if he did. But the other two men, especially the lanky one Luc had seen with Luis Sebastian, were still horrified by Sugden's callous dismissal of Sebastian. Now they were equally concerned with their own safety.

Nonetheless, Luc knew they'd go for the whiskey. Bear's Blood might keep his promise to hunt them down if they didn't return, and they'd hope against hope their leader wouldn't betray *them*.

Hope and fear were potent incentives. Almost as potent as

the rotgut that didn't exist anymore. What would the three men do upon discovering that their cache had been raided?

Before Luc could even make a calculated guess, Bear's Blood gestured toward Rebecca. The irascible chief's expression revealed no friendliness, no hospitality, but no immediate threat, either.

With a dismissive wave, Bear's Blood told four braves to escort Horse-tamer and his woman back to the lodge . . . and keep them there.

"If they bring lots of whiskey into this camp, things are going to get a whole lot worse, aren't they?"

"Sugden's followers won't be bringing back *any* whiskey, Rebecca. Unless they have some in reserve, which I doubt." Luc honed his knife on a rock, somewhat surprised it hadn't been confiscated, especially after Follows-the-Badger's death. He could only assume that his whistling arrival and his knowledge of the Sioux language had secured his benevolent-visitor status. "That, too, is going to make things worse. Six of one, half a dozen of another. Bear's Blood will either be cranky because he has no whiskey or cranky because he's drunk out of his mind."

"What are we going to do?"

"You are going to stay here and try to rest a bit more. I am going to water our horses, for starters, then see if I can figure out some sort of plan."

"You must hate me."

Her remark came out of the blue, and for an instant Luc couldn't gather it in his mind. How could he hate the woman he loved, even if she didn't know he loved her and now might never know?

"Nothing to hate *you* for," he said. "Trying to rescue your sister was always a chancy business at best, and downright dangerous no matter how you slice it."

"I think it's been sliced far too thinly, Lucas. I should have listened to you from the start."

"That's only because you're here and you've seen what we're up against. Hindsight can be amazingly transparent. But it isn't over yet," he added. "Not by a long shot."

"You won't be long, will you?" she asked, as he turned to leave the lodge.

"Only as long as I have to be. Please try to rest. It'll be a damned long day for everybody, I reckon, although Sebastian has more to worry about than we do right now."

"They'll kill him, won't they? Horribly."

It wasn't precisely a question and Luc knew a detailed answer would make her sick to her stomach. With a shrug, he pushed aside the flaps and stepped into the morning.

Rebecca just sat there, alone in the lodge, all her nightmares swarming towards reality.

Eyes like chips of obsidian watched as the three outlaws rode in hopelessly confused circles around the place where their whiskey had been so carefully cached.

"Fools," Sleeping Fox muttered to himself. These white men were so stupid he began to wonder if they could have found the whiskey had he *not* bothered to move it. They had gone round and round the area a dozen times, effectively destroying any tracks that might have helped them, and now they argued about what to do next.

Though difficult to follow with his imperfect command of their language, their debate fascinated Sleeping Fox.

"Are you sure this is the place?" asked the tall, scrawny one.

"Of course I'm bloody sure," the short, one-eyed man replied, his nose twitching like a rabbit's. "Look for yourself, Williams. You can see where the kegs *were*."

"Then what the hell happened to them?"

"Shit! How the hell would I know? They're gone, that's for sure. And if we've a lick of sense, we'll be gone, too . . . and quickly."

"Gone where? We have to ride back and report this. Sugden will have someone's head for it."

"Are you crazy? The hell with Sugden! He threw Sebastian to those bloody savages and he'd do the same to us. I say we ride out of here now. Ride north and try to get across the line before them Injuns even know we're gone."

"What? Just leave the boss? Christ, Harrigan! We can't do that!"

"Maybe you can't, Williams, but I sure as hell can. He'd do the same to us and don't you believe otherwise."

Sleeping Fox could hardly contain his amusement. All the time the two men talked, they rode round and round, destroying more and more tracks.

The third man, only a boy, seemed not altogether there in his head. He followed them patiently, staring slack-jawed at whomever spoke.

Finally he said, "We go back."

The boy's tone was flat, as expressionless as his eyes, but the rifle in his hands embodied his message.

The tall, thin man and the one-eyed man both stared at the boy. Then they shook their heads so emphatically, Sleeping Fox was surprised their sweat-stained hats stayed atop their scalps.

"Christ, boy, what the hell's all this about?" Williams pointed a shaky finger at the rifle.

"We go back. Now. Tell boss."

Harrigan's face revealed his disgust. "We should have shot this idiot in Kansas!" Reaching for his revolver, he paused as the rifle shifted to line up squarely with his belt buckle.

"It's okay, boy," said Williams. "We'll go back and tell the boss. We know you're a dead shot, don't we Harrigan? *Don't we,*

Harrigan? It's why the boss likes you so much, damn it!"

Williams slowly turned his horse around. After a scowl at the impassive boy, Harrigan followed.

Sleeping Fox's shoulders shook with silent laughter. The boy had surely saved all their lives, at least for the moment. Williams and Harrigan were too stupid to know, as Sleeping Fox knew, that a dozen Sioux had been stationed to cut off any other route they might have taken. Each patiently waiting Sioux had his bow strung and his arrow fully knocked.

The tall, thin man, the one-eyed man, and the boy were hardly out of sight when an ugly Sioux atop a big painted gelding emerged to do some scouting of his own. A far better reader of sign than the white outlaws, he circled the copse several times, each time moving farther and farther outward, his hooded eyes scanning the ground then glancing upward.

Despite the growing warmth of the day, Sleeping Fox remained in position, motionless, watching the warrior from his peripheral vision lest his own interest draw attention. He knew he could easily deal with a single Sioux, but he didn't want to alert the rest of the party, and that might be difficult.

The Sioux stared directly at where Sleeping Fox lay hidden, and the stare went on too long for the old Peigan's comfort.

Just as Sleeping Fox prepared himself for the inevitable assault, the foolish warrior turned, kicked his gelding into a canter, and followed his back trail toward the encampment.

Soon *Le Carcajou* and Bear's Blood would know about the missing whiskey. What would happen then? Sleeping Fox couldn't decide if such knowledge would benefit Horse-tamer and his sunset woman, or threaten them.

Either way, he might be the only one who could do anything about the situation.

When Luc returned with the Appaloosa and buckskin, the

sentries were still posted outside the lodge. Luc asked for permission to tack up his horses. That granted, he said, "Will my new friends allow my woman to help me?" The braves looked uncertain so he nudged one with his elbow. "My worthless woman does not know very well how to saddle a horse properly, and she could use the practice."

The sentries laughed and nodded.

"I don't know if there's a chance in hell for us to ride out of here," Luc said to Rebecca, after they'd finished saddling her buckskin and his Appaloosa. "But it can't hurt to be ready."

As he draped his stallion's hackamore over his saddle horn, her eyes widened. "Would they *let* us ride away?" she asked.

"Maybe, maybe not. I expect I'll have to square things with Sun Eagle, first. I just hope I've convinced him my stallion would be more trouble than it's worth. I'd hate for us to leave on foot, especially with Sugden's crew on the loose."

"Your stallion! You mean you . . . you'd give up your stallion? I know he's only a horse, Lucas, but . . . well, he's *more* than that, to you."

"I would give my life to save you, Rebecca."

She didn't appear to hear him, her mind miles away, perhaps behind the clouds that scudded across the sky.

"I wonder," she said. "Can a horse be the essence of a man?"

"I'm not sure where the greatest danger to you comes from," Luc said, ignoring a question he didn't know how to answer. His mother's people would have said yes, his father's no. "Without whiskey, Sugden has no real bargaining power, and Bear's Blood might very well punish . . . retaliate . . ."

"You can say the word torture, Lucas. That's what Sugden did to my father."

She was with him now, listening.

"I don't think *we* have much to fear from Bear's Blood, Rebecca, but we have to appease Sun Eagle. He captured you;

therefore he owns you."

"No one owns me!"

"Sun Eagle does. He found you, seized you, and . . ."

"Owns me. Yes, I know." Momentarily, her chin jutted. "He's made a mistake, Lucas, a *big* mistake. If he thinks your stallion rebelled, he need only wait until . . ."

"I'm serious, Rebecca!"

"So am I! The first time he caught me off guard. Like . . . like Amy did."

"I think she's the biggest danger of all."

"My father begged me to kill her if I couldn't rescue her. Begged me on his death bed. Do you suppose he knew?"

"I doubt it. He merely expressed the usual opinion that any white woman who's been . . . touched . . . by savages is better off dead. You have to see it from his point of view, Rebecca. He'd probably feel the same about . . ."

"Savages? Those savages are almost civilized, compared to Amy."

"She's insane." Luc made the comment flatly, dispassionately, thankful to have been interrupted, but plagued once more by his need to set things straight. He'd almost said it, almost said that her father would feel the same about himself and Rebecca . . . white and Métis.

"She's evil, Lucas."

"Yes, but I doubt you'd want her death on your conscience."

"That's what I thought, in the beginning, but now . . . what did you say . . . before . . . when I was talking about your stallion?" Her eyes widened again. "Did you say you'd give your life for me?"

He reached out, grasped Rebecca's hand, and led her inside the lodge. Now was the time to reveal his dual identity! Now, when she couldn't turn away. Now, when they were united against a common enemy. Her sister. The very same sister Otis

260

Bennett had begged Rebecca to shoot because he couldn't stand the thought of his daughter cohabiting with Indians.

How much of her father's attitude had rubbed off on Rebecca? During her long pilgrimage, she'd admired Medicine Horse, justified Sleeping Fox's vengeance, even condoned the brutality aimed at Sebastian—at least for the moment. And yet . . . the thought of cohabitation might provoke an entirely different reaction.

Luc could articulate his feelings, and suspected she might already have guessed them from his impulsive *I would give my life for you.* But he was, and always would be, Métis. Could her inborn fears ease with time? Assuming they had time?

He gathered her against him, comforted by the fact that she came willingly into his arms. "Rebecca, there are things I must say to you," he began. "Things I must explain that you may find difficult to understand."

She snuggled against him. Unguided, almost unmanageable, his hands roamed along the contours of her back, her shoulders, the outthrust swelling of her rump. She sighed and moved closer. He lifted her chin with his finger, forcing her head up.

"I . . ." He got no further. Her gaze pulled at him, tugged at him, drawing his mouth against hers to drink in the sweetness of her breath, the taste of her. The upsurge of his ardor fairly staggered both of them, and they swayed together, fighting for a balance Luc knew would never come as long as he held her.

She tried her best to flow into him, to become a part of him, to merge hips and lips and loins. "Rebecca," he said, forcing himself to relinquish her mouth, seeking enough sanity to say what had to be said. Dammit, she needed to hear the truth, needed to know he loved her, perhaps had always loved her. She was his medicine vision come alive, complete. "Rebecca, we must talk. Must!"

"L'Hirondelle, you bastard! I'll kill you for this!"

261

The sheer savagery of the voice outside their lodge brought Luc and Rebecca apart, and she looked up at him with genuine confusion.

"L'Hirondelle! Damn you! Come out of there!"

The tent flap was thrust aside to reveal the florid, scowling face of Dover Sugden, his hands clenching and unclenching.

"What have you done with my whiskey, you bloody sneaking half-breed? You'd better explain yourself to the goddamn chief, and you'd better do it now!"

Luc wasn't intimidated by the outlaw's threat. He could tell Bear's Blood about the stolen cache. But he could never explain away the pain in Rebecca's eyes, as sudden realization came to her, and with it the brutal stench of betrayal.

19

L'Hirondelle!

The name thundered through Rebecca's head like a herd of wild horses, scurrying here and there, leaving in their wake a welter of shock and confusion.

Luc L'Hirondelle! The Métis boy! The Métis boy her father had found, along with the dead grizzly bear! *Lucas Swallow's* scars now made perfect sense. Should have, she thought bitterly, right from the start!

But why had the Métis *man* deliberately deceived her? He had known her identity from the very beginning, had known she was Otis Bennett's daughter when he saw the bear claw round her neck.

As Rebecca followed Lucas Swallow . . . *Luc L'Hirondelle . . .* she recalled his behavior at the Helena soirée.

The look in his pale green eyes when he studied her talisman. The touch of his strong fingers when he returned the carved claw to her bodice. The muted hum of the crowd inside the governor's mansion. The tangy scent of his cheroot . . .

Everything raced through her mind and sparked her senses, even as her gaze darted left and right, taking in the scenario outside the lodge.

A calm L'Hirondelle regarded an agitated Sugden, flanked by Bear's Blood and a host of his warriors.

"You stole my whiskey, you goddamn half-breed! Who the hell else could have done it?"

Lucas addressed his reply to Bear's Blood. "You saw me ride into your camp. There was no whiskey with me." He turned his face to Sun Eagle, who stood near the chief. "And you, my friend, you brought in my woman and the goods from my camp. Surely if I had any whiskey you would have found it, would have brought it with you. If there had been whiskey, I would have offered you that for helping my woman, rather than the buckskin pony, my many-shoots gun, and my saddle."

Rebecca could easily follow his hand gestures, especially the *my woman* parts, which struck her with a blend of emotions she had no ability, nor desire, to evaluate.

Sun Eagle's quandary seemed almost palpable. *He still considers me his property,* Rebecca thought wryly. *He had never claimed the gun, pony, or saddle, much less any whiskey, but the speed of events has left him off balance. All he can do is scowl.* It would have been funny under different circumstances.

"I do not know what this one's problem is," Lucas said, gesturing toward Sugden, "and I wonder why the Minniconjou would allow a guest in their camp to be threatened by such a man."

Rebecca hid her tight-lipped smile within a discreet cough. What a cunning ploy! "Guest" denied their captive status, and if accepted might improve their future prospects substantially. If accepted . . .

Sugden's roar of objection was silenced by an abrupt wave of Bear's Blood's massive hand. His gaze ranged from Lucas to Sugden and back again, and Rebecca could almost read the chief's mind. One man had to be lying, perhaps both.

He fixed his stare on Sugden. Rebecca couldn't understand the chief's furious words, but his hand movements clearly conveyed the message. Sugden had promised whiskey and not delivered. No whiskey had been promised by Horse-tamer.

Rebecca instinctively flinched when Amy pushed her way to

the forefront, effectively bringing the confrontation to an impasse.

Filthy and disheveled as ever, ignoring her twin, Amy pointed to the sky, then the edge of the camp where Luis Sebastian had been lashed to the cottonwood stump. Rebecca couldn't even hope to understand the gibberish Amy mumbled and whined, but Bear's Blood apparently suffered no such difficulty.

Amy's drivel seemed to solidify his intentions. He growled a brief command and waved his arm in a curt, harsh gesture. Warriors surrounded Sugden and his men, while others closed in around Rebecca and Lucas.

Both groups marched through the camp toward Sebastian and a pack of small naked children, all of whom were pelting the prisoner with rocks.

"Stay close."

Rebecca shot a glare at Lucas. Stay close? What choice did he think she had?

The small boys scattered like quail at their approach, but as the two groups halted, another, different element of dissension emerged.

The mother of the slain youth stalked forward to stand defiantly in front of the chief. Behind her, bearing her son's body on a litter, were several women. In fact, Rebecca thought, it looked as if the entire Sioux camp had assembled. When the woman spoke, it was into a well of reverent silence.

"She says they must have the funeral first," Lucas said.

This morning the slain boy's mother had slashed her arms. Now Rebecca could see that one finger had been hacked off. Horrified, yet impressed at the depths of the woman's suffering, Rebecca ignored the impulse to shut her eyes.

Bear's Blood listened in sullen silence, but his gaze roamed amidst the throng as if he wanted to estimate which way the mood might be strongest. Evidently, most sided with the bereaved woman because Bear's Blood spent no time arguing. A brief gesture sent the funeral party on its way. Another directed the white "guest" captives to separate areas of shade.

"They're telling us to sit down, Rebecca."

"I can *see* that, Lucas . . . Luc. What the hell should I call you?"

"Luc."

"Now what?" she asked. Most of the Sioux, including Sun Eagle and Bear's Blood . . . and Amy . . . had followed the litter.

"Now," Luc said, "we wait."

Only a few of the Sioux warriors remained, but it was clear from the way the two groups had been separated that Bear's Blood wanted to keep them apart. Dover Sugden, a tall, lanky man, a one-eyed man, and a vacant-eyed boy squatted in malevolent, low-voiced consultation, occasionally casting a baleful glance toward Luc.

Deliberately ignored by his outlaw cohorts, Luis Sebastian showed no sign that he recognized the shun, or even cared.

"He's dead already," Luc said, reading her mind. "All he can hope for is a quick death, and there's damned little chance of that. Lord, Becky, I wish I could have spared you this."

Becky. The sound of her nickname on his lips seemed to flow through her mind like music, but it was discordant music when linked to his deceit.

"You couldn't help this," she said. "But why did you lie to me? Why did you deliberately deceive me? Why . . ." She heard her voice rising. "Why couldn't you have told me who you were, right from the beginning?"

"Would it have mattered?"

"Well, of course, it would have mattered."

His question made no sense at all. She wasn't bothered by the content of Luc's deceit, but by the fact of it.

The facts were, the man she had fallen in love with had deceived her. She loved him, and his deception spit upon that love. Worse, she didn't even know *why* she'd been deceived!

"I wanted you to believe I helped you by choice," he said.

The illogical statement silenced her, stunned her. What on earth was he talking about?

"I don't remember holding a gun to your head," she finally stated, staring at her moccasins. "I didn't *force* you to come with me. I could just as easily have made the attempt by myself!"

What a ridiculous thing to say. She wouldn't have made it past Fort Benton without Luc's help. She knew it, and he knew it.

"This is perhaps not the best time to discuss this, Becky."

She blinked with surprise, not because he'd used her nickname again, but because he had slipped into a sort of French *patois*. Did he do that when emotionally shaken? She found the characteristic endearing, and wanted to tell him so, when another sound intruded.

A lamentation for the dead, so primitive and . . . elemental. Rebecca shivered. The keening sound came from a distance, but she could feel needles of ice prickling along her spine, could feel the small hairs at the back of her neck rising, as if lifted by the chant.

"Has it occurred to you that we may never have another time?" she asked.

The distant moans continued, and she wanted nothing more than to move closer to Luc, to huddle against him, to draw upon his warmth and strength.

"We'll survive this," he promised. "But you must understand that we have no chance whatsoever of rescuing your sister. None!"

"I realize that," she said, and shivered again.

Rebecca also understood that she could not fulfill her father's dying wish, even if the opportunity arose. It wasn't in her to kill Amy. And she couldn't ask Luc to do it, either.

"If you can escape," he said, "try to head north by west. It might not be easy, in fact it damned well won't be, but if you can make your way to the Cypress Hills you should be safe. I expect the Berubes are there now, with your wagons, but even if they aren't, others of the Métis are."

"What about you? Where will you be while I'm escaping?"

"I'll be doing whatever it takes to help you escape. Just remember, the Sioux might not be your worst problem. Sugden still believes you can lead him to your father's gold, although I don't think he's overly preoccupied with that notion at the moment."

"You still haven't told me why you agreed to help me rescue Amy. I know you didn't want to, at first. What made you change your mind?"

"Your father saved my life, Rebecca. To my people, such a thing makes a debt of blood, a debt of honor. When it became clear that you'd try and rescue Amy on your own, I had no choice. I had to help you, or at least try to keep you . . . safe."

"That's all? Nothing more than a debt?"

"Far more, now. I think you know that, or at least you should. But it's . . . difficult."

"Difficult?" She looked around, her ears still half attuned to the wailing, primitive lament that came from the next ridge. "I would certainly agree it's difficult, but that isn't what you mean, is it?"

"No."

"Well for goodness' sake what *is* it, then? Damn you, Luc! Don't you think I have the right to know?"

"Of course you do, Rebecca. It's just that I would have picked a better time and place."

"*This* is the time and place. We could be *dead* by tomorrow."

"You've said you hated it out here, that all you wanted to do was rescue your sister and go back to civilization."

"You're changing the subject!"

"True, but I have a reason."

"Many times I've said I hate it here, Luc, but it's only partly true. I hate the violence, but I love the country."

"There's violence everywhere, even in places you might think are civilized. You've coped remarkably well here, Rebecca. You've defended your principles and your friends. You've even earned yourself a war name."

"What are you saying, Luc? That I should forget about going back to civilization? That I should stay out here? Marry and raise a dozen children for the Indians to slaughter or capture? Start up a freight business with two wagons? Maybe I should go into competition with *them*." She pointed to where Sugden and his men still huddled in muted conversation.

"You're being evasive, Rebecca."

"*I'm* being evasive?" She heard her voice rise to a strident screech and didn't care. "I never lied about my name, lied about who I am and what I am! How dare you say I've been evasive, you . . . you . . ."

"Métis," he said, his voice as cold as his eyes. "I am Métis. Don't you understand what that means . . . why it is such a problem?"

"Of course."

"No," he said. "No, I don't think you do. Here, south of the medicine line, it means I'm a half-breed, neither Indian nor white. I'm a person to be spat upon, treated like dirt. You saw the way the men of the vigilante posse looked upon the Berubes."

"Those men were drunken pigs!"

"True, but their attitude toward anyone of Indian blood was obvious."

"They didn't look askance at *you.*"

"Because I was dressed as a white. Those men would have shot me as soon as look at me if they'd come across us traveling together, just the two of us, clothed the way I am now. And if we'd run into a cavalry patrol, the result might have been the same."

"Are you telling me . . . trying to tell me . . . that this is the real you, that you consider yourself more Indian than white, that this is the way you would choose to live?"

"I *have* lived like this, Rebecca. I grew up with the Peigan, in the foothills west and north of here. But, unfortunately, the way of the plains Indian is over. There are fewer buffalo each year. Already the hide-hunters have almost wiped out the southern herds. Without the buffalo, the plains Indians cannot survive. It is the center of their culture, their very existence."

"And yours, as well?"

"No. But I'm Métis, and the days of the Métis are also numbered. The Métis in Canada live by the buffalo, if not quite as strongly as do the plains tribes. Yet they face much the same changes for the future, and it will be difficult for them . . . very difficult. They've been a binding force between two cultures, but I think the time will come, has to come, when they must choose between the two."

"And have you chosen, Luc?"

"I've made . . . some choices. I believe in the end all the people, both Indian and Métis, will end up taking the white road, at least to some extent. I've learned to do that, over the years."

"You do it rather well," she said, aware that the vestiges of grief from his deception tinted her voice. "But you're not telling me if it's what you *want* to do. In fact, Luc, you aren't even telling me *what* you want to do."

"I've started to build a horse ranch. I managed to find a good place for such a venture, a place with excellent water, year-round grazing, everything I need. But . . ."

Rebecca watched him take a deep breath, as if preparing to dive into deep waters.

"My ranch occupies an area adjacent to where I believe land will be set aside for the Peigan, should a treaty be signed. The Canadian government is considering it. Nothing has been settled, but there's been talk."

"Would this treaty be a problem for you?"

"For me, no. But . . . you see . . . I . . ."

Luc's mind stuttered. Rebecca's accusation had been fair. He *was* being evasive. How could he question her about her inherent fear of Indians when she was about to be introduced to Sioux barbarism at its very worst?

And was this really the time to tell her that he wanted to marry her? The time to tell her that her father's gold didn't exist anymore? That the boy whose life her father had saved had used the gold to buy the grassland and horse ranch he'd just described?

"I haven't told you how I purchased my ranch," he said.

Rebecca looked at him expectantly.

Before he could continue, Amy Bennett hurtled herself into the clearing and glared at the helpless figure of Luis Sebastian.

"Blood Hand!"

The cry began as a murmur, then grew louder as additional voices joined in. The chant rose until it filled the sky, only to cease abruptly when the chief waved his arm and directed his men to bring the two groups of guest-captives closer.

"This one has killed a Minniconjou," he said, pointing at Sebastian. "He is evil and cowardly, like all whites, but perhaps even worse than most. Now we must see if he can die bravely . . . like a Sioux."

Bear's Blood's harsh glare at Sugden and his followers

271

implied that Sebastian's reaction to the torture might well affect their own futures. The chief didn't even glance at Luc and Rebecca, his anger wholly directed toward the whiskey trader and his entourage.

"Blood Hand!"

Once again the chorus started slowly, then rose to a fierce furnace of frenzied fury, and hatred, as Amy Bennett danced around Sebastian, seeking his attention, *demanding* it.

In her hand she held one of his own razor-sharp throwing knives, and she began the persecution with a series of small jabs, aimed at his arms and shoulders. A few of the perforations didn't even draw blood, and Sebastian showed no reaction whatsoever.

"Blood Hand! Blood Hand!"

Through the singsong chant, Rebecca heard her sister's voice: "Pat-a-cake, pat-a-cake, baker's man. Make me a cake as fast as you can." Amy's words wouldn't be comprehensible to anyone else, not even Luc, which was perhaps the very reason why Rebecca not only heard the babble, but understood it.

"Pat it and prick it and mark it with a 'B' . . . and put it in the oven for Becky and me . . ."

With a maniacal laugh, she stabbed at Sebastian's genitals in a carefully measured motion devised to cause severe pain. Her dance took on distinct sexual connotations as she attempted to arouse him, pain or no pain.

Sebastian cursed her, his words a polyglot mixture of border Spanish and gutter English. Then he spat at her, a heroic venture, considering he had been tied up all morning in the sun without anything to drink.

Amy howled with delight. Any reaction, it seemed, was preferable to none at all. Her prancing dance continued, clearly guided by some music only she could hear, for there was a definite rhythm to her movements, a kind of warped sensuality that couldn't be ignored.

"Three blind mice. See how they run," she recited. "They all run after the farmer's wife, who cut off their tails with a carving knife . . ."

Sidling behind Sebastian, she rubbed her crotch against his bound hands and tickled his ear with the knife.

Rebecca shifted closer to Luc. She wanted to hide herself against him. She felt sorry for her sister, a deep, empathetic sorrow, a commiseration that overrode all antipathy, but faced with this . . .

"What the hell is she saying?"

"Nursery rhymes . . . nonsense verse." With an effort, Rebecca held back the desire to laugh hysterically. Or cry. "My father made us memorize a map while my mother insisted we memorize poetry . . . all sorts of . . . poetry. She . . . my mother called it elocution . . . elocution lessons. She was desperate for us to become well-bred ladies . . . oh, God, Luc, I can't watch this. Amy is insane, and evil, but she's a lost little girl, and this . . . this display . . . is break . . . breaking my heart."

"I know, but don't cry. Don't show any weakness."

"I can't help it. I don't care."

Rebecca turned her head away, but a growl and gesture from Bear's Blood said she must watch, or she and Horse-tamer would suffer the consequences.

Amy danced around to face Sebastian, only this time she used her hand to fondle him, rubbing, stroking, squeezing in an effort to arouse him. He tried to spit again, but his mouth was too dry.

The Sioux were impressed. Their Blood-Hand chant rose in tempo, matching Amy's rhythm, accelerating it, enhancing it.

She seemed to glory in the attention. Her dance became more feverish, more erotic. Behind Sebastian again, she forced herself firmly against his bound hands as she ran her fingers down along his shoulders and arms. He cursed louder, then spasmed. Then his fingers grabbed at her, clenching in the most vicious pinch he could manage.

Amy gave an anguished scream and stabbed at his wrists with the knife. Now it was she who cursed, and if her nonsense verses were pathetic, the way she mixed her curses with English words from her childhood sounded even more pitiful.

"Bad man . . . bad, bad, bad!" she raged, flinging down the knife and rubbing herself where his fingers had pinched. Then she scuttled around until she found two good-sized stones.

Sebastian couldn't see her. She sneaked up behind him like a child playing hide-and-seek.

"Bad," she hissed. "Badbadbadbad . . . bears are bad . . ."

"Dear God," Rebecca breathed. Instinctively, she knew what would happen next.

"Bad man, bad bear," Amy said.

Clack! The stones came together with a noise that rang like a gunshot. Again! Only this time there was no "clack." This time the stones met with one of Sebastian's fingers between them, and his face contorted as he held back a shriek of agony.

Amy laughed in the haunting voice of a loon, a voice devoid of humor but alive with madness. Her laughter rose in volume and tempo as she systematically smashed the rocks together, destroying each of Sebastian's fingers and thumbs until all ten were bloody mush. But she still couldn't draw any sounds from him.

Rebecca slumped against Luc, certain she'd faint, terrified she would and equally terrified she would not. She breathed in short, harsh gasps, but couldn't seem to get enough air. Luc's arm curled around her shoulders.

Amy circled Sebastian, taunting him, teasing his genitals with the knife. This time, he didn't look at her. Through stubbornness, or from pain, his eyes were firmly shut.

She slapped his face, screeched in his face, but he remained stolidly impassive, even though Rebecca could see his jaw clench.

And when he did speak, it was not to his torturer. Sebastian turned his head to where Sugden stood. "Damn you, *Le Carcajou!*" he screamed. "I will come back from hell to get you for this!"

He tried his best to spit at the prancing figure in front of him, but could muster up only enough moisture to wet his own lips. Amy squealed with fiendish delight, then began her evil-erotic sway again, prodding at Sebastian's genitals with her fingers and the point of the knife.

Rebecca sagged against Luc, certain she'd be sick, not caring anymore if it might get her killed, if it got them both killed.

"If you have to throw up," Luc said, "do it now, and do it quickly. Bear's Blood is watching your sister, not us."

"No! I won't vomit. I swear I won't," she said, even though her tummy lurched and sweat beaded her brow.

Around them, the Sioux's yells and cheers resounded along with Amy's mad keening.

"They're showing approval," Luc said, raising his voice to be heard above the din. "Sebastian is a brave man. He's giving them a good show and they respect him for it."

Luc's loud comments drew an enigmatic scowl from Bear's Blood and a pleading look from Sebastian.

"L'Hirondelle!" he shouted, then lapsed into French. He managed to get out the words "For the love of God, kill me!" before a smashing blow from Amy brought him around to face her again.

"I would if I could," Luc said, also in French. Sebastian gave no sign of having heard him.

But Amy did, and Luc could have kicked himself as she turned to stare at him—and Rebecca.

"Becky Sue," she said, and Luc stiffened, prepared for anything, knowing he would die if he interfered, but prepared for that, too.

"Amy and Becky went up the hill to fetch a pail of water," Amy recited. "Amy fell down and broke her crown . . ."

"And Becky came tumbling after," Rebecca said.

"Yes! Yes, yes, yes!" Gleefully, Amy turned away.

Luc sighed with relief.

Amy returned to her macabre dance. She reached out to flick with the knifepoint at Sebastian's groin. Despite the pain he must have suffered, the little *mestizo* ignored her, although his muscles were strongly delineated as he fought for control.

He's dying well, Luc thought, then sensed a new restlessness. The Minniconjou wanted more than their shaman was giving them. Amy sensed it, too. She whirled and made a slash with the knife, drawing a fine red line just below Sebastian's waist. As Luc watched, as they all watched, the line thickened until blood welled to the surface.

Amy reached out one filthy finger and touched the flowing red line. Then, to Luc's astonishment, she began to draw with the blood, her canvas the sweat-sheened chest of her victim.

Rebecca gasped as a definitive map emerged, drawn in Sebastian's blood!

Sugden pushed his way forward. The outlaw's piggy eyes were riveted to the gruesome chart. Then he turned and fixed his gaze upon Rebecca.

Slowly, Luc put his hand on his knife hilt.

Amy scowled at her drawing. Then she rushed over, grabbed Rebecca's arm, and dragged her from Luc's side.

"Becky Sue draw map," Amy demanded, pushing Rebecca's hand toward the still-flowing line of red.

Rebecca couldn't speak, could hardly think. She stared as her own fingers became smeared with the life of Luis Sebastian, then looked into the eyes of the girl who had once been her sister.

"Becky Sue draw *map!*" The command, harsher now, brooked no argument, allowed no refusal. Amy held Rebecca by one hand, but her other hand hefted Sebastian's knife in an obvious threat.

Rebecca looked down at her red-stained fingers. "No," she said.

"Do it!" Luc shouted. He tried to move forward, but three Sioux halted his advance. "Rebecca, draw the goddamn map!"

Amy's eyes flashed to meet his, then she waved a filthy, bloody hand and waiting, willing warriors moved to her bidding. Luc had no chance to resist as he was dragged over and bound back-to-back with a still-silent Luis Sebastian.

Rebecca was dragged closer, Luc's own knife forced into her hand as her mad sister stared at her.

"Map. Becky Sue draw map."

Gripping Rebecca's hand with a madwoman's strength, she forced the knife closer and closer to Luc's stomach, her intention all too obvious. Rebecca resisted, but it was a struggle and she was clearly losing.

"Becky Sue such a baby," Amy crooned, a lilting, evil sound. But her strength was greater than Rebecca's.

"No-o-o-o-o-o-ooooo!" Rebecca shrieked, and her fingers flashed in a slap that turned her sister's head halfway round.

Amy's response was quick as a rattler's strike. A fist smashed Rebecca back, down, into the suddenly silent crowd. Two warriors lifted her to her feet, held her at a gesture from Amy.

"Bad! Becky Sue *baaaad!*"

Amy hissed like a malevolent snake as she approached Luc, the knife now a deadly serpent's fang. Then she paused, head cocked in a curiously childlike posture, her attention seemingly diverted by the scars on his back and shoulders.

"Bear?"

Her voice lost all harshness, became almost plaintive. Her grubby fingers reached out to touch at the scars with a strange, eerie gentleness.

Luc nodded silently.

"Bear . . . bad."

Amy's fingers continued to stroke the scars for a moment, then her attention wandered again, and she began idly to trace designs across the muscles of Luc's chest. Her eyes looked down at the knife, back at Luc, down again.

It was the map, all over again, and Rebecca could see his stomach tense as he, too, realized what was going on.

The Sioux began to show impatience; this was not the spectacle they had come to see. Rebecca's captors, engrossed in the curious situation, absently released their grip. She couldn't . . . didn't believe it at first, but then was quick to take advantage. She moved backward, her hand scrabbling at the ripped side-seam of her doeskin frock.

She had the revolver in her hand, then, the hammer back, both hands shaking as she raised it and aimed at her sister. And nobody even seemed to notice! Except Luc, whose eyes widened as he realized what was about to happen.

He mouthed a silent "no," but it served only to catch Amy's notice, and she turned to stare at Rebecca with blank, feral eyes that seemed to dismiss the threat of the shaking weapon.

The gun shook; sweat streamed down to blur Rebecca's vision. She lowered the revolver, gasped in a huge, deep breath, then raised it again. Amy merely held her feral stare.

"Baaad. Becky Sue baaaad." Her voice was a serpentine hiss that lifted to a shriek as she turned, then, knife upraised, the target—Luc's chest—not in question.

Rebecca's eyes closed for an instant as she anticipated the recoil, her finger squeezed, then jerked on the trigger. She heard the discharge, felt the thrust of the gun against her hands, opened them to see splinters flying from the stump just above Luc's head.

Then saw, as if in a dream, the strange, feathered *something* that seemed to grow from her sister's throat.

The impact of the feathered object twisted Amy, turning her. The knife struck, not at Lucas, but into the softness of Luis Sebastian's neck, as his torturer embraced him in her dying . . . and his.

20

The wild ululation of the Peigan war cry seared into the clearing like a wind from the gates of hell, and hard behind it, the thunder of hooves as half a dozen ponies stampeded down off the ridge.

Before the ponies had struck level ground, the Sioux scattered like a covey of pheasants. Even the armed sentries around Sugden and his followers broke ranks and ran.

Bear's Blood was not among them. As the body of Amy Bennett crumpled to the ground, a second feather-fletched arrow took the chief squarely in the heart. A third, hastily aimed at the fleeing figure of Sugden, sliced a wicked cut from the top of the outlaw's shoulder but failed to slow him.

Rebecca saw it, and didn't see it. She thrust the revolver back into its holster, then rushed to grab up Luc's knife, using it with fumbling fingers to cut him free. All she wanted then was the safety of his arms, but there was no time for that now.

Pandemonium ensued. The Minniconjou sped toward the village while the stampeding ponies plunged through them, dispersing them and hampering their retreat. From the other direction, Luc's big blue roan Appaloosa, broken tether flying, galloped into the fray. He wasn't terrorized by the war cry, but called by it, and he charged furiously through the oncoming Sioux. Flailing out with his deadly hooves, he snapped his enormous teeth at any warrior who happened to get in his way.

Behind the stallion, the buckskin pranced, snuffling through his nostrils, shaking his mane, trying to keep the picket rope from tripping him—as it did some of the Sioux he passed.

Cradled in Luc's arms, Rebecca saw the flurry of rising dust. She saw Amy, throat pierced by an arrow, embracing Sebastian as her body slid down the front of his in a mingled welter of blood.

"Are you all right? Can you ride?"

Luc's voice was reassuring, despite the urgency in it. "No . . . yes," she managed.

He flung her onto the buckskin's saddle, then turned, picket rope in hand, and fairly flew onto the back of his stallion.

The stallion led as they charged up the ridge, and Luc screamed out his own war cry to add to the confusion. His cry joined with that of a figure who galloped past them and rode into the clearing, a rifle in one hand, a scalping knife in the other.

Sleeping Fox! Who would surely find them later, Luc thought, but not before the old man had counted coup on his enemies.

Bravery beyond the point of foolishness!

Alone, Luc would have joined his friend. But Rebecca's safety came first, would always come first.

Sleeping Fox would know that, too.

Luc rode for half an hour, weaving his way through the coulees, going flat out across the occasional sections of prairie, and in his mind he thanked his gods for having given him the sense to tack up the horses.

Rebecca rode behind him, bouncing like a sack of grain, her fingers clenched round the saddle horn. Her face looked ashen, and she seemed to have no idea where she was.

Luc found a shallow creek and slowed to walk the horses upstream, using the respite to refresh them, trusting the current would wash away their tracks. At his insistence, Rebecca dismounted and laved her face and arms with the cool water.

Silent, she clambered back onto her buckskin.

"Keep Governor Potts on a short rein," Luc said, using the absurd name she'd bestowed upon the horse, hoping he could rouse her.

Expressionless, she gathered up the reins, looked at them as if she'd never seen them before, but then dropped them. He tightened his grip on the buckskin's rope.

Sleeping Fox found them later in the day, and waved silently from just out of gun range before leading several horses tied nose-to-tail, cantering his pony down a slope.

"I wanted you to see me clearly," he said. "I did not want your sunset woman to shoot at me again."

"After saving us? I cannot imagine her wanting to shoot you for that. We are in your debt, grandfather."

"I am three ponies poorer because of you, Horse-tamer. And many kegs of whiskey poorer, too. I should have kept them, but there was not time to unload and hide them again before I realized I must rescue you, so I had to leave the whiskey on the ponies."

Luc hit his forehead with the heel of his hand. "*You* moved the cache! I must be getting old. I was certain I knew that little pinto's tracks, but I couldn't remember . . ."

"You are not old, Horse-tamer. Your brain is mixed up because of this sunset woman, that is all. Is she fit to ride? Because we should keep on riding until it is too dark for the Sioux to follow us. I do not believe they will, now that their chief is gone, but it is better to be prudent."

Luc looked at Rebecca, slumped in the saddle, her head down, her entire attitude one of exhaustion and numbness.

"I think she is in shock," he said. "This has been very hard on her, and then to see her sister die like that . . ."

"She will recover. She is a strong woman, that one. You have chosen well, I think. If you can tame her, she will bear you many strong sons. But now is not the time for talk. We should go from here quickly, just in case some of the Sioux are bold enough to chase us."

"You have counted a mighty coup, grandfather, killing their chief and their evil shaman."

"I did not intend to kill her. You must tell the sunset woman that. I was aiming for her arm, but it had to be very fast, and I am old. My eyes are not what they once were."

"Intent or not, I believe it is a good thing you killed her."

"She had a sickness inside her, and it was not one of being in touch with the Old Man Above. Now you can understand why the Bloods were happy to trade her."

"I am only sorry the Bloods did not kill her. It would have saved many lives, I think. All that Blood Hand business must have been going on for a long time, and I expect many people died because of it."

"It was not all her doing, Horse-tamer. That Bear's Blood has always been a bad one. He, too, was . . ." The old man swirled his finger round his ear. "But it does not matter now. Let us ride and try to make some distance before the day is over."

After an hour, Sleeping Fox said, "Your woman and I must change horses. The buckskin is not strong, and the way the sunset woman is riding hurts him. She only hangs on. She is not helping him."

Rebecca mutely accepted the exchange. Luc splashed water on her face while the old Peigan switched the saddles on her horse and his. But the Indian pony didn't like the leaden burden any more than the buckskin. They had hardly set out again when it began to bunch its muscles into a bucking stance.

Luc yanked at its lead, then pulled it in close so that he—and the Appaloosa—could control it better.

Holding both horses down to a slow, steady walk, Luc reached out to Rebecca with his voice, murmuring words of encouragement. He used the same tone he would have used with a fractious colt, except, of course, the words were vastly different.

At first the words *swooshed* and rumbled in Rebecca's ears, as if she held her head underwater.

Gradually, some of the words became clearer, although she heard them in fragments; short bursts that made little sense.

Even the words she could hear sank into the blackness that was her mind—the empty, colorless, formless void, which she recognized as a barrier, a protection, a blanket against the thoughts that could harm her.

". . . not your fault . . ."

". . . nothing else you could do, Becky . . ."

". . . can ride better than this . . . killing that poor horse . . ."

". . . love . . ."

". . . without you . . ."

". . . Damn it! How can I marry . . ."

". . . Fox wasn't aiming to . . ."

Lucas Swallow's voice! The sound of his voice drew her mind back to when she'd first met him. To when she'd first noticed him, standing like a wolf among sheep. A wolf *disguised* as a sheep!

". . . knew from the start I couldn't live without you . . ."

". . . you in my medicine dream . . ."

". . . the color of a sunset, the red mare I never chased, never caught . . ."

Her pony stumbled, then shambled back into a plodding walk. But the stumble seemed to shake something loose, a vague segment of memory that hovered just beneath the surface of her consciousness.

". . . strong sons. If I can persuade you to marry me. But how can I do that? I am Métis. And you are . . ."

". . . father's gold . . . gone . . ."

". . . used it to buy my ranch. The most beautiful place you can imagine. High in the foothills, grass to a horse's belly, plenty of water . . ."

She snapped her head up, somehow sensing evil, like a whiff of rotting meat.

Amy?

No. Amy was dead.

Suddenly, Rebecca heard a different voice, and this one did what the other voice could not. It brought her back to reality in a single, blinding instant of awareness.

Luc had loosened the rope on her pony and it walked nose-to-tail with his stallion. Rebecca felt the pony tense. Leaning forward, she stroked its forelock, poll and mane. At the same time, she carefully gathered up the slack reins.

". . . and I told you they'd head west instead of north, didn't I, boys?"

Dover Sugden slouched in his saddle, flanked by his scummy band of jackals. Blood stained Sugden's left shoulder, but it didn't seem to hinder the pistol in his right hand . . . a pistol aimed squarely at Luc.

The tall, lanky man, the one-eyed man, and the half-witted boy hadn't bothered to draw their guns. Both Sleeping Fox and Luc had put their rifles in their saddle scabbards, the old warrior's hands were empty—no bow, no arrows—and Luc wore no sidearm.

"Nice of you to bring us the girl." Sugden gave Luc a vicious sneer. "Right convenient, I'd say."

"She can't help you." Luc sounded calm, yet Rebecca could see that his body was rigid. "She has no more idea where the gold is than you do."

"I've got a more than halfway idea. I saw the map her sister drew, same as you did. And this little bitch here has the rest of it in her pretty head. Don't bother lying to me about that!"

Luc shrugged. "Map's one thing, knowing the country's another. You could spend years searching, just like Otis Benn—"

Sugden snorted his interruption. "At least we'd have something to entertain us while we looked, eh, boys? 'Specially at night. Nights get cold in the mountains. Might be fun to have something warm and shapely in our blankets."

"Wouldn't it be better to have the gold? Women wear out, eventually. This one does not know where the gold is, map or no map. But I do!"

Luc's last three words fell like a huge rock into a small pond, and Rebecca used the distraction to slide her hand through the slit in her doeskin frock. Only partially hidden behind Luc, she tried to make the gesture casual, as if she scratched her hip. Her fingers found the pistol's butt and she began to ease it out of the holster.

Sensing danger, the one-eyed man sniffed the air. Rebecca's heart skipped a beat and she stilled her fingers.

"You?" Sugden snorted. "How the hell would you know?"

Again, Luc shrugged. *He's playing for time,* Rebecca thought. *He wants to choose his words as carefully as he'd choose an arrow.* His knees controlled his stallion, the Appaloosa's eyes narrowed, great nostrils wide with tension.

"I was there, or at least nearby, when Bennett found the gold," Luc said. "Or haven't you heard that part of the legend? The part about the Métis boy he doctored? The boy the grizzly damn near killed?"

Turning sideways in the saddle, very *very* slowly, he showed off the long white scars that ran like a sunburst along his shoulder and back. Then he lifted his leg to display his puncture wound. It took less than a minute, but that was enough for Re-

becca. Luc's motion put her squarely behind him, out of sight.
She freed the pistol and placed it in her lap.

"I suppose your price to show us the gold is to let the girl
go," Sugden said. "Would that be about right?"

Rebecca surreptitiously cocked the pistol and curled her
finger round its trigger. Dear God, it was so slippery. She wanted
to wipe her sweaty hands on her saddle blanket, but didn't
dare. And would it matter? She couldn't shoot straight anyway;
she'd too recently proven that. But this time . . .

The one-eyed man kept sniffing. He looked like a feral dog,
and Rebecca felt a crawling sensation in her belly.

The tall, lanky man picked at his fingernails with something . . . a knife. When had he drawn his knife?

The slack-jawed boy seemed unaware . . . maybe not. His
gaze seemed to go straight through Luc and . . .

"Want the red girl," he said, apparently taking his leader's
words at face value.

Red-*haired* girl, Rebecca silently admonished, as if she cor-
rected one of her former students. Something hit her leg,
something that felt like a whisk broom. Startled, she nearly fell
from the saddle, but it was only her pony's tail, swishing
impatiently. *Only?*

Hurry, please hurry, she begged mutely. *Soon this damn pony
will toss me off its back.*

As if he'd heard her plea, Luc said, "Yup, that's the deal. Let
the girl go, and my old friend here. He has no part in this."

"The hell he doesn't!" Sugden reached up toward his
shoulder. His gun's muzzle pointed at the sky as the knuckle of
his little finger gingerly touched his wound. "That Indian
damned near killed me!"

Rebecca's heel nudged her pony to the right. At the same
time, she raised her pistol and fired. It belched and bucked
against her wrist, but she saw a splotch of scarlet erupt from

Sugden's chest.

Luc's stallion dashed forward as if drawn by the bullet, his great hooves lifting as he smashed between Sugden's horse and that of the half-witted boy.

Sleeping Fox's buckskin galloped between the other two men. The old warrior yelled his piercing, haunting, paralyzing Peigan war cry as he surged forward with a knife in his hand . . . a knife that flashed silver and then scarlet in the evening light.

Rebecca steadied her spooked pony and cocked her revolver again, although the tangle of horses and bodies made a clear shot impossible. Sugden was down, as was his horse. The boy had also hit the ground, thanks to a clout from Luc's fist.

The other two outlaws sprawled in the dirt, one on top, one on the bottom, their arms and legs spread like a giant squid. They'd reached for their guns, but Sleeping Fox's cry had given them pause, and his dexterity from a lifetime of battle made their momentary immobility permanent. The one-eyed man's chest bled profusely and the lanky man had landed belly down, impaled by his own knife.

Rebecca dropped her revolver. Then she leaned over the side of her pony and was promptly, thoroughly sick to her stomach.

21

The last camp Luc and Rebecca shared with Sleeping Fox was just south of the Cypress Hills, and the medicine line . . . the border with Canada.

"I will not go into the Grandmother's country," the old warrior said. "The Grandmother's red-coats would ask too many questions about these horses, and also about . . ."

He bit back the rest of his words, but Rebecca knew he referred to the scalps he carried; both Indian and white. Although he had been persuaded, for her sake, to ignore the scalps of Sugden and his band, the scalp of the wolfer was with him, and would be until his death.

She and Luc and Sleeping Fox were in a snug little coulee, one which offered a deep, clear-flowing stream that bottomed into a pond, suitable for swimming or bathing. They had, in fact, all bathed there. Rebecca's hair felt gloriously clean, along with the rest of her, and she had manipulated the strands into thick braids.

Luc had his "white" garments spread over a bush, drying after a wash in the clear water. For the moment, however, he was as he had been since they'd begun their quest, clothed in a breechclout and his high-topped, buffalo-soled moccasins. She had changed into what remained of her proper clothing, needing something to wear while she found a way to repair her doeskin frock.

Sleeping Fox walked over to her. His hands, gnarled by age

but still flexible, wove an eagle feather from his own hair into one of her braids.

"You must wear this always," he said in both sign language and Peigan, expecting Luc to translate, even though she had no trouble following his words.

"You are not only the sunset woman who defeats her enemies with an empty gun, but a warrior woman, a woman who deserves to wear the feather of an eagle for the enemy you have slain. You are much woman. And if this one . . ." He gestured toward Luc. ". . . if this one does not appreciate you, come to me and I will offer many ponies, more than those I have already offered."

Rebecca smiled at the old man's tease. He would be going west, not north, with the horses he had taken from the Sioux, plus those of Sugden, the tall man, and the one-eyed man—now buried in shallow graves. And, of course, the booty from his earlier exploits. By Peigan standards, he would return to his people a wealthy man, and, even more important, a man redeemed, a man who had wrought vengeance upon his wife's despoiler and upon many other enemies of his people.

Luc and Sleeping Fox had stayed out of sight when, riding alone and wearing her bedraggled gingham gown, Rebecca had left the half-witted boy with a small wagon train they'd come upon the day before. She had told the settlers why the boy was rope-tied hand and foot, and a woman who looked and sounded like her old friend Mattie Holmes had said she'd care for him until he could be brought to justice.

Would there be justice out here? Rebecca didn't know . . . or care. Luc and Sleeping Fox couldn't kill the boy—knocked unconscious in the fight—in cold blood; as Peigans, they believed his madness came from God.

Or so they said; Rebecca privately thought he'd been spared solely because of her, because they both thought . . . she would wish it so. Amy had been a different situation, given her obvious menace, but even then, the elderly warrior had aimed his arrow at Amy's arm. Rebecca wanted to believe she, too, would only have wounded her sister . . . but she knew in her soul that might be a lie. Neither of the men had ever mentioned her mis-aimed shot at Amy. Neither, she knew, ever would.

The settlers had begged Rebecca to join their wagon train, and she felt her mouth stretch in a secret smile as she wondered what Mr. Luc L'Hirondelle would have thought of her reply.

"We owe our lives to you," she told Sleeping Fox, and waited while Luc translated.

The old man grinned, creasing his wrinkled face even more. "Your man gave me back my life, and then you, yourself, saved it by not hitting me with your many-shoots gun," he said in a curious mixture of Peigan, sign language and, surprisingly, a few words of English.

Rebecca leaned forward to kiss him on the cheek and had the pleasure of realizing that, even at his age, he could blush.

Then she faced him and slowly, laboriously made her final remarks in sign language. It wasn't easy, especially with Luc looking on.

"I will bring you my children," she signed, "so that you can teach them the proper ways."

As the old man grinned again, she sneaked a peek at Luc . . . but couldn't decipher his expression.

Then, standing next to the man she loved, she watched the elderly warrior disappear over the rim of the coulee, his string of horses trailing behind him.

"Are you all right?" Luc asked, as if perhaps a sudden illness had been responsible for her farewell to Sleeping Fox.

"I would be a lot better if I had a proper needle," she said, keeping her voice deliberately low, her eyes averted. "It really wasn't very thoughtful of you to ruin the seam on my beautiful doeskin dress."

Luc didn't respond, and when she finally looked up at him, she saw that *he* had turned his eyes away.

"Did you mean what you said to the old man, Rebecca?"

"Please call me Becky, and I don't see why anything I said would suggest I'm not all right. Sleeping Fox is a wonderful man, and his own children are . . . gone."

She knew she was being evasive, but her parting words to Sleeping Fox—and the fact that Luc had heard them—suddenly overwhelmed her. She wanted to retreat, but where would she go? *Should I hide under a horse blanket, or dive into the pond?*

"And just how many of your children do you plan to take to him, Miss Bennett?"

"Well that's a silly question. How can I possibly know how many children I might have? I'm not even married. Indeed, Mr. Swallow . . . or Mr. L'Hirondelle, if you prefer, I haven't even been asked. Recently."

"I am Luc L'Hirondelle . . . or Lucas Swallow . . . or Horse-tamer, whichever suits you," he said.

He sounded stunned and, perversely, that made her feel better. Her moccasins raised a modest cloud of dust as she fanned out her tattered gown. "I'm not likely to be asked, either, Mr. Horse-tamer. Not looking like this, at any rate. I'm not fit for the wilderness, much less civilization, and you can't even find me a simple little thing like a needle."

His snort came back over his shoulder as he strode to where the camp gear lay. Then he rummaged through his own saddlebags before returning to hand her, not one, but two needles, along with a small coil of fine sinew.

"I don't think you *are* all right," he said. "I know you, Rebecca Susan Bennett, and this business of playing seamstress is very much out of character, especially at a time like this."

"Out of character? When the only decent dress I own has half the side ripped out of it?"

"Are you sure you want to wear that dress? Soon we'll cross the medicine line to where there are . . . people."

She put down the sewing utensils, and reached up to touch the eagle feather in her hair. "Why . . . that's right! Didn't you say the Berubes might be there? If so, isn't this what I wore the last time they saw me? I can't see what has happened to change things all that much."

"*Everything* has changed!"

"Not to a woman who defeats her enemies with an empty gun."

"Thank God it wasn't empty last time, although Sugden mightn't agree. And in the Indian camp . . ."

She cut him off; that subject needed no further discussion. "And when I have my stock and wagons back . . . well, I suppose Sleeping Fox could find me a decent husband should I want one. Four horses might not be enough, but if you throw in my wagons . . ."

"Damn it, Rebecca! The *man* is supposed to offer the horses!"

"So what you're saying is that I cannot be wed until a man offers horses for me? Many horses, I would think, for a woman warrior?"

She waited, eyes downcast. Waited through his silence, which really wasn't all that silent, considering the way his breath moved in and out. *Exasperated gasps,* she thought, but couldn't stop teasing. This was . . . fun. The first fun she'd experienced in a long, long time.

"How many horses do *you* have?" she asked, and had to fight to keep the laughter from her voice, to keep from glancing up at him, even though she wanted to see the look on his face.

"Only one, and you damned well know it."

The words seemed to come from some great distance, so

softly did he speak, but there was no distance in the words themselves.

"One?" She *tsked* her tongue against the roof of her mouth. "But you couldn't even get that young, beautiful Berube girl for only one horse. What was her name, again?"

"Enough!"

Luc's strong arms picked her up, and she flew through the air to land with a splash in the deepest part of the pond. She was still gurgling with breathlessness, and laughter, when he slid into the water beside her.

"There are limits, you know," he said, reaching out to pull her against him, his fingers already fumbling with her buttons while his lips led the way along the hollow of her throat.

Rebecca threw her arms around his neck, her mind traveling back to another pond, another time. "Yes," she said. "I suppose one horse might limit things a bit."

"There aren't enough horses in the world to meet your value, Miss Bennett. But my stallion has the potential to create the best of what there will be. I'm an honorable man, and if I promise many horses, then many horses is what I'll deliver."

"Yes, Luc," Rebecca managed. His fingers had finished with the buttons on her gown, and it slid down her water-slick body, then floated up beside her in a shapeless gingham blob.

Hanging onto his shoulder with one hand, she took off her moccasins and tossed them toward the bank. Finally, she looked into his eyes, ice-green but far from ice-cold.

His body was even warmer than his eyes as he crushed her against him. She pulled away, removed his breechclout, and tossed that, too.

"Are there likely to be any other people in the Cypress Hills?" she murmured. "Besides the Métis, I mean?"

"It's possible, I suppose. There are several forts, and with Sitting Bull expected to cross the line, the red-coats . . . mounted police . . . should be there. Why do you ask?"

A silly question. Luc thought he knew the answer. Father Jules De Corby, priest of the large Métis community, could very well be in the Cypress Hills. Most of the Wood Mountain people had moved West the year before, to winter where the hunting would be better. Luc hoped Father De Corby *was* in the area, although he knew that among the Métis the timing of a wedding was usually irrelevant.

"It would be nice to see some proper women again," she said, surprising him. "There are things I'd like to . . . to talk about."

"You can talk to me."

Despite his earnest suggestion, which Rebecca thought very dear, his lips stopped all conversation, then slid down along her throat to capture her breasts as he lifted her upward so that he could lick the droplets of water from her nipples.

She could feel increasing evidence that talking was the last thing he had in mind, which suited her just fine. She had learned to shoot a gun, hadn't she? Surely a warrior woman could learn to make love.

But when he scooped her up and carried her in his arms to the shore, she felt more like the woman who'd bluffed with an empty rifle.

Luc placed her on the spread blankets, his hands caressing, his gaze devouring her as tangibly as his fingers. And even as her own hands moved down to explore, to marvel at the erect thickness of him, at the warmth and strength of him, she couldn't help saying, "Luc . . . what if somebody sees us? I mean—"

"There is no one who could, my love," he replied, and her heart sang with the sound of that word; that one word she'd begun to think she'd only imagined during their flight from the Sioux.

After an eternity in which he roused her, he went into her, gathering her around him with a unique combination of gentleness and passion that spurred her past the initial pain and into the sunrise country beyond. Waves of pleasure throbbed through her, not unlike the sun's rays at dawning.

They cried out together. And later, again, as their needs were more urgent then respite.

Much later, Luc said, "Eventide has begun to draw its curtain across the Western skies, my love, and the skies reflect the color of your hair. No wonder Sleeping Fox calls you my sunset woman."

They were still without clothing. Rebecca hadn't had the time nor the inclination to repair her doeskin frock, and her only other dress was still floating in the waters of the coulee pond. At least she hoped it was.

"Becky?"

"Yes, Luc?"

"Back in the camp of the Minniconjou, you quoted Lord Byron. Do you happen to have another quote that fits this occasion?"

"I don't know. I've always used the wisdom of others when I'm frightened. But, for the first time in my life, I'm not the least bit frightened."

She dug through her memory. "Lo, the poor Indian, whose untutor'd mind, sees God in clouds or hears him in the wind."

"Alexander Pope. *Essay On Man.* Perfect. Thank you."

"You're welcome," she said, and even to her own ears, her voice sounded torpid with pleasure; somnolent; replete.

As she gathered her lover back down to her, Rebecca looked across his shoulders at the red-strewn sky that heralded their union.

ABOUT THE AUTHOR

Gordon K. Aalborg, under his pseudonym of Victoria Gordon, is the author of *Finding Bess* (Five Star Expressions 2004) and more than twenty Harlequin/Mills & Boon category romances.

In his own name, he is the author of the Five Star Publishing thrillers *The Specialist* and *Dining with Devils,* (set in Tasmania, where he lived for many years) as well the animal survival epic, *Cat Tracks.*

Raised in Alberta, he grew up listening to tales of the Wild West as it really was. His maternal grandfather cowboyed with the famous Western artist Charles M. Russell in Montana, where this novel is set.

Gordon is married to mystery/romance author, Denise Dietz, and lives on Vancouver Island, in Canada.